"Why is it that you beguile me so, Tess Stuart?

"Is it that you taste like wine and smell of roses, even in the most god-awful heat of the day? Is it that fall of golden hair of yours, or your eyes, like wild violets? No . . . it must be the tender words that you're always whispering so gently to me. Words like *scurvy rat*."

"Lieutenant, will you please—"

"I do want you."

"What?" Tess cried.

"Very much. And you might wake up one night and realize that it's going to be, that there's just something there. I feel it when I touch you, when I'm near you."

"You're a fool!"

"Am I?"

He leaned closer. He was going to kiss her again.

"Don't!" she cried out.

He ignored the warning, taking her lips with his own, and though she rumbled a second protest in her throat, her mouth was already parting for his. She trembled against the sweet savagery of his kiss, and she hated him for it. But she needed him still, and she wanted him. . . .

Dear Reader:

Harlequin offers you historical romances with a difference. Harlequin Historicals have all the passion and excitement of a five-hundred-page historical in three hundred pages, and stories that focus on people—a hero and heroine you really care about, who take you back to and make you part of their time.

We have some great books for you this fall. I've highlighted a few, and I'm sure you'll want to look for these and our other exciting selections. Here's what you can look forward to in coming months: *Rose Red, Rose White* by Marianne Willman is a passionate romance set in medieval England. *Texas Heart* by Ruth Langan is the story of a young woman who goes in search of her father and finds love along the way. *Apache Summer* is the third and final book in Heather Graham Pozzessere's miniseries, and it features Jamie Slater. Lastly, in December, look for *Chase the Thunder* by Patricia Potter, which is an exciting Western romance and a sequel to *Between the Thunder*.

We appreciate your comments and suggestions; our goal is to publish the kinds of books you want to read. So please keep your letters coming. You can write to us at the address below.

Karen Solem
Editorial Director
Harlequin Historicals
P.O. Box 7372
Grand Central Station
New York, New York 10017

Apache Summer

Heather Graham Pozzessere

Harlequin Books

TORONTO • NEW YORK • LONDON
AMSTERDAM • PARIS • SYDNEY • HAMBURG
STOCKHOLM • ATHENS • TOKYO • MILAN

Harlequin Historical first edition November 1989

ISBN 0-373-28633-3

Books by Heather Graham Pozzessere

Harlequin Historical

Dark Stranger #9
Rides a Hero #19
Apache Summer #33

HEATHER GRAHAM POZZESSERE

This award-winning author of historical romances written under the names of Heather Graham and Shannon Drake now begins a new series of historicals for Harlequin as Heather Graham Pozzessere, the name under which she has won popular acclaim for her contemporary romances. In addition to being a multitalented novelist, Heather has worked as a model, actress and bartender. Now a full-time wife and mother of four, she considers herself lucky to live in Florida, where she can indulge her love of water sports, such as swimming and boating, year-round.

Chapter One

Western Texas, 1870

Look, Lieutenant! Fire, rising high to our left!''

Jamie Slater reined in his roan stallion. With penetrating silver-gray eyes he stared east, where Sergeant Monahan was pointing. Across the sand and the sagebrush and the dry dunes, smoke could indeed be seen, billowing up in black and gray bursts. Tendrils of flame, like undulating red ribbons, waved through the growing wall of smoke.

"Injuns!" Monahan breathed.

To Jamie's right, Jon Red Feather stiffened. Jamie turned toward him. The half-breed Blackfoot was a long way from home, but he was still one of the best Indian scouts around. He was a tall, striking man with green-gold eyes and strong, arresting features. Thanks to a wealthy white grandfather, Jon Red Feather had received a remarkable education, going as far as Oxford in England.

Jamie knew that Jon resented the ready assumption that trouble meant Indians, even though he admitted readily to Jamie that trouble was coming, big trouble. The Apache hated the white man, the Comanche despised him, and Jamie was convinced that the great Sioux Nation was destined to fight in a big way for all the land that had been grabbed by the hungry settlers.

Through Jon, Jamie had come to know the Comanche well. He didn't make the mistake of considering the Comanche to be docile, but, on the other hand, he'd never known a Comanche to lie or to give him any double-talk.

"Let's see what's going on," Jamie said quietly. He rose high in his saddle and looked over the line of forty-two men presently under his command. "Forward, Sergeant. We ride east. And by the look of things, we'd best hurry."

Sergeant Monahan repeated his order, calling out harshly and demanding haste. Jamie flicked his reins against the roan's shoulders, and the animal took flight with grace and ease. His name was Lucifer, and it fitted the animal well. He was wild—and remarkable.

That was one thing about the U.S. Cavalry, Jamie reckoned as they raced toward the slope of the dune that led to the rise of smoke. They offered a man good horses.

He hadn't had that pleasure in the Confederate cavalry. When the Confederacy had been slowly beaten into her grave, there hadn't been many mounts left. But the war had been over for almost five years now. Jamie was wearing a blue uniform, the same type he'd spent years of his life shooting at. No one, least of all his brothers, had believed he would last a day in the U.S. Cavalry, not after the war. But they had been wrong. Many of the men he was serving with hadn't even been in the war, and frankly, he understood soldiers a whole lot better than he did politicians and carpetbaggers.

And he had liked the life in the saddle on the plains, dealing with the Indians, far better than he had liked to see what had become of the South. This was western Texas, and the reprisals from the war weren't what they were in the eastern Deep South. Everywhere in the cities and towns were the men in tattered gray, many missing limbs, hobbling along on crutches. Homeless and beaten, they had been forced to surrender on the fields, then they had been forced to surrender to things that they hadn't even understood. Taxes forced upon them. Yankee puppets in place where local sheriffs had ruled. The war was horrible—even after it was over.

There *were* good Yanks, and Jamie had always known it. He didn't blame good men for the things that were happening in the South—he blamed the riffraff, the carpetbaggers. He liked his job because he honestly liked a number of the Comanche and the other Indians he dealt with—they still behaved with some sense of honor. He couldn't say that for the carpetbaggers.

Still, he never deceived himself. The Indians were savage fighters; in their attacks, they were often merciless.

But as Jamie felt the power of the handsome roan surge beneath him as he raced the animal toward the rise of fire and smoke, he knew that his days with the cavalry were nearing an end. For a while, he had needed the time to get over the war. Maybe he'd needed to keep fighting for a while just to learn how not to fight. But he'd been a rancher before the war had begun. And he was beginning to feel the need for land again. Good land, rich land. A place where a man could raise cattle in wide open spaces, where he could ride his own property for acres and acres and not see any fences. He imagined a house, a two-story house, with a great big parlor and a good-sized kitchen with huge fireplaces in each to warm away the winter's chill. Maybe it was just time for his wandering days to be over.

"Sweet Jesus!" Sergeant Monahan gasped, reining in beside Jamie as they came to the top of the rise of land.

Jamie silently echoed the thought as he looked down upon the carnage.

The remnants of a wagon train remained below them. Men had attempted to pull the wagons into a defensive circle, but apparently the attack had come too swiftly.

Bodies lay strewn around on the ground. The canvas and wood of the wagons still smoldered and smoked, and where the canvas covers had not burned, several feathered arrows still remained.

Comanche, Jamie thought. He'd heard that things were heating up. Seemed like little disputes would eventually cause a whole-scale war. Monahan had told him he'd heard a rumor about some whites tearing up a small Indian village. Maybe this was done in revenge.

"Damnation!" Sergeant Monahan breathed.

"Let's go," Jamie said.

He started down the cliff and rocks toward the plain on which the wagon train had been attacked. It was dry as tinder, sagebrush blowing around, an occasional cactus protruding from the dirt. He hoped there was no powder or ammunition in the wagons to explode, then he wondered what it would matter once he and his men looked for survivors. The Indians had struck sure and fast, then disappeared somewhere into the plain, up the cliffs and rock. Like the fog wisping away, they had disappeared, and they had left the death and bloodshed behind them.

"Circle carefully!" he advised his men. "A half-dead Comanche is a mean one, remember!"

Riding behind him, Jon Red Feather was silent. Their horses snorted and heaved as they slowly came down the last of the slope, trying to dig in for solid footing. Then they hit the plain, and Jamie spurred his horse to race around and encircle the wagons. There were only five of them.

Poor bastards never had a chance, he thought. He reckoned that someone had been bringing some cattle north, since there was at least a score of dead calves lying glass-eyed and bloody along with the human corpses.

There was definitely no one around. And there was not a single Indian left behind, not a dead one, or a half-dead one, or any other kind of a one.

He dismounted before the corpse of an old man. There was an arrow shaft protruding from his back.

Jamie touched the man's shoulder, turning him over. He swallowed hard. The man had been scalped, and a sloppy job had been done of it. Blood poured down his forehead, still sticky, still warm.

It hadn't happened more than a half hour ago. If they had headed back just a lousy thirty minutes earlier, they might have stopped this carnage.

His men had dismounted too, he realized. At a command from Sergeant Monahan, they were doing the same as he, searching through the downed men for any survivors. Jamie shook his head, standing. Hell. He had just been to see the local Comanche chief. Running River was the peace chief, not the war chief, of the village, but the white men and Running River's people had been doing just fine together for years now.

Jamie liked Running River. And though he had never kidded himself that any Comanche couldn't be warlike when provoked, he couldn't begin to imagine what in hell would have provoked an attack like this one. If the Indians were hungry, they would have stolen the calves, not slaughtered them.

Jon Red Feather was next to him, investigating the body.

"No Comanche did this," he said.

Jamie frowned at him. "Then what do you think? A band of Cheyenne? Maybe a wandering tribe of Utes. We're too far south for it to be the Sioux—"

"I promise you, Lieutenant, no self-respecting Sioux would ever do such a careless job. And the Comanche are warriors, too. They learn from an early age how to lift the hair."

"Then what?" Jamie demanded impatiently. His blood ran cold as he realized that Jon was insinuating that it hadn't been Indians who had made this heinous attack.

It wasn't possible, he told himself. No white man could have killed and mutilated his own kind so savagely.

"Hey, Lieutenant!" Charlie Forbes called to him. Jamie swung around. Forbes was on the ground beside one of the dead men, an old-timer with silver-gray whiskers.

"What is it, Charlie?"

"Looks like this one was hit by an arrow, tried to rise and got shot with a bullet, right in the heart."

He could feel Jon standing behind him. Jamie adjusted his plumed hat and twisted his jaw. "Don't try to tell me the Comanche don't have rifles."

"Hell, I'm not going to tell you that. They get them from the Comancheros—the Comancheros will sell rifles to anyone. Of course, you've got to bear in mind that the Comancheros do buy them from your people."

Jamie didn't say anything. He stepped past Jon and stared at the one wagon that seemed to have had little damage done to it. He thought he heard something.

He had to be imagining things. The job here had been very thorough. Still, he watched the wagon as he straightened his back, trying to get out all the little cricks and pains.

He felt queasy about this thing. And he hadn't felt queasy about anything in quite some time.

He'd grown up on bloodshed. Before he had been twenty, his sister-in-law had been slain by Kansas jayhawkers. Then war had been declared, and though he had fought in a decent regiment under the command of John Hunt Morgan, he had never been able to escape the horror of the border war. From his brother Cole he had learned that the Missouri bushwhackers could behave every bit as monstrously as the jayhawkers.

And a Southern boy called Little Archie Clements had gone around doing a fair bit of scalping in his day. He and his men had stripped down men in blue and shot them without thought, and when they'd finished with the killing they'd gone on to scalping.

He had no right to think that the Indians were any more vicious than the white men. No right at all.

He exhaled slowly. Knowing that the Southern bushwhackers had been every bit as bad as the Northern jayhawkers was one of the reasons he was able to wear this uniform now. A blue cavalry uniform, decorated in blue trim, with a cavalry officer's sword at his side. He didn't carry a military-issue rifle, though. Through four years of civil conflict he had worn his Colts, and he wore them to this day.

His eyes narrowed suddenly. He could have sworn that something in the wagon had moved.

He glanced over his shoulder. Jon was behind him. Jon nodded, aware instantly of Jamie's suspicions. He circled around while Jamie headed straight for the opening at the rear.

He looked in. For a second he could see only shadows in the dim light. Then things took form. There were two bunks in the wagon. Ironically, they were neat and all made up—with the sheets tucked in, the blankets folded back at an inviting angle and the pillows plumped up. Beyond the bunks were trunks and boxes. Everything seemed to be in perfect order.

But it wasn't. He felt just a flicker of movement again. He didn't know if he really saw it or if he felt it, but all his senses were on edge. He hadn't worked in Indian country and spent all this time with Jon Red Feather not to have learned something of his senses. There was someone near. He could feel it in his gut, and he could feel it at the nape of his neck, and he could feel it all the way down his spine. Someone was very near.

"Come on out of there," he said softly. "Come on, now. We don't want to hurt anyone here, we just want you to come on out."

The movement had ceased.

Jon was moving up toward the front of the wagon. The horses, still smelling smoke, whinnied and nickered nervously. Jamie leaped to the floor of the wagon.

His eyes flickered to the left bunk. There was a long, soft white gown lain out by the side. It was sleeveless, low-bodiced and lacy, a woman's nightgown, he thought. And a pretty piece for the dustiness of the road. It did belong with the perfectly made and inviting beds, but it didn't really belong on a wagon train. Was she alive? Had she been some young man's bride? He hadn't seen a woman's corpse, not yet, but then his men were still moving among the bodies.

"Is anyone in here?" he said, moving past the bunks. There were boxes and trunks everywhere. There was a coffeepot, cast down as if someone had been about to use it. There was a frying pan in the middle of the floor, too. He paused, crouching on the balls of his feet, looking at the floor. Coffee was spilled everywhere.

"Come on out now," he said softly. "It's all right, come on out."

He kept moving inward. The shadows in the wagon made it difficult to see. There seemed to be a swirl of soft mauve taffeta, fringed in black lace, set in a heap before him. He reached down carefully, hoping he hadn't come upon another corpse.

He touched a body. He touched warmth. He moved his hand, and it was filled with fullness and living warmth. Instinctively his fingers curled over the full, firm ripeness of a woman's breast. He could feel the shape and weight and the tautness of the nipple with his palm right through the taffeta. She was warm, but very still. Sweet Jesus, let her be alive, he thought, still stunned by the contact his fingers had made.

She was alive. Beyond a doubt, she was alive. She burst from her hiding place with a wicked scream of terror and fury. Startled, he moved back. He had been prepared for danger, for a wounded Comanche, but when he had touched the softness and striking femininity of her form, he had relaxed his guard.

Foolish move.

He backed away, but she screamed again, high and shrill and desperate, a sound like that of a wounded animal. He started to reach for his Colt, but his hand fell quickly as he reminded himself that it was just a woman. A small, delicate woman.

"Ma'am—"

She cast herself upon him with a vengeance, pitting her body against his with a startling ferocity and strength.

"Hey—" he began, but she didn't heed him. She slammed her foot against his leg and brought a fist flailing down upon his shoulder, trying to throw him off balance. He braced himself as she slammed against him, but still she brought them both down upon the floor.

"Hey! Damn, stop!" he yelled, aware of her fragile size, her wild mane of honey-colored hair. Nor could he forget the full feel of her breast within his hand. She was exquisite. He had to be gentle.

Her foot slammed against his shin again. She thrashed with the fury of ten Comanche. Her flailing fist caught his jaw so hard that his teeth rattled.

Gentle . . . hell!

She was a monster. There was no way in hell a man could possibly be gentle and survive. Gritting his teeth harshly he caught her wrists, trying not to hold them in a painful vise.

She screamed again incoherently, freeing her hands to grope on the bunk. He should have held her in a vise! There was just no being nice here. She was like wildfire atop him, raging out of control. He saw a smile of triumph light her features as her fingers curved around something, and she lifted it high.

"Whoa, wait a minute, ma'am—" he began, seeing that she held a long-bladed and lethally sharp bowie knife. Damn! She was going from fists to steel. "Lady, I'm warning you, stop!"

She didn't pay the least bit of attention to him. Rather, she fought on with desperation, drawing up her arm again, preparing to slash the blade across his throat.

Jamie swung out, catching her by the middle, his hands resting beneath the swell of her breasts. He cast her far away from him and struggled to his feet. "I'm the cavalry!" he snapped out. "Damn it, I'm the good guy."

She didn't seem to hear him, or really even see him. Her huge, violet-blue eyes were glazed, he saw, and she barely blinked at his words. She certainly didn't seem to understand them. She screamed again and flew at him. The blade slashed the air uncomfortably close to his windpipe.

He clamped down grimly on his jaw and caught her arm with a stunning blow, sending the blade flying out of the wagon. She gasped, but when he lunged for her, she was ready to fight again, her nails gouging for his eyes. He swore again, capturing her wrists and falling down hard with her upon the floor of the wagon. Struggling to hold her still, he looked up to see that Jon Red Feather was looking in from the driver's seat of the wagon.

"I could have used some help here, you know!" he thundered.

Red Feather grinned. "You—against one little honey-haired girl? Honestly, Lieutenant."

She was no little girl. Lying atop her, Jamie was very aware of that. She was small and slight, but the sweet, provocative fullness of her breasts was now crushed lushly against his cavalry jacket, reminding him that it had been some time since he'd last been to Maybelle's House of Gentlemanly Leisure Pursuits. She fought him still, writhing like a wildcat, and with every twist and turn of her body, he realized more fully just how grown up the woman was, how evocatively mature. She stared at him with death-defying hatred, and as he gazed at her, she lunged against him again, trying to bite his shoulder.

"For the love of God!" he snapped, rolling with her to retain his hold without bringing bodily injury to her or losing a hunk of flesh himself. She freed one wrist from his grasp and began tearing at him again. Their momentum was taking them closer and closer to the rear of the wagon, and then suddenly they were outside it, plunging down to the dirt together.

She shrieked, and he realized then that she was fighting to free herself from his hold rather than fighting to harm him. But he wasn't about to let her go. She was too unpredictable. Their limbs entangled, and her petticoats rode around them. He could feel the slender length of her legs, warm and alive, scantily clad in pantalets, against his own. She reached up to strike him again, and he caught her hand with a serious fury as his patience snapped.

"Enough!"

He drew her hands high over her head and straddled her hips, pinning her down at last. Her hair lay spread out over the dirt in a majestic fan while the Texas sand smudged her beautiful features. She gasped desperately for breath, her breasts rising and falling with her effort. She was down, subdued at last. He released her wrists, remaining straddled upon her, careful to maintain his own weight.

"It's all right—" he tried to tell her, but to no avail. She tried to twist, lashing out, clawing for his face. She caught his chin and drew blood.

"Woman, no more!" he shouted. His hand raised high and with determination, and he caught himself right before he could slap her in return. He saw her eyes close tightly in expectation of the blow, but it did not fall. He held her tight, trying to check his temper, staring at her hard. Then he caught her arms and dragged them high above her head, leaning close and hard against her. His anger faded at last as he saw her eyes go damp with tears she fought to control. She was hysterical, he realized, and yet she had really come at him with an attempt to kill.

She shuddered and gasped, and a trembling rippled through the entire length of her body. Still, he could not trust her to release her. "We're the damned cavalry!" he repeated. "Listen to me! No one is going to hurt you. The Indians are gone. We're the cavalry. We want to help you. You do speak English, don't you?"

"Yes!" she snapped furiously, and the trembling ceased. "Yes, yes, I understand you!" Her eyes beheld him, then glazed over again. "Bastard!" she hissed to him, "Murdering, despicable bastard."

"Murdering bastard? I'm trying to help you."

"I don't believe you!"

Startled by her words, Jamie fell silent. Her eyes remained locked with his, the tears she would not shed highlighting the deep blue color. Her hair fell in tangled streams around them both, like a pool of sunlight just before twilight fell. Watching her, he nearly forgot why he straddled her.

She didn't believe him. He had come to rescue her from the Comanche, and she didn't believe him.

"Listen, now, lady, I am with the cavalry—these men, all of us, we're with the United States Cavalry—"

"Your uniform doesn't mean anything!"

"Lady, you are crazy!" That was it, she had lost her mind. She had watched the savage attack and she had retreated into some fantasy world of fear. "You're all right now, or you will be if you quit trying to hurt me."

"Hurt you! Oh!"

"The Indians are gone—"

"There never were any Indians!"

"No Indians?"

"They dressed like Indians, but they weren't Indians. And you were probably in on it! The law is corrupt, why not the cavalry?"

"Lady, I don't know what you're talking about. I'm Lieutenant Slater out of Fort Vickers, and we've just stumbled upon your present difficulty."

She blinked, and her gaze went guarded. He still held her locked beneath him. His men were coming near, alerted by the commotion.

She gazed around her, past his head, and it seemed that she slowly realized that they really were a cavalry company. Everyone was staring at her with silence, with sympathy.

She looked at Jamie, and a slow flush spread into her features. They were now both painfully aware of the way their bodies came together. Her legs and hips burned against his, bare beneath the thin cotton shield of her pantalets. She wore no corset, he knew that very well, and her breasts seemed to swell, as if with realization of their intimate contact against his chest. She touched her dry lips with the tip of her tongue, and even that seemed an intimate gesture. She squirmed beneath him, but he wasn't about to give her any quarter. He had tried to be as gentle as possible and he was bleeding as if he had been gouged by a mountain cat because of it. A drop of blood from his chin fell upon her bodice even as he thought that he should show her some mercy.

"Lieutenant, let me—"

"What's your name?"

"If you would just—"

"What's your name?"

Her eyes flashed with a silver-blue annoyance as she realized that he was going to hold her until he chose to let her go. "Tess," she snapped. "It's Tess."

"Tess what?"

Her eyes narrowed. "Tess Stuart."

"Where were you going and where were you headed from?"

"Wiltshire. We were bringing some cattle and a printing press. We were heading home from a small town called Dunedin, nearly a ghost town now. That's why we bought the printing press. They didn't need it anymore."

"You said we. Who were you riding with?"

"My—" She hesitated just a moment, her lashes rising and falling swiftly. Tears burned behind her eyelids. She must know that everyone was dead.

She wasn't going to shed those tears. Not in front of him. "My uncle and I. We were heading home to Wiltshire."

He eased himself up a little. He saw her swallow as his thighs tightened against her hip, then she lifted her chin, determined to ignore him, determined to be as cool as if they were discussing the matter over tea in a handsome parlor.

She had inestimable courage. No matter how she was beaten, she would never surrender but would fight it out until the very end. It was there in her eyes. All the silver-blue fire a man could imagine. She was either a complete fool or one of the most extraordinary women he had ever met. Despite her warm honey spill of hair, her large, luminous eyes and her perfect fragile features, she had a spine of steel.

Courage could kill out here in the West. That, he told himself, was why he held to her so tightly. She needed to learn that she could be beaten.

"You're lucky as hell that the Indians didn't see you, you know," he told her hoarsely.

She lifted her chin. "I told you—they weren't Indians."

"Who were they?"

"Von Heusen's men."

"And who the hell is von Heusen?" He was startled when he heard a curious rumble in someone's throat behind him. Still holding her, he whirled around. He looked at the faces of the young men in his company.

"Well? Does someone want to answer me?"

It was Jon Red Feather who drawled out a reply. "Richard von Heusen. Calls himself a rancher sometimes, an entrepreneur at others. You never heard of him, Lieutenant?"

"No, I never heard of him."

"You spend all your time on Indian affairs, Lieutenant," Jon said. "You've been missing out on the shape of things down here."

It was true, Jamie thought. He hadn't wanted to know a lot about the ranchers. He didn't want to see the carpetbaggers, or talk to them.

"You're telling me a guy named von Heusen did this?" he said to Jon.

Jon shrugged. "I can't tell you that."

"I can tell you that he owns a hell of a lot of Texas," Monahan said softly. "It's a good thing it's a big state, else he might own a good half of it."

Jamie looked curiously at the girl. Tess. Her eyes were upon him as she watched him in silence, scathingly. Then she hissed with all the venom of a snake. "He's a carpetbagger, Yank. You ever heard tell about the carpetbaggers down here? They're vultures. They came down upon a defeated and struggling South, and they just kicked the hell out of us. Bought up land the Southern boys couldn't pay their taxes on 'cause the Union didn't want any Confederate currency. Well, Lieutenant, von Heusen bought up Wiltshire."

"You're trying to tell me that a Yankee named von Heusen came out here and shot your wagon train full of arrows? In broad daylight, just like that?"

"No, not just like that," she retorted. "And I doubt that he came out here himself. He had his men all greased down and painted up like Comanche, just in case someone didn't die."

"So you did see Comanche attack the wagon."

"No. That's not what I'm telling you at all. I'm no fool, Lieutenant. I was born and bred out here and I know a Comanche when I see one. And I know a fraud when I see it, too."

"You're saying a group of white men came out here and did this to their own kind?"

"Yes, Lieutenant, how wonderfully perceptive of you. Why, you must have studied at West Point! That's exactly what I'm telling you." Her lashes flicked again. "Von Heusen masterminded this whole thing. You need to arrest him, Lieutenant. Arrest him for murder."

"You said yourself, von Heusen himself probably wasn't even here."

Her eyes widened, her fury seemed to deepen, but she kept her voice low and controlled. "You're not going to arrest him?"

"I'm not a sheriff to begin with, Miss Stuart. And if I were, I'd have to have some kind of proof."

"I'm your proof!"

"It would be your word against his!"

"He wanted our land!"

"Lots of men try to buy land. It doesn't make them murderers!"

She looked as if she wanted to scream, or at least gouge out another pound of his flesh.

"You're a fool!"

"Thank you kindly, ma'am," he retorted.

She gritted her teeth. Tears stung her eyes again. "Get the hell off me."

He realized he was still lying against her, still holding her down. She wasn't trying to kill him anymore. She just looked as if she wanted to escape him, the touch of him, the sight of him.

"I can't go bringing in a man for something without some kind of proof!" he told her furiously. "And not at the word of a half-crazed girl."

"Oh!" She raked out at him again. He caught her hand, then he rose to his feet, dragging her up with him. His jaw twisted hard against the loathing he saw in her eyes.

"Lady—"

"Lieutenant!" Charlie called to him, walking around from the field of corpses. "Shall I start a burial detail?"

She was staring past Charlie, staring at the white-haired man who had been hit by the arrow then shot through the heart.

"Oh, God!" she gasped. She stumbled forward, trying to reach the corpse. The blood fled from her face, and her beautiful features became as ashen as the smoke-charred sky. She paused suddenly, unable to go any farther. "Oh, no, oh, God. Uncle Joe," she whispered, reaching out a hand.

She did not take another step. Even as she reached out, she was falling. Her lashes fluttered over her beautiful eyes, and she began to sink toward the ground.

Instinctively, Jamie rushed forward. He caught her as she fell, sweeping her into his arms. She was as cold as death itself, and remained every bit as pale as he stared down at her.

There was silence all around him. His men looked on.

"Charlie, yes! For God's sake, yes! Get a damned burial detail going, and get it going quickly!"

The men turned around, hustling into action.

And Jamie stared at the girl, wondering just what in hell he was going to do with her. He needed to set her down, to let her lie somewhere. She was a slight burden, weighing practically nothing, or so it seemed.

Yet she was a burden. A definite burden.

He hurried toward her wagon, maneuvered up to the floor of it and laid her on the bed. He meant to turn around and leave her and call for the company surgeon, but for some reason he paused and found himself smoothing out her sun-and-honey hair and brushing her cheek with his knuckles.

He felt a sensation down his back and looked up quickly. Jon Red Feather was just below him, looking into the wagon. "She's still out cold."

"I'll call Captain Peters. He doesn't have much hope, but he's still checking to see if there is any breath remaining in any of the bodies."

"Maybe she's better off being out for a while anyway," Jamie said softly.

"Yeah, maybe." Jon hesitated. "What are we going to do with her?"

"Take her back to the fort. Then someone can escort her on home."

Jon nodded. He smiled suddenly. "Someone, right?"

"Yeah, that's right. Someone."

"She's your responsibility," Jon said. "Your burden—she fell into your arms."

"What? She's a burden I've just set down, Jon."

Jon shook his head. "I don't think so. I don't think so at all. I think that you've taken something upon yourself, Jamie, and I don't think that you can ever really let it go."

Jamie arched a brow. "Yeah? Well, I don't believe you, Jon, and I don't believe her. This von Heusen may be a carpetbagging monster, but I don't believe he can be guilty of this."

"You're just going to have to find out, aren't you?"

"That's not my job, Jon."

"That's not going to matter, is it? 'Cause you see, if the girl is right, then she's in danger. You're going to have out the truth—or you'll be signing her death warrant."

"That's ridiculous, Jon."

"No, it's not. You really can't let her go."

"The hell I can't."

"Oh?" Jon arched a raven-dark brow. "Is that so?" He inclined his head toward Jamie. "Your fingers are still all tied up in her hair, Lieutenant. All tied up. Silken webs maybe, but seems to me that you're all tied up."

Jamie gazed at his hand. His fingers were still hovering over her hair. It was truly the color of honey just kissed by the sun. Much deeper than blond. Too touched by light to be brunette. Golden red.

He pulled his hand away and turned toward Jon with a denial. But Jon, smiling serenely, had already turned away.

"Doc Peters should be free by now," he said quietly, then he was gone.

Jamie stared at the girl. Silken webs . . .

He clenched down hard on his jaw because Jon was right about one thing. Someone would have to discover the truth about her accusations. He didn't believe them. He couldn't believe them.

And yet . . .

If they were true, to leave her alone in the town of Wiltshire might very well be to sign her death warrant.

He swore softly and leaped from the wagon. His leg still hurt from where she had kicked him, and his chin still ached. He could feel it bleeding. Damn her. She was as quick as a sidewinder, as ornery as a mean bear. He could still remember her fury . . .

He paused, for he could remember more. The alluring fullness of her breast beneath his fingers, the softness of her hair, the warmth of her legs entangled with his.

He clenched his fists at his sides and unclenched them, knowing Jon was right, that he was going to have to somehow stick beside her until he could find the truth. She was a hostile little witch . . .

And he already wanted her. Craved her. Ached to touch her, feel more of her.

He swore softly, determined to behave like an officer and a Southern gentleman and solve this dilemma with no more thought for his unwilling companion.

Then he heard her . . . weeping, crying very, very softly as if she were muffling the sound in her pillow. She had come back to consciousness, and it seemed to be a bitter awakening. She cried and cried. He felt her agony, felt it rip and tear into him, and it was terrible. The horror of it reached inside him and touched his heart as it had not been touched in years. He had thought his emotions were stripped away by war.

The girl's wrenching sobs brought them back.
He started to turn, to go to her. He stopped himself.
No. She would not want him.
He stiffened his shoulders and walked on.

Chapter Two

By dusk, all the graves had been dug. By the light of lanterns and camp fires, Reverend Thorne Dryer of Company B read services over the graves.

Tess Stuart stood near the reverend. Her eyes were dry now, and she was silent. Something about her very quietness touched Jamie deeply; she was small, but so very straight, her shoulders square, her lustrous hair hidden beneath a black hat and sweeping veil, her form encompassed in a handsome black dress with gray pearl buttons on the sleeves and at the throat. Dust to dust, earth to earth, ashes to ashes. The reverend called on God to claim His own, to show mercy upon their souls, to give solace to those who remained behind.

Tess stepped forward to drop a single flower on her uncle's grave. She was still silent, and not a tear marred the perfect and tragic beauty of her face.

Then she swung around and headed for her wagon. Jamie didn't mean to follow her, he just discovered that he was doing so. She sensed him just before she reached the wagon and swung around.

"Yes, Captain?"

"Lieutenant, miss. Lieutenant Slater."

"Whatever," she said coolly. "What do you want?"

Hostile! he thought. More hostile than any full tribe of Indians he had come across. She made him itch to set a hard hand against her behind, but she had experienced great pain today. He was a fool to have followed her. He should let her be. He didn't want her as a burden, and she didn't want him as her protector. If she needed a protector.

"Miss Stuart, I just came by to offer my condolences. To see if you were all right, if you might need anything for the night."

"I'm just fine, Lieutenant." She hesitated. "Thank you." She whirled around in her black skirt, then crawled into the wagon. Jamie clenched his hands tight at his sides and returned to the group. The funeral was just about over. Jon and Monahan and a few of the others were stamping down the last of the dirt and erecting wooden crosses over the graves.

The crosses wouldn't stay long. The wind would take them, the dust would wear them away, and in time animals then men would tramp upon them. The West was like that. A man lived and died, and little but bones could be left behind. Bones and dreams.

"I ordered the men to set up camp, Lieutenant, just like you said," Monahan told him.

"Thank you, Sergeant."

"Is that all, Lieutenant?"

"No. Split them even, Monahan. Half can sleep while the second half stay on guard. Just in case."

"In case the Injuns come back," Monahan said.

"In case of anything. This is the cavalry, Sergeant!"

"Yes, sir!"

Monahan saluted sharply. He shouted orders, his voice loud in the night. The men at the graves hurried after Monahan as he started toward the fires where the others were already setting up camp. As Jamie watched, he saw his men melt into the rocks and crevices around them. They were a crack troop. They had campaigned through the most rugged Indian territory in the West and they had all learned their lessons well. They could walk as silently as any brave, shoot with the same deadly accuracy and engage in lethal knife play with ease.

It hadn't been easy for Jamie, not at first. Some of the men had resented the Rebel who had won his promotions so easily. Some hadn't thought a Reb ought to be given a gun, and many had had their doubts about Jamie in Indian country. He had been forced to prove his way at every step, in battle or in negotiations. They'd met up with a tribe of warring Apache once near the border, and he had shown them something of his mettle with his Colts as the battle had begun. Later he found out there had been some whispering about all the Slater brothers, and how deadly he and Cole and Malachi had been during the war. Overnight, it seemed, his reputation had become legendary.

He smiled in the darkness. It had been worth it. He had gained a loyal following, and good men. Nothing would come slipping through his lines tonight. He could rest with ease.

If he could rest at all.

Despite himself he felt his eyes drawn toward the wagon that stood just outside the circle of small cavalry-issue A-frame tents.

"What a burden," Jon said quietly from behind.

Jamie swung around, arching a brow. Jon wasn't the usual subordinate, nor did Jamie expect him to be. "Why don't you quit making the comments and start telling me something about this von Heusen fellow."

"You really interested?" Jon asked.

"Try me. Come on. We'll get some coffee and take a walk up by the ridge."

Monahan gave them coffee from a tin pot at the fire, then the two men wandered up the ridge. Jamie found a seat on a flat rock and rested his boots on another. Jon stood, watching the expanse of the prairie. By the soft light of the moon, it was a beautiful place, the mountains rising like shadows in the distance, the sage rolling in ghostly fashion and the camp fires and stars just lighting up the darkness around them.

"She's telling the truth," Jon said.

"How can you know?" Jamie demanded.

Jon shrugged, scuffed his boots against the earth and turned to hunker down near Jamie. "I know because I've heard of this man before. He wanted land further north during the war. He was a cattle baron up there then, and he was ordered by the government to provide members of the Oglala Sioux on reservation land with meat. He gave them maggot-riddled beef that he wouldn't have fed to his own sows. The Indians formed a delegation to speak with the man. He called it an Indian uprising and soon every rancher in the area was at war with the Sioux. Hundreds, red and white, died. Uselessly, senselessly. And von Heusen was never punished."

Jamie was quiet for a moment. He stared toward the remnants of the wagon train.

"So he's got property now in Wiltshire. And he wants more. And he likes to rile up the Indians. I still can't do anything, Jon. Even if I believed Miss Stuart, there wouldn't be anything I could do."

"Because you can't prove anything."

"Exactly. And no sane white man is going to believe it."

"That's too bad," Jon said after a moment. "That's really too bad. I don't think Miss Stuart can survive very long."

"Come on, Jon, stop it! No matter how powerful this von Heusen is, he can't just out-and-out murder the woman! The whole town would be up in arms. He can't own the whole damned town!"

Jon shrugged. "He owns the sheriff. And we both know that he doesn't have to out-and-out murder the girl. There are ways."

"Damn!" Jamie stood up, dusting the dirt off the rump of his breeches with his hat.

"So what are you going to do?"

"I told you. We're riding back to the fort—"

"And then?"

"Let's get there, eh?"

Jon stood. "I just wanted you to know, Jamie, that if you decide to take some of that time the government owes you, I'll go with you."

"I'm not taking any time."

"Yeah. Sure. Whatever you say, Slater."

Jamie paused, grinning. "Thanks, Red Feather. I appreciate it. But believe me, I'm sure I'm not the escort Miss Stuart has in mind."

Jon pulled his hat low over his eyes, grinning. "Well, Jamie, me lad, we don't always know just exactly what it is that we need, now, do we? Good night." Without waiting for a reply he walked down the ridge.

Jamie stayed on the ridge a while longer, looking at the camp fires. He'd stay up with the first group on watch; Monahan would stay up with the second.

But even when he saw the guard change and the sergeant take his place silently upon a high ridge, he discovered he couldn't sleep. The cot didn't bother him—he had slept on much less comfortable beds—nor did the night sounds, or even the nightmare memories of the day.

She bothered him . . .

Knowing that she slept not far away. Or lay awake as he did. Perhaps, in private, the tears streamed down her face. Or perhaps she was silent still, done with the past, determined to think of the future. She believed what she was saying to him. She believed that the wagon train had been attacked by white men dressed up like Indians. She wouldn't let it rest.

He groaned and pulled his pillow over his head. It wasn't exactly as if she was asking for his help. She'd made it clear she didn't even want to hear his voice. He owed her nothing, he owed the situation nothing.

Yes, he did.

He owed the people who had died here today, and he owed the Comanche, who were going to be blamed for this. And he owed all the people who would die in the bloody wars to follow if something wasn't proven one way or the other.

Still, he didn't sleep. He lay awake and he wondered about the woman with the sun-honey hair who lay not a hundred yards away in the canvas-covered wagon.

Sometime during the night Tess slept, but long before dawn she was wide awake again, reliving every moment of what had happened. Her grief and rage were so deep that she wanted to scream aloud, but screaming again would do no good, and she had already cried until she felt that her tears were a river that had run as dry as the plain with its sagebrush and dust.

She cast her feet to the floor and stared across the darkened wagon to the bunk where her Uncle Joseph should have been sleeping, where he would sleep no more. Joe would lie out here in the plain for eternity, and his body would become bone, and in the decades to come, no one would really know that a brave and courageous man had died here fighting, even if he'd barely had a chance to raise a weapon. Joe had never given in, not once. He couldn't be intimidated. He had printed the truth in the *Wiltshire Sun*, and he had held fast to everything that was his.

And he had died for it.

Tess pulled on her shoes and laced them high up her ankles, then silently slipped from the wagon. The cavalry camp fires were burning very low. Dawn couldn't be far away. Soldiers were sleeping in the A-frame tents, she knew, and more soldiers were awake, on guard, one with the rocks and cliffs that rose around the edge of the plain.

They were on guard—against Indians!

She clenched her jaw hard, glad of the anger, for it helped to temper the grief. What kind of a fool did they think she was? Not they—him! That Yank lieutenant with the deep, soft drawl.

The one she'd like to see staked out for the ants.

Walking silently through the night, she came upon the graves at last. She closed her eyes and she meant to pray, but it wasn't prayers that came to her lips. Goodbye, Joe, I loved you! I loved you so very much! I won't be able to come back here, I'm sure, but you're the one who taught me how special the soul was, and how little it had to do with the body. Uncle Joe, you were really beautiful. For all that grizzled face of yours and your broken nose, you were the most beautiful person I ever knew...I won't let you have died for nothing, I swear it. I won't lose. I'll keep the paper going, and I'll hold onto the land. I don't know how I'll do it, but I will, I swear it, I promise. I promise, with all my heart...

Her thoughts trailed off and she turned around, uncannily aware that she wasn't alone.

She wasn't.

The tall lieutenant with the wicked force to his arms was standing not far behind her, silent in the night. In the haze of the coming morning, he seemed to be a towering, implacable form. He wasn't a heavy man, but she had discovered in her wild fight with him that his shoulders were broad, that his arms and chest were well and tautly muscled, that he was as lean and sleek and powerful as a puma, agile and quick. His eyes were a most interesting shade of gray, remote, enigmatic, and yet she felt their acuteness each time they fell upon her. She realized, in the late shadows of night, that he was an arresting man. Handsome . . . but not because of perfect features or any gentleness about him. His face was ruggedly hewn, but with clean, strong lines. His jaw was firm and square, his cheekbones were high, his eyes were wide and well set, his forehead was broad. He had a look of the west about him, and a look of the war, perhaps.

Something seemed to stir within her, startling her. He was compelling in his very masculinity, she decided. His mouth could be hard, controlled, grim, but then again, when his lips did move, they were strikingly sensual. And then there was the color of his eyes, and the way they could fall upon her. She discovered that her palms were damp and her lips were dry. It was difficult not to wonder about the man. She'd already touched him. She knew the hot feel of his muscles beneath her fingers, she knew the warmth and tension of his body stretched over hers. She hadn't realized it until this moment. She had been fighting him.

But now she remembered. Every sensation.

She clenched her fingers into fists at her sides, remembering that this was the man in charge. The man who refused to believe her. She'd lived here all her life. She knew the difference between a white man and a Comanche. She definitely knew the difference between von Heusen's men and Comanche.

The Comanche had morals—and a sense of honor.

"What are you doing here?" she asked, determined to keep her chin high, her voice level, her dignity intact. She'd already scuffled with him once—but he wouldn't find her in such a tempest ever again. He could doubt her from here to eternity. She'd give him no opportunity to find her hysterical or babbling.

"I heard you come here. I didn't mean to intrude, I just wanted to make sure that you were all right."

She couldn't help it—she felt as if the hackles rose on her neck just like those of a wolf, as if every nerve ending in her body had come alive to scream. Things seemed to snap and crackle in the air, and she longed to kick him in the shin again. He was worried about her. Because he considered her to be unhinged!

"I'm just fine, Lieutenant."

"Look, Miss Stuart—"

"You look, Lieutenant. You have your opinions, I have mine. And they don't seem to coincide in any way. I'm fine. Your men are guarding the camp. I'm quite sure that a ferret couldn't slip by them. They are, after all, your men, and I'm quite sure that they've got the fear of God whipped deeply into them."

"Oh, really? The fear of God is whipped into them?"

He cocked his head at an angle, and his mouth moved. Sensual. When it wasn't cast into one of those grim lines, it was wide and generous, and she discovered that she was staring at his lips.

Tess stepped back, almost as if he had reached out to touch her, which he had not. He was keeping his distance. His feet were firmly planted on the ground, his arms were crossed over his chest, and the look he gave her was one of amusement.

"Yankee discipline," she said sweetly. He didn't answer her, but something seemed to fall over his eyes, something very hostile. Well, they'd all survived the war. Hostility died hard.

She hadn't meant to continue hating the North. The war had been exhausting. It had been good to hear that it was over, that no one else was going to die. But then the carpetbaggers had descended. Von Heusen, in particular, and more of his ilk. Men who bought the land from decent people who couldn't pay their taxes.

Von Heusen went further. When he wanted a ranch, the cattle had a habit of disappearing. When the rancher tried to buy feed, it was moldy and bad. And sometimes even the rancher disappeared. Von Heusen had hired guns to go with him every time he moved.

Hired guns . . . who could be painted bronze and wear buckskin and attack with tomahawks and rifles.

She was hostile, she realized. Really hostile. Maybe this Yankee lieutenant wouldn't do the things von Heusen had done, but he hadn't promised her a lick of help in righting things. He didn't care.

The only people who cared were the citizens of Wiltshire, and there weren't really all that many left. Even the sheriff was one of von Heusen's men, put into office during one of the shadiest elections imaginable.

It was light, Tess realized. The daylight had come as they had stood there, staring at one another. Against the pink of the sky, Lieutenant Slater suddenly seemed a towering menace. A pulse beat at the base of his throat as he watched her. His jaw seemed cast into a slight twist, then locked as if it held back his temper. There was a good ten feet between them, and still she felt his heat, body heat. Her heart was beating too quickly, and something warm churned deep within her abdomen while little touches of mercury seemed to dance along her back. She needed to break away from him. She despised his attitude; she couldn't help but despise him for the blue uniform that reminded her so completely of the war.

He wore it well, his dark, plumed hat pulled low over his eyes, his shoulders broad in the navy blue cavalry shirt, his legs long, his hips trim . . .

She had to walk past him. She swallowed hard and forced herself to smile. "If you'll excuse me, Lieutenant, I'm sure that you're anxious to ride as quickly as possible."

She started to walk. The closer she came to him the harder her heart beat. She was almost past him.

Then his arm snaked out and he caught her elbow. Her heart slammed against her chest as she looked into his smoke-gray eyes, sizzling into hers beneath the sun. His eyes were still shadowed by the brim of his hat.

"I am sorry, Miss Stuart. I'm very sorry."

She wanted to speak. Her throat was dry. She felt his fingers upon her as if they burned. She was acutely aware of the warmth and strength of his body.

She stared at his hand upon her and pulled from his grasp. "Thank you, Lieutenant," she managed to say, then she forgot her dignity and fled.

In an hour they were ready to start out. Lieutenant Slater ordered the downed and useless wagons burned. He almost ordered her new printing press burned, but Tess forgot all about a low-toned and well-modulated voice and dignified behavior and came bursting from her wagon to demand that the press be carried into something that was still capable of rolling.

"What in hell is it?" the lieutenant demanded impatiently.

"A press! A printing press! I need it for the *Wiltshire Sun*!"

"Your uncle's newspaper? But he's—dead, Miss Stuart."

"The *Wiltshire Sun* is not dead, Lieutenant, nor do I intend to let it die. I will not take a step without that printing press."

A spark of silver touched his eyes as they narrowed upon her. "Don't threaten me, Miss Stuart."

"I'm not threatening! I'm telling you what will and will not happen."

He took a step toward her and spoke very quietly. "Miss Stuart, you will move when I say so, ma'am, because I'll set you upon your pretty little—er—rump within the wagon, and one of my men will drive."

"You wouldn't dare! I'll tell your superiors—"

"You tell them anything you want. Want to test me?"

She gritted her teeth and stared into his eyes. "I need that press, Lieutenant."

He stood still, hard, cold, immobile.

"Lieutenant, please! I need that printing press! It would only take your men a few minutes. Please!"

For a moment he continued to stare at her. Then he turned around, calling to Sergeant Monahan. The men were ordered to move the press into one of the wagons that could still roll. "Private Harper!" Slater called. "Hitch your horse to the rear and drive the extra wagon."

"Yes, sir!"

Tess exhaled slowly. Lieutenant Slater cast her a hard glare, then turned around. He strode away, calling for his men to see to the last of the fires, then mount up.

When he had gone, Tess realized that the handsome Indian with the striking eyes was silently watching her. He saluted with a smile, as if she had managed very well. Then he, too, turned away.

Tess was certain it was a long day for the cavalry. The men were accustomed to moving quickly—now they were burdened down by the wagons. The landscape was beautiful—and monotonous. The land was a constant pale, dusty brown, the little bit of color against it the dull green of sage and cactus.

She was determined not to complain, but the dust soon covered her, and after endless hours of driving the six mules that pulled her wagon, she was exhausted. Her arms hurt in places where she hadn't realized she had muscles. She could have said something, she was certain. The majority of the young cavalry men were kind and solicitous, riding by her whenever they could, asking her if she needed anything.

But each time a man drove by, she saw Lieutenant Slater in the distance beyond him, and so she smiled sweetly and said that she was doing very well.

He had to stop. He had to stop sometime.

He finally called a halt when the sun began to fall into the horizon and the whole world went pink again. He stayed away from her, but she knew he was watching her. Was he judging her? Trying to decide if she was crazy or if she was having female whimsies? She had to keep a tight lid on her temper. No matter what he did or said, she had to keep quiet. When she reached his fort she would speak calmly and rationally with the commander, and she would make him understand.

"Miss Stuart!" Sergeant Monahan rode over to her, then dismounted from his horse. "Let me help me you down, miss. I'll see to your mules and the wagon."

"Thank you, Sergeant. I can really—"

She broke off, nearly falling as he helped her from the wagon. He held her steady as her feet touched the ground, and she smiled for him. "Thank you again. I guess I do need some help."

"At your service."

She felt she was being watched. She looked over Monahan's shoulder and there was Slater, still mounted on his huge horse, overseeing his men as they broke their formation to make camp. He tipped his hat to her, and she felt something run hot and liquid inside her. He was watching her in Monahan's arms, and very likely acknowledging a feminine ability to draw others to handle her own responsibilities. Her temper started to soar.

Monahan stepped back, and his wide baby blue eyes were full of gentleness and kindness and maybe just a bit of adoration. He was a wonderful man, just like a great big shaggy bear. The devil to Lieutenant Slater. If his men wanted to behave like gentlemen, she had no intention of stopping them.

"Miss Stuart, Lieutenant Slater rode this far because we know this place. If you go just past that ridge yonder, there's the prettiest little brook. It's mostly surrounded by dry rock, but the water runs pure and clean. There's an area up there far from where we'll water the horses. You can take a walk up there and find all the privacy you might desire."

"Thank you again, Sergeant," Tess said. "I would dearly love a bath. I'll take you up on your suggestion." She hurried to the back of the wagon and found clean clothing, a bar of soap and a towel. When she emerged again, Sergeant Monahan was unharnessing the mules. He pointed toward the ridge. She could see that some of the soldiers were headed in the other direction. She smiled again and hurried toward the ridge. She was puffing slightly when she walked over it, but then she gasped with delight.

The brook was surrounded by boulders and high rocks, but there were little tufts of grass growing between the rocks, and a few wildflowers had managed to eke out an existence there. The evening was pink and gold and very beautiful, and she could hear the sound of the water as it ran. It looked so cool and delicious after the dry dust of the day.

She clambered down the rocks to a broad ledge, dropped her towel and soap and clothing and sat down, hurriedly untying her shoes. Staring at the clean, fresh water, she pulled her blouse from her skirt and quickly shed it, then her skirt and shift and pantalets and hose. She stepped down the rock, so entranced by the water that she never once realized she wasn't alone.

Barefoot and bare-chested, his cavalry trousers rolled above his ankles, Jamie Slater sat in the shadow of a rock, swearing softly. His own bath had just gone straight downhill. And he didn't mean to be a voyeur, but she had stripped so damned quickly, and he'd been so darned surprised that he had just stayed there.

Watching.

She was like a nymph, an angel cast out from the evils of the heat and the plain. Her skin was alabaster, her breasts perfect. Her waist was very trim, her derriere rich and lush and flaring out from that narrow waist, and her legs were so long and shapely that they suggested the most decadent dreams, the most sensual imaginings. Angel...vixen...her hair streamed around her like the sunset, thick and cascading, falling over her bare shoulders, curling around her breasts, haunting, teasing, evocative.

He fell back, groaning slightly.

Tess didn't see him. She plunged into the water, amazed that she could still draw such simple pleasure when the pain of Joe's loss was still so strongly with her. But she was still alive, and the water was so cool and clean after the dust and filth of the plains. It came just to her ankles at first, and there were little rocks and pebbles beneath her feet, so she had to be careful walking. Then the water became deeper, and she sank into it, stretching out, soaking her hair, float-

ng, shivering, delighted. The sun was still warm, the water
almost cold, and together they were marvelous. She swam
around in the shallows, careful not to hit her arms and legs
on the pebbles, then found a smooth shelf to stand on and
scrubbed herself thoroughly with the soap, rising to form
rich suds, sinking beneath the surface again to rinse them
away. She scrubbed her hair, feeling wonderful as she re-
moved the dirt and grime from her scalp. Finally she rose
from the water. She paused, ringing out her hair, then hur-
ied to where she had left her things. She picked up her towel
and studiously rubbed herself dry, then sat upon the ledge
to dry her hair before donning her clean clothing.

She stretched, closing her eyes and leaning against the
rock, which was still warm from the sun. The last of the
dying rays touched her body, and she closed her eyes for a
moment.

When she opened them, she nearly screamed.

Lieutenant Slater was standing above her. His shirt hung
open over his chest, and he was barefoot and grim. She
opened her mouth to protest. She was stark naked, and he
was staring down at her without the least apology.

But when she opened her mouth, he suddenly drew his
gun and fired off several shots.

She'd never seen a gun move so fast or heard anything like
the way the Colt spit and fired in fury.

She didn't gasp; she didn't scream. She thought he had
lost his mind, but when she twisted to grasp her towel, she
paused, stunned, staring at the carcass of the dead moccasin that had been barely a foot away from her.

She looked up at the lieutenant, unable to speak, unable
to move. He had saved her life, she realized. She had been
completely unaware of the snake that she had so carelessly
disturbed.

He didn't say anything, just looked at her, his gray eyes sliding over her body, and everywhere they touched her, she felt fire coursing through her. She felt her nipples harden, and she was horrified that they did so, but still she didn't manage to say a word.

He slid his Colt into his hip holster and spoke at last. "You need to be more careful about the rocks you choose, Miss Stuart," he said.

She heard running footsteps. He quickly reached for her towel and handed it to her. She clutched it to her breasts as a young private suddenly appeared.

"Lieutenant! I heard the shots!"

"It's all right, Hardy. It was me. A snake. Nothing that could shoot back."

The private was staring at them, wide-eyed.

"That's all, Hardy."

"Yes, sir, Lieutenant."

The private saluted. Slater saluted in return. Then he tipped his hat to her and turned around. Tess reddened to a dark crimson and watched as he picked his way upstream. She saw his socks and boots on a flat boulder, and her breath seemed to catch in her throat. He had been there all the time.

She leaped to her feet and hurried into her fresh clean clothing with shaking fingers. She could barely tie her pink-ribboned corset, and she had to do the buttons on her blouse twice. She pulled on clean hose and her shoes and looked at the rock.

He was waiting. Waiting for her to leave. He sat on the ledge, his toes in the water.

He looked up as if he felt her watching him. "It's almost dark, Miss Stuart, if you don't mind."

"If I don't mind! You—you sat there through my bath, Lieutenant!" she sputtered.

"Lucky I did," he replied pleasantly.

She was alive. Maybe she was lucky. But that wasn't the point, and he knew it.

He shrugged, rising, casting off his shirt. "It really doesn't matter that much to me, Miss Stuart. You're welcome to stay. Maybe you'll even want to join me... ?"

She swung around, furious. He was ready to strip down with her standing right there. He'd sat and stared at her while she had been completely naked, assuming she was alone...

She'd given him a whole damned show in the water!

Swearing softly, she plodded away, anxious to quit the brook. She hurried to her wagon and sat on the bunk, hugging her arms to her chest.

Damn him. Just remembering his eyes upon her made her breasts swell again and her nipples harden to taut peaks. When she closed her eyes it didn't help. She remembered the way that his shirt had hung open over his chest, and the sandy dark hair that grew in rich profusion there, the ripple of tight muscle on his abdomen, the swell of it at his breast and shoulders.

"Miss Stuart?" It was Sergeant Monahan.

"Yes?" She almost shouted the word.

He was at the rear of the wagon, smiling. "Wasn't that just the prettiest little brook you've ever seen?"

"Absolutely beautiful," she said evenly. But it didn't matter—apparently word of the shots had gotten out. Another one of the men stepped behind Monahan, nodding respectfully to her.

"Monahan! Hardy says she almost got it from a moccasin. Luckily the lieutenant was near and blasted the thing to kingdom come. Ma'am, it is the prettiest little brook around, but you be careful from here on out, you hear? You've become pretty important to all of us."

"Thank you, that's very kind," she murmured, but she knew that she was blushing again. Everyone knew what had happened.

But they didn't really know. They didn't know what it had felt like when his eyes had touched her naked flesh . . .

"Rations aren't much, ma'am, but one of the boys brought in a few trout. May I fix you a plate and bring you some coffee?" Monahan asked her.

"Please," she agreed. "That would be very nice."

Monahan brought her a plate of food, the other young man brought her coffee. She thanked them both. Then, as she ate, it seemed that every man in the company came by to see how she was, if she would like anything, if she needed anything, anything at all, for the night.

She thanked them all, and when they left, and the darkness fell, and the camp became silent, she smiled. They were Yanks, but a good group of them. Maybe there was hope. She believed again. There were von Heusens in the world but there were others, too, good people. She just had to keep fighting. She had to hold on to the ranch and she had to keep the Wiltshire newspaper going.

"Miss Stuart."

She started, feeling every nerve within her body come alive. She knew the voice. Knew the deep tone, low and husky and somehow capable of slipping beneath her skin. It was a sensual, sexy voice, and it awakened things in her she was certain had died beneath the rifle fire of the last years of the war.

She inhaled quickly. If she was silent, he might just walk away. He might believe that she slept and just walk away.

But he wouldn't. He knew she was awake. She sensed it, and she resented him for his easy knowledge of her.

"Yes?" she asked crisply.

"I just wanted to make sure that you were all right."

"I'm fine, Lieutenant."

"Is there anything you need?"

"I want you to believe me, Lieutenant. And you're not offering me that."

He was silent. She hoped he would turn away, but she sensed he was smiling.

"You didn't thank me. For saving your life."

"Ah, yes. Thank you for saving my life." She found herself crawling the length of the bunk, then defying him over the rear edge of the wagon. "Lieutenant?"

"Yes?"

"Come closer, please."

He took a step nearer. Tess let her hand fly across his cheek. He instantly caught her wrist, and she was glad of the surprised and furious fire in his eyes as they caught hers. She kept smiling, even if his fingers did seem to be a vise around her, even if the air seemed charged with electricity.

Even if she was just a little bit afraid that he was going to drag her out of the wagon and down beneath him into the dirt.

"I do thank you for saving my life, Lieutenant. But that was for the ungentlemanly way in which you did so."

She pulled on her hand. He didn't let go. His eyes glittered silver in the moonlight.

"I'll try to remember, Miss Stuart, that you are most particular about the way a man goes about saving your life," he told her.

"You know exactly what I'm saying."

"I never meant to give you offense."

"Never?"

"I do swear so, Miss Stuart. I kept my presence quiet because you were as bare as a baby before I realized it. And then, well, I do admit, I was caught rather speechless."

"You weren't speechless on the rock!"

He smiled slowly. "No."

"Oh, you . . . Yank!"

She tugged on her wrist again. He didn't release her at first, then his fingers slowly unwound. He was smiling, she realized. And his eyes fell over her again, and she felt as if he was burning the sight of her into his memory. A flame shot high within her, and she didn't know if she was horrified—or fascinated.

"Good night, Miss Stuart," he said softly.

Then he did walk away. She didn't move, and after a moment he turned back.

"Miss Stuart?"

"What?"

He hesitated. "You're a very beautiful woman. Very beautiful."

He didn't wait for an answer. He walked away and disappeared into the night.

Chapter Three

Two days later, they reached the fort.

It was, Tess thought, a typical military fort in Indian country. The walls of the stockade were high, maybe twenty-five feet high, and built of dark sturdy logs. She heard the sound of a bugle while they were still some distance from the fort, then the huge wooden gate swung open to allow their party to enter. Looking up as they went into the compound, Tess saw armed guards in their cavalry blue lined up on all the catwalks and staring down at them.

She was grateful to have reached the fort. She was driving her mules, swearing to them beneath her breath, and wondering if the calluses would ever leave her fingers. She'd gotten them right through Uncle Joe's heavy leather gloves. She was sweaty, salty and sticky, and her hair was coming loose from the neat braid she'd twisted at her nape. She had said that she could manage—and Lieutenant Slater had let her do just that.

His men had continued to be very kind, and she had continued to smile and be as gracious as she could in return. He had kept his distance since he had left her that night, but she had felt his eyes on her.

Always... his eyes were on her. When she drove the wagon, she would suddenly feel a warmth, and she would look around to discover that he was no longer at the head of the column, but had ridden back and was watching her. And at night, when one of the men would bring her coffee or food, he would stare across the distance of the camp fire. And by night she heard footsteps, and she wondered if he wasn't walking by to determine if she was sleeping. If she was safe. Or did he walk by to discover if she might still be awake?

He infuriated her, but she was also glad, and she realized that she felt safe. Not because she was surrounded by thirty or so cavalry men, but because he was walking by, because he was near.

But now they had come to the fort. He would turn her over to his commander and disappear from her life. Someone would be assigned to see her to Wiltshire, and she need never see him again. Never feel his eyes again, the touch of smoke gray and insinuation that warmed everything within her and seemed to caress her as if he saw her again as he had by the brook.

They were in front of the command post. Tess pulled hard on the reins, dropped them and started to leap from the driver's seat. She smiled, for Jon Red Feather was there to help her. She had grown to like the man very much: his striking, sturdy appearance, his silence and his carefully chosen words. And she sensed that he believed her when others might not.

He set her upon the ground. She thanked him then looked at all the confusion around her. Wives, children and perhaps lovers had spilled from the various buildings in the compound to greet the returning men. Monahan had called out an order dismissing them all, and the band was quickly breaking up. Lieutenant Slater was striding up the steps to the broad porch that encircled the command post, saluting the tall, gray-haired man who awaited him. Jon indicated the steps. "Miss Stuart, I believe the colonel will want a statement from you as soon as possible. I'll see to your accommodations for the evening and return shortly."

He walked her to the porch. Apparently Slater had already explained something about her, for the colonel was quick to offer her a hand and guide her up the steps. "Miss Stuart, our most sincere condolences on the loss of your uncle, but may I say that we are heartily glad that you have survived to be here today."

"Thank you," Tess said. It was strange. It already seemed like the whole thing had happened in the distant past. Days on the plains could do that, she decided. And yet, when the colonel spoke so solicitously of Uncle Joe, all the pain and the loneliness rushed back.

She tried to swallow them down. She needed to impress this man with intelligence and determination, not a fit of tears. She didn't want to be patted on the back. She wanted to be believed.

"Miss Stuart, if you would be so good as to join us inside, the colonel would like to speak with you," Slater said. There was a startling light in his eyes as they touched her. Not amusement, but something else. Almost a challenge. He wanted to see if she would back down, she thought.

Well, she wouldn't.

She walked past both men and into a large office with file cabinets and a massive desk and a multitude of crude wooden chairs. Slater pulled out a chair for her, and she sat down as regally as she could manage, pulling off her rough leather gloves and letting them fall into her lap. She felt Slater's eyes, and she looked up then looked quickly away. He had seen the blisters and calluses on her hands.

The colonel took his seat behind the desk. He was an elderly man, whose gentle blue eyes seemed to belie his position as a commander of such a post. His voice, too, was gentle. Tess thought he was genuinely grateful to see her alive, even if he had never met her before. "Would you like coffee, Miss Stuart? I'm afraid I've no tea to offer you—"

"Coffee will be just fine, thank you," Tess said.

She hadn't realized that there was another man in the room until a silent young corporal stepped forward to bring her a tin mug of black coffee. She thanked him and an awkward moment followed. Then the colonel sat forward, folding his hands on the desk. "Miss Stuart, Lieutenant Slater informs me that you have claimed that it was not Indians who set upon your band."

"That's right, sir."

"Then who?"

"White men. Hired guns for a man named von Heusen. He is trying to take my uncle's property and—"

"He'd have men attack a whole wagon train to obtain your uncle's property? Think now, Miss Stuart, is that logical?"

She gritted her teeth. Slater was watching her politely. She wanted to kick him. "It wasn't a large wagon train, Colonel. We've had good relations with the Comanche in our area, and my uncle wasn't afraid of the Comanche! We were traveling with a very small party, a few hired hands, my uncle—"

"Maybe, Miss Stuart, the Indians weren't Comanche. Maybe they were a stray band of Apache looking for easy prey, or Shoshone down from the mountains, or maybe even an offshoot of the Sioux—"

"No Indian attacked that wagon train."

Tess swung around. Jon Red Feather had come into the room. He helped himself to coffee, then pulled up the chair beside Slater. He grinned at his friend, then addressed the colonel. "I'm sure that Miss Stuart does know a Comanche when she sees one, sir. And it wasn't Apache. Apache usually only scalp Mexicans—in retaliation." He turned and smiled at Tess. "And I can promise you that what was done was not done by the Sioux. A Sioux would never have left Miss Stuart behind."

A shiver ran down Tess's spine. She didn't know if Jon meant that the Sioux would have taken her with them—or that they would have been sure to kill and scalp her, too.

The colonel lifted his hands. Even with Jon corroborating her story, he didn't seem to believe her. Or if he did believe her, he had no intention of helping her. "Miss Stuart, I have heard of this von Heusen. He has big money, and big connections, and I understand he owns half the town—"

"Literally, Colonel. He owns the judge and the sheriff and the deputies."

"Now, Miss Stuart, those are frightful charges—"

"They are true charges."

"But don't you see, Miss Stuart, you'd have to go into a court of law against this man. And you'd have to charge him in Wiltshire, and like you said . . ." His voice trailed away. "Why don't you think of heading back east, Miss Stuart?"

She was up on her feet instantly. "Head back east? I have never been east, Colonel. I was born here in Texas. My grandparents helped found Wiltshire. And the little bit of town that von Heusen doesn't own yet, I still do. I have no intention of turning it over to him! Colonel, there's nothing else that I can tell you. I have had a rather trying few days. If there's some place where I might rest, I'll be most grateful to accept your hospitality for a night or two. Then, sir, I have to get home. I have a ranch and a paper that need my expertise."

The colonel was on his feet, too, and she sensed that, behind her, Jon and Slater had also risen. She spun around, feeling Slater's eyes, certain that he was laughing at her again.

But he wasn't laughing. His eyes were upon her, smoky and gray and enigmatic. She sensed that she had finally gained a certain admiration from him. What good it could do her, she didn't know. The colonel had been her last hope. Now the battle was hers, and hers alone.

"Miss Stuart, I'd like to help you if I could—"

"Nonsense, Colonel. You don't believe a word I'm saying," Tess told him sweetly. "That's your prerogative, sir. I am very fatigued..."

"Miss Stuart can take the old Casey place while she's here," Jon said. "Dolly Simmons is there now, with linens and towels."

"I shall be most grateful to the Caseys," Tess said.

"No need," Slater drawled. "Casey is dead. Caught a Comanche arrow last year. His wife went on back east."

He was taunting her, and she smiled despite it. "I have told you all, Lieutenant, I've never been east—"

"Oh, not that east, Miss Stuart. Mrs. Casey and the kids went to live in Houston, that's all."

"Well, I rather like the area I live in," she said sweetly, then she turned to the colonel. "If I may, sir...?"

"Of course, of course! Jamie, you and Jon will please escort the young lady to her quarters. And Miss Stuart, if it's Wiltshire you're insisting on reaching, I'll arrange you an escort just as soon as possible."

"Thank you."

Jon opened the door. Tess sailed through it. Slater followed her. "It's this way, Tess," Jon told her. He'd never used her first name before, and certainly not as he did now, intimately, as if they were old friends. There was a bright light to his striking green eyes, and she realized that it was for the benefit of Jamie Slater. Jamie. Silently, she rolled the name on her tongue. "Lieutenant" seemed to fit him better.

Not always...Not that day he had looked down at her on the rocks after shooting the snake. His hair had been ruffled, his shirt had fallen open, and she had wanted to touch him, to reach out and feel the vital movement of his flesh, so bronze beneath the setting sun. Then, then the name Jamie might have fit him just right. It was an intimate name, a name for friends, or for lovers.

He was behind her still. Jon Red Feather was pointing things out to her. "That's a general store, and there's our one and only alehouse, we don't dare call it a saloon. And down there is the coffeehouse for the ladies. We've a number of women at the fort here. The colonel approves of the married men having their wives with them, and since the fort is strong and secure..." He shrugged. "Then, of course, we have the stores and the alehouse and the coffeehouse, so we've a few young and unattached ladies, which makes it nice for the soldiers at the dances."

"Dances!"

"Why, Miss Stuart, we do try to be civilized out here in the wilderness."

"Desert," Jamie Slater said from behind them. "I think it's really more a desert than a wilderness, don't you, Jon?" He didn't wait for an answer, but continued, "There's the Casey house right there." He strode up three steps to a small house that seemed to share a supporting wall with the structure beside it.

The door burst open suddenly. There was a large buxom woman standing there. She had an ageless quality about her, for her features were plump and clear, her eyes were dark and merry, and it was difficult to see if her hair was blond or silver. "You poor dear! You poor, poor dear! Caught up in that awful Indian attack—"

"Miss Stuart doesn't believe that it was Indians, Dolly," Jamie Slater said evenly.

Dolly waved a hand in the air. "Don't matter who it was, does it? It was awful and heinous and cruel and this poor girl lost her friends and her uncle. It was your uncle, right, dear?"

"Yes," Tess said softly.

Dolly had a hand upon her shoulders, drawing her into the house. Jon and Jamie Slater would have followed except that Dolly inserted her grand frame between them and the doorway. "Jon, Jamie, get on with you now. I'll see to Miss Stuart. I'm sure you were right decent to her on the trail, but she's had a bad time of it and I'm going to see to it that she has some time to rest, and I'm going to give her a nice long bath, some home-cooked food, and then I'm going to put her to bed for the night. She needs a little tenderness right now, and I'm not so sure you're the pair to provide it!"

"Right, Dolly," Jon said. Amused, he stepped back.

Jamie Slater tipped his hat to Tess over Dolly's broad shoulder. His lip, too, was curled with a certain amusement, and Tess felt that, for once, she could too easily read the message behind his smoke-gray eyes. He thought that she needed tenderness just about as much as a porcupine did.

"Good evening, Miss Stuart. I do hope that you'll be feeling better soon."

"If you're lucky, Jamie Slater, she'll be up and about for the dance tomorrow night."

"If I'm lucky—" Jamie started to murmur.

"Well, hell, there's no lack of young men around here, Lieutenant!" Dolly said.

Tess could feel a brilliant crimson flush rising to her cheeks. She wasn't sure who she wanted to bat the hardest—Dolly for so boldly putting her into an awkward situation, or Jamie Slater for behaving as if escorting her to a dance would be a hardship.

"There's absolutely no need for anyone to concern himself," she said quietly, a note of steel to her voice. There—she'd given Slater his out. "I consider myself in mourning. A dance would be completely out of the question."

"Would it?" There was a core of steel to Jamie's voice, too. He managed to step past Dolly and catch her shoulders, and she thought he was furious as he gazed into her eyes. She couldn't understand him in the least. "I don't think so, Tess. Your uncle was a frontiersman, a fighter. I don't think he'd want you sitting around crying about what can't be changed. He'd know damned well that life out here was hard, and sometimes awfully darned short and sweet, and he'd want you to live. And that's what you're good at, isn't it? Fighting—living?"

"Lieutenant Slater, really, I—"

"Maybe it's just the fighting that you're so good at. Maybe you don't really know how to live at all."

She cast back her head, ignoring the grip of his fingers upon her shoulders. She gritted her teeth hard, then challenged him hotly. "And you think you're the one who could teach me how to live, Lieutenant? Why, I'm not sure that you're more than a perfect Yankee mannequin yourself, Lieutenant."

His lip curled. His grip on her shoulders suddenly relaxed. "Why don't you test me then, Miss Stuart?"

"Jamie Slater, that young girl is vulnerable right now—" Dolly started to warn him, but Jamie and Tess both spun on her.

"As vulnerable as a sharp-toothed cougar," Jamie supplied.

"Never to the likes of him!" Tess promised.

Dolly was silent. Soft laughter sounded, and Tess saw that it was Jon Red Feather laughing, and that he seemed quite pleased with the situation.

"No wonder white men don't like Indians!" Jamie muttered darkly.

"Sure. Keep the white folks at war with themselves, and half the battle is solved," Jon said pleasantly. "Jamie, come on. It's settled. You can pick up Miss Stuart right after sunset."

"Nothing is settled—" Tess began.

"Sunset!" Jamie said. He seemed to growl the word. And he didn't give her another second to protest, but slammed his way out the door. It closed with such a bang that even Dolly jumped, but then she smiled benignly.

"I do just love that man!" Dolly said.

Tess stared at her blankly. "Why?" she demanded.

"Oh, you'll see, young lady. You'll see. And that Jon! He does like to stir up trouble. But then, maybe it's not trouble this time. Jon can be plain old silent as the grave when he wants, too. I think that he's just delighted to put Miss Eliza's nose out of joint. She thinks she just about has her claws into Jamie, and who knows, it is lonely out here. But she isn't right for him, she just isn't right at all. You'll see."

"Miss Simmons—"

"Dolly. We're not very formal out here. 'Ceptin' the men, when they're busy playing soldier, that is."

"Dolly, I have no intention of going to a dance with Lieutenant Slater. I don't really like him. He's self-righteous and hard as steel and cold as ice—"

"Hard maybe, cold, no. You'll see," Dolly predicted.

"But—"

"Come on, I've got a steaming bath over there in the corner. You just hop in, and I'll make you some good strong tea, and pretty soon dinner will be ready, too. And you can tell me all about yourself and what happened, and I'll tell you more about Lieutenant Slater."

"I don't want to know anything more about Lieutenant Slater," Tess said firmly. But it was a lie. She wanted to know more about him. She wanted to know everything about him.

And she did want to go to the dance with him. She wanted to close her eyes and feel his arms around her, and if she thought about it, she wanted even more. She wanted to see him again as she had seen him that morning with his shirt hanging open and his hair tousled and his bare feet riding the rocks with confidence and invincibility.

"Let me help you out of those dusty travel clothes," Dolly said. She was quick and competent, and Tess felt immediately at home with her, able to accept her assistance. In seconds she was out of her dirt-coated clothing and into a wooden hip tub with a high back that allowed her to lean in comfort. Dolly tossed her a bar of rose-scented soap and a sponge, and she blissfully squeezed the hot water over her knees and shoulders.

"What did you do to your hands, young lady?" Dolly demanded.

Tess looked ruefully at her callused palms. "Driving. I can do it, of course. It's just Uncle Joe usually did most of the driving."

She didn't know what it was about saying his name, but suddenly, tears welled in her eyes.

"You should cry it out," Dolly warned her. "You should just go right on ahead and cry it out."

Tess shook her head. She couldn't start crying again. She started talking instead. "He raised me. My parents died when I was very young, both caught pneumonia one winter and they just didn't pull through. Joe was Father's brother. He sold Father's land and put the money into trust for me, and he took me to live with him, and he made me love the land and reading and Texas and the newspaper business, and most of all, he made me love the truth. And he never gave up on the truth or on fighting. And that's why I have to keep it up. He always gave me everything..."

Her voice trailed away. So much, always. She remembered learning how to ride, and how to ink the printing press, and then how to think out a story, and what good journalism was, and...

And what it was like to live through pain, and stand up tall despite it, and to learn to carry on. Joe had been there when she had fallen in love with Captain David Tyler back in '64, when his Confederate infantry corp had been assigned to Wiltshire. She had been just seventeen, and she'd never known what it was like to love a man in that mercurial way until she'd met David. They'd danced, they'd taken long walks and long rides and they'd had picnics out by the river, and he had kissed her, and she had learned what it was like to feel her soul catch fire. They'd known the war couldn't go on much longer, and they planned to marry as soon as it was over.

But then David's company had been assigned to Kirby-Smith. Most of the other men, Rebels and Yanks, had lain down their arms and started on the long trek home, but David had been killed by cannon fire because Kirby-Smith fought to the bitter end. And when Tess had felt as if her heart had really broken and that there was no way to go on any longer, Joe had been there. He had been silent. He hadn't tried to tell her that she was young, that she would get over it, that she would love again. He had just held her, and he had been there to comfort her whenever she had needed him. And he had given her more and more assignments on the newspaper. She had discovered that although she never forgot David, she could learn to live with the pain, that she could even smile at his memory. There had been warm, good things between them, and she never wanted to forget them. Because of Joe, she had learned that she could remember them with a smile.

But now Joe was gone, too. And in his way, Jamie Slater was right. Joe wouldn't have wanted her to stop living.

Stop living...

Who did the Slater man think he was? She had always lived, and lived hard and with boldness and determination!

Maybe it had been a while since she had had fun. She was twenty-four years old. Most men would consider that rather over the hill, she realized. But then, times had changed. Many women were over the hill these days. The war had taken so many of the young men the women her age would have married.

She'd never cared about that. She'd never believed that marriage was a market, that a woman had to be married. Joe had given her her independence, too. She could manage the paper without him—she had done so often enough when he had traveled. He had taught her to take care of things herself. And when David had died, she hadn't wanted anyone else; she had wanted to work, and to listen to Joe. Then it had become all-fired important to fight von Heusen. Just as it was important to fight him now.

She touched her cheek with her damp fingers, and despite herself, she wondered if she looked old, like a spinster. She hadn't given her appearance much thought in a long time, and yet she had still known how to play the sweet young girl with Slater's men. She had even managed to do a little innocent flirting to irritate him. Not that he seemed to notice. He'd never come around insisting that she needed help...

But he had asked after her, he had walked by her wagon. And he had looked at her in that way.

In the warmth of the water, she felt her body grow hot and she wondered with some dismay at the effect that thoughts of the man had upon her. She hadn't felt this surging pulse of heat when she had been in love with David.

She wasn't in love with Slater. She disliked him. He was self-righteous, and he didn't believe a word she was saying. He was the type of man she needed to fight, a Yankee carpetbagger, scalping what he could from Texas.

"You all right now, Tess?" Dolly asked her.

Tess opened her eyes and smiled. "I'm fine, Dolly, I'm really just fine. I appreciate your caring, and your help."

"Oh, maybe I have a bit of Jon Red Feather's streak of mischief in me. You're a beautiful young thing—"

"Miss Simmons—"

"But you are!" Her dark eyes sparkled. "And by tomorrow night we'll have that pinched look gone from your face and your hair all clean and in ringlets and you'll be a rare challenge to Miss Eliza!"

"Dolly, I don't want to be a rare challenge to Miss Eliza. I've work to do. I must return to Wiltshire just as soon as possible. I've got a good foreman at the ranch, and the paper has a fine editor, but the ranch and the paper are both mine now, and I've got to make them work."

Dolly sniffed, apparently uninterested in a woman running a paper or a ranch. "There's things a young lady should be doin', and things she shouldn't! Now you, you need to be married. You need yourself a man."

Tess sank back into the water wearily. "I need a hired gun, that's what I need."

Dolly was quiet for a moment, then she said enthusiastically, "Well, then, you really do need Lieutenant Slater."

"What?"

Dolly came around the side of the tub and perched on a stool. "Why, he was claimed to be an outlaw, him and his brothers! There was a big showdown, and the three of them shot themselves out of an awful situation. Then they surrendered, and all went to trial, and the jury claimed them innocent as babes! But those Slater boys—why, it was legendary! He's as quick as a rattler with his Colt.''

He was, Tess thought. She couldn't forget the way he had killed the snake. She might have died, except that he was so fast with that gun.

She shivered suddenly. Maybe he wasn't what she needed. He was what she wanted. A man good with a gun. A man with hard eyes and a hard-muscled chest and hands that were strong and eyes that invaded the body and the soul.

"Someone's got to escort you to Wiltshire," Dolly said flatly. "And Jamie, he's got time coming. And he really ain't no fool. I know there's this big thing going on about whether it was Indians or white men attacked you, but Jamie, he'll find out the truth."

"He didn't believe a word I said."

"Oh, but he could discover the truth! He knows the Shoshone, the Comanche, the Cheyenne, the Kiowas and even the Apache better than most white men—most white men alive, that is! Why, he speaks all their languages! He can tell you in a split second which tribes are related to which, and he knows their practices, and how they live. Sometimes he even knows the Indians better than Jon Red Feather, 'cause you see, Red Feather is a Blackfoot Sioux, and he thinks that the world begins and ends with the Sioux! If you're telling the truth—oh, my dear! I didn't mean that! I know you're not telling fibs! But if you're right about it being white men, why, Jamie will find that out. He won't let the Comanche be blamed for some atrocity they didn't commit!"

Tess was silent. Dolly spoke again, softly. "If it isn't Lieutenant Slater who takes you, it might be the colonel himself. His wife was killed by Pawnees before the war, and he ain't ever forgiven any Indian since. Or else there's Sergeant Givens, and he's an Indian hater, too. Or Corporal Lorsby, and he's a lad barely shaving, he won't be too much good to you. Oh, wait just a minute, I've got some shampoo here, all the way from Boston.''

''I don't want to use your good—''

''Come, come, what good does it do to this old head of mine? Use it! Your hair will smell just like spring rosebuds, and every bit as sweet as sunshine.''

Tess accepted the shampoo. She disappeared beneath the water to soak her hair, then she scrubbed and rinsed it. As she rose from the water again, Dolly was still talking to her.

''Lieutenant Lorsby, he's a good boy. He's just untried. He's never been in a battle. He came from the east, and I'm sure he's a bright and wonderful boy, but he don't know a Kiowa from a Chinaman, and that's a fact. You really need to think about this, you know.''

Tess nodded, feeling a chill as the steamy water cooled. Maybe she did need Lieutenant Slater after all. She smiled at Dolly. ''Could I have the towel, please?''

Dolly held it, and Tess stepped from the bath, wrapped the towel around her and took a seat before the fire as she started to dry her hair. ''All right, Dolly, so tell me, please, just what is it about this Miss Eliza that's so horrible.''

''Why, I'm not quite sure. 'Ceptin' she seems to think that she's God's gift to the men of the cavalry. Jamie's the only one who's never fawned over her, and I think that's exactly why she's set her cap for him! He seems to be amused most of the time, but the woman does have a wicked fine shape, and a wicked heart and mind to go along. You'll see. Now sit back, and I'll bring you your tea, and then some of the finest Irish stew you'll ever taste. Then I'll see to getting the rest of your things brought in. I have a nightgown for you, right over there on the bed. Once you're all tucked in, I'll see to the rest. You need to get some sleep."

Dolly brought her tea, then the stew, and it was delicious. Tess hadn't felt so warmed and cared for since...

Since Joe had died. The thought brought her close to tears again, but she didn't shed them. She finished eating and put on the nightgown Dolly had provided for her. She crawled into the bed, more exhausted than she had imagined. As Dolly started to leave the darkened room, Tess called her back.

"Thank you, Dolly. Thank you, so very much."

"It's nothing, child."

Tess sat up. "Dolly?"

"Yes?"

"I didn't take you from your family, did I?"

She smiled. "Me? No, child. I sit around most of the day and remember Will. My husband. He was with the cavalry, killed just a few years ago. He made it home, though. Jamie Slater brought him home to me. He rode through an ambush to bring Will home. So now I mind the store a few hours a day, and I try to look after the soldiers that need a little mothering. And now you. It's been my pleasure, dear, so you go on and get some sleep."

Dolly was gone then. Tess yawned in the luxurious warm comfort of the clean bed. She stretched out, thinking that she would sleep. If she wasn't plagued with memories of Joe.

But it wasn't memories of Joe that kept her from sleeping. Even in the darkness and the warmth, she felt strange chills snake along her body. It was Jamie Slater's face she saw before her in the darkness, the dry amusement in his gray eyes. Then she remembered the feeling of wicked, surging heat as his gaze fell over the length of her. He had stayed away...

And he had been drawn back. Almost as if he was feeling the same thing.

She didn't need a lover, she told herself. She needed a hired gun. Maybe she would have to barter to gain what she wanted . . .

Barter! she charged herself.

And in the darkness she admitted that he could be as cold and hard and ruthless as stone, he could care for her not at all, or perhaps even want her with a curious interest.

It didn't matter. She hadn't thought about any man in over five years.

But she wanted this one. That he could deal well with a gun was all the better.

When she finally did sleep that night, it was with the stern reminder that she ought to be saying her prayers. That she ought to hope that Jamie Slater wanted nothing more to do with her, that the stoic colonel would take her to Wiltshire.

She could fight von Heusen, and she would. She just wasn't sure if she could fight von Heusen and all the decadent and shameful things she felt for Jamie Slater at the same time.

It was wicked.

It was true. If Joe had taught her anything, it was wisdom. She couldn't change what she was feeling, even if what she was feeling could only cause her pain.

Exhaustion overwhelmed her, and she slept. Slept, and dreamed. Of smoke-gray eyes, of a man with broad shoulders, taking her into his arms.

Naked, as she had been by the brook.

He was moving into a trap, Jamie thought the next night as he walked along to the Casey house, where Tess Stuart was. He was definitely moving into a trap, because he couldn't call Tess a liar. He did know the Indians well, and he couldn't let a huge war get started because everyone was unjustly blaming the Comanche. He was going to have to find out what had happened.

He paused at the door before knocking upon it, swallowing down a startling, near savage urge to thrust the door open and sweep the challenging and all too luscious Miss Stuart into his arms. No matter how he tried, he could not forget everything that he knew about her. No matter what gingham or frills or lace or velvet adorned her, he kept seeing beneath it.

He'd lied to her. She was very much alive. She spoke of passionate life and living with her every breath, her every word. Her spirit was ever at battle, never ceasing. She would stay on in Wiltshire, he was certain, no matter how stupid it would be for her to do so. She was determined to fight this von Heusen, and she would fight him even if they met on the plain and he was carrying a shotgun and she was completely unarmed.

If...if... Was the man really so dangerous?

He didn't want to believe her. He wanted to be a skeptic. But there was truth in her passion, in her determination. There was truth in the honesty of her beautiful, sea-shaded eyes, eyes that entered into his sleep and made him wonder what it would be like if she looked at him with her hair wound between them and around them in a web of passion.

Every time he was near her he felt it more. Something like a pounding beneath the earth, like a rattle of thunder across the sky. Every time...

And if he didn't watch out, the day would come when he would thrust wide a door and sweep her hard into his arms. He wouldn't give a damn then about Indians or white men or the time of day or even if the earth continued to turn. All that would matter would be the scent of her and the feel of her silken flesh beneath his fingers . . .

He was going to a dance, he reminded himself. And every officer in the post would be there, and the enlisted men, too. He gritted his teeth and willed his muscles and his body to cease tightening with the harsh and ragged desire that seemed to rule his every thought. He knocked on the door.

"Come in, Lieutenant."

He pushed open the door, irritated that he should want her so badly, determined that he would control himself. She was probably late, women always were. She was probably trying to pin up her hair, or fix her skirts or petticoats.

She wasn't. She was standing silently by the small fire that burned in the hearth. She didn't need to change a thing about her hair—it was tied back from her face with a blue ribbon, then exploded in a froth of sun-colored and honey ringlets. The tendrils curled over her shoulders and fell against the rise of her breasts.

Her gown was soft blue, with a darker colored velvet bodice over a skirt of swirling froth. The sleeves were puffed, baring much of her arms, and the velvet bodice was low, but just low enough to show the rise of her breasts, the beautiful texture of her flesh, the fascinating way the soft curls of her hair lay upon it. She was even more beautiful than he had seen her before, her eyes bright and fascinating with the light of challenge, her smile soft and untouched by tragedy this night.

"You're ready?"

"Yes, of course. You did say sunset, didn't you?"

He nodded. She reached for a blue silk stole and handed it to him. Woodenly he took it from her fingers and set it around her shoulders. The sweet scent of her hair rose against his nostrils, and the essence of it seemed to fill him. Damn. He'd tried so hard to gain control before entering the house. Now the scent of her was tearing through his senses, exciting his temper as well as his passions.

"Shall we go?"

"Yes, of course." Her smile, he decided, was a wanton's. Miss Stuart was not entirely innocent, but rather a woman completely aware of her power. She hadn't become a fluttering belle. Her intelligence was apparent, along with her rock-hard strength, in her steady gaze.

And still...her beauty, her femininity...they were breathtaking. Jon had seen it even when Jamie hadn't.

"Where is the dance?"

"In the alehouse," he said curtly. But then he determined that he knew the game himself; he would play it, too. He smiled graciously, capturing her hand and slipping it around his elbow. "The rest seems to have done you quite well. You're looking wonderfully—healthy."

"Why, thank you, Lieutenant. With such flowery compliments a girl could surely lose her head."

"What a little liar. You wouldn't lose your head if the entire Apache Nation was staring you down, would you, Miss Stuart?"

"There you go again, Lieutenant, what a dazzling compliment."

"Do you need compliments?"

"Maybe."

They had reached the open doors to the alehouse. Already music could be heard, the strains of a lively jig. The notes of the fiddle seemed to be loudest, and for a moment Jamie thought that Tess's smile wavered. He was suddenly displeased with the night, and with himself. She had gone through a harrowing experience, and she had come through it with tremendous spirit.

No more platitudes for this chit! he warned himself. But her eyes met his in the dim light spilling from the open doorway. So deep a blue they were mauve in the darkness, so wide and unwavering upon his. He wished suddenly that she hadn't been young, that she hadn't been beautiful. That she hadn't been different from any other woman he'd ever met in his life.

"Maybe you shouldn't have come tonight," he said softly.

She smiled. "I'm fine, Lieutenant, truly I am. Shall we go in?"

He nodded and escorted her on into the room. Dancers filled the floor, soldiers in uniform, officers with epaulets and brightly colored sashes, women in their sparkling finery. The floor seemed alive with the blue and gold of the uniforms, and with brilliant reds and greens and soft pastels, lovely silks and brocades, satins and velvets.

But none compared with the blue gown that Tess Stuart was wearing. No other garment seemed to so fit a woman, to cling to her shape, to conceal and enhance, to so artfully combine both purity and sweetly simmering sensuality. Like the touch of her fingers upon his arm. Like the scent of roses that seemed to fill him and make him mindless of what else went on.

Jamie saw Jon Red Feather coming toward them, and he swore softly beneath his breath. Normally the darned half-breed was as silent as the night. Suddenly these days he was expounding away with his Oxford eloquence.

"Miss Stuart! Jamie. Ah, you've made it at last. Miss Stuart, please don't think me too bold—Jamie! I dare demand the first dance!"

"Jon—" he began in protest.

"Jon! Good evening!"

The delight in Tess's voice was so obvious that Jamie wanted to spit. If the two of them were so damned all-fired eager to be together, Jon should have escorted her tonight. It wouldn't have made the least bit of difference to him.

The hell it wouldn't. She was his.

He'd found her, he'd touched her and he'd brought her back here. It might be a trap, but he was deep within it now, and there was no crawling out. Still, he had to be civil. Too bad they weren't out on the plain. He and Jon could go to it like savage kids. They'd done it before.

He smiled and bowed with the best of the Southern chivalry he could remember from the days before the war. "Jon—Miss Stuart, please. Just return her in one piece, Jon."

"He's trying to pretend that I take scalps. I don't, you know," Jon informed her gravely.

Tess smiled again—brilliantly. Everything about her lit up. Smiles for him, and taunts for me! And still, Miss Stuart, we are irrevocably bound, aren't we?

"Evenin', James," the colonel addressed him.

"Evenin', sir."

"I see that Miss Stuart has been whisked away." He nodded toward the dancers. "Well, she's lovely. A very welcome addition to our little soiree, eh?"

"Yes, sir."

"Ah! Well, you shan't be lonely long. There's Eliza coming to whisk you away, I dare say."

Eliza was on her way over. She had stopped to chat at the punch table, but now, with her fan fluttering against the heat of the night, she was hurrying around the dancers to greet him. He hadn't seen her since he'd come back with Tess.

But she knew. She knew that he'd come back with a woman, and she knew that he was with Tess tonight. He could see it in her velvet dark eyes. She was smiling, but it seemed that the curve of her lip hid a snarl.

She was still something to behold. Her neck was long and swanlike, her hair as dark as ebony, and though she was slender and graceful, a man could get lost for hours in her voluptuous breasts. Her skin was ivory and flawless, her lips red, her face lovely. Jamie knew she'd had her mind set on tormenting him for some time. He usually enjoyed her company because she was such a brazen piece of baggage. He'd seen her break half a dozen hearts before she'd determined to stomp on his, but he'd always managed to hold his distance from her. To take care that he never spoke a word that sounded like commitment.

He hadn't been able to refuse her constant seduction. He hadn't been her first lover, and he was sure that he wouldn't be her last.

She was especially seductive this evening, her ink-dark hair caught to one side of her head and plunging in a black cascade over one shoulder, her bodice so low-cut as to reveal the endless depths of the valley between her breasts, her kelly-green gown contrasting beautifully with the darkness of her hair and the perfect ivory of her complexion.

"Jamie, darlin'! Well, you have saved the first dance for me. I've missed you so!"

In full view of the company she slipped her arms around him, rose on tiptoe and kissed his lips.

He waited for something to stir inside him. He swore inwardly. It was Tess. He was obsessed, and any other touch would leave him cold until he had quenched that newfound fire...

"Eliza, nice to see you," he murmured, catching her arms and unwinding them from around him. She pouted prettily, but he barely noticed. He was looking past her, toward the dance floor where Tess smiled and laughed, swirled and dipped and whirled in his best friend's arms. They were striking together, the tall half-breed and the exquisite blond who looked so delicate but had a will of pure steel.

"Dance, yes!" he muttered, and he swept Eliza into his arms and onto the floor.

"I was afraid that you hadn't missed me!" she told him, her eyes growing dark.

"What? Of course I missed you," he said.

"You didn't come to see me last night."

"No, I had reports to fill out."

"I waited for you. Very late. Into the night."

"I'm sorry."

"I'll wait again."

It was promising. Maybe he could close his eyes and imagine that he held Tess's sun-honey blondness.

No. It wouldn't be fair.

He smiled. "Eliza, I brought Miss Stuart to the dance."

"Miss Stuart? Oh, yes! I heard about her! The zany woman who thinks white men are Comanche." She shuddered. "Honestly, Jamie, I understand how you might feel responsible, but just walk her home and then come on over."

"Can't, Eliza. Not tonight."

She looked furious for a moment, as if she was about to argue. But she fell silent, pressing closer to him. The musky scent she was wearing rose around him. He felt the pressure of her breasts, the flash of a thigh. She wanted to excite him.

"I'm glad to find you so understanding, Eliza," he said pleasantly.

"Of course. I'm always understanding," she told him gravely, sweetly.

Like hell, he thought. But he smiled. Jon was no longer dancing with Tess.

She'd already danced with half the men in the regiment, Jamie thought irritably. She was in the arms of a young sergeant now, a handsome towhead stripling! A kid who probably hadn't even shaved yet. And he was gushing all over her.

Just about to trip over his own darned tongue.

Jon reclaimed her. Jamie gritted his teeth, determined to watch his date for the evening no more.

He had no way of knowing that Tess Stuart was watching him every bit as covertly. Those strange stirrings rose inside her as she watched the ebony-haired enchantress laughing, pressing against him, heaving her bovine breasts beneath his nose. She was very anxious to be retrieved by Jon, and managed to dance her way over to the tall Sioux.

He promptly cut in and swept her around, smiling like the devil's own disciple.

"Mr. Red Feather?"

"Yes?"

"Who is the massive mount of mammary glands?"

He laughed and bent low to whisper against her ear. "That, Miss Stuart, is Eliza."

He lifted his head again and smiled benignly toward Jamie. "Keep an eye on that one," he warned Tess.

"I certainly intend to," she told him sweetly, then she tossed her hair and laughed, and the sound of her voice was like a melody on the air.

And every man in the place seemed to turn to her.

Including Jamie Slater.

Chapter Four

Tess didn't see how or when Jamie extricated himself from Miss Eliza, but within a few minutes, he was tapping on Jon's shoulder, claiming her for a dance.

She smiled serenely as they moved to the music. He must have attended many of these little balls. He was as accomplished at dancing as he was with riding and shooting. She felt suddenly as if she walked on air herself, as if the room and the people all around them faded, as if they shared more than a simple touch. Maybe they did. His eyes were boring into hers.

"Enjoying your conquests, Miss Stuart?"

She widened her eyes. "Whatever do you mean?"

"I mean every snot-nosed young trooper here is ready to lie down and die for you."

"Really?" she asked with a sweet note of astonishment. "Well, how very genteel of the lads, how kind! But tell me, Lieutenant, how am I doing with the others?"

His jaw twisted slightly, but there was still amusement to his smile.

"The graybeards, Miss Stuart, are quite willing to dig their own graves, if need be, for your cause."

"Oh, dear! Ah, well, let's hope that it need not be. But I'm curious, sir, how am I doing with the men between nineteen and ninety?"

"Would it please you to know that a number of them were probably quite ready to slit one another's throats for the mere bounty of your smile?"

She didn't know if he was teasing. Not anymore. The smoky quality was in his eyes again. She lowered her lashes, shivering slightly, wondering if he was really a man to play with so freely. Then she raised her eyes with a bold and sweeping challenge. "Thank goodness, sir, that you would not participate in such a skirmish! I mean, as one could see how heavily involved you are..."

"What?" he demanded, scowling.

"The bountiful brunette, Lieutenant. Miss Eliza."

"Oh, Eliza."

He said the name dismissively. Too dismissively. He knew Eliza well, maybe better than he wanted to at the moment.

"Yes, Eliza," she said pleasantly. "Are you engaged, Lieutenant?"

"Good heavens, no!"

"Ah, was the horror of that statement over the possibility of engagement, or over Eliza?"

"Miss Stuart, you are very presumptuous."

"Sir, no one is forcing you to dance with me."

His arms tightened around her. He was smiling, but there was a sizzle to the smile, and it sent little shock waves rippling all along her system. Maybe she was playing dangerously. It was delightful. Maybe she risked igniting his temper to extremes she had yet to know. She realized that she was willing to do so, that the storm taking place within her own heart and body was demanding that she do so.

"Miss Stuart, I am your escort to this dance, remember?" he said bluntly.

"Oh . . . yes, well, I suppose that I had forgotten. When I saw the way your lips became pasted together with Eliza's . . ."

"Jealous, Miss Stuart?"

"Well, how could I be? I have just entered into your life. I couldn't possibly mean to dissuade you from, er, liaisons you have been nurturing."

She heard the clenching of his teeth. The scowl that tightened his handsome features seemed to reach inside her and take her breath away. She felt his hand upon her waist, warm and powerful, and the fingers of his other hand so tightly entwined with hers that the pressure nearly caused pain. She inhaled a clean scent from him that also seemed to speak of the plain, of the rugged vistas, of the horseman, the marksman. Everything rugged, and everything striking.

He was a real son of a bitch, a small voice warned her.

It didn't matter . . .

"Do you always hop so recklessly into the fray, Miss Stuart?"

"Whatever do you mean? What fray, Lieutenant?"

"You've barbs on your tongue, ma'am."

"Why, Lieutenant! I'm only speaking frankly."

"Um. I still say there are barbs there. Perhaps I should discover if I am right . . ."

He was swift on his feet, agile and sure. In a moment he had danced her out the door and into the shadows on the porch. He swept her against a supporting pillar, then his mouth descended upon her, lips parted, parting hers. She had wanted this . . . this very thing. She had teased and goaded him, and now she had him. But the kiss was no casual dance-floor brush. It was a thing so searingly intimate that she lost all hope of breathing, all hope of standing upon her own two feet. His mouth encompassed hers, drawing from her all strength and will. The heat of his mouth filled and infused her, and his tongue swept by all barriers to ravage and invade.

And she did nothing to stop him, nothing to fight back, nothing to protest even the shocking intimacy of the invasion. He kissed her mouth as if he kissed all of her. His tongue touched every little crevice and nuance of her mouth and thrust with a rhythm that entered into her pulse, into her bloodstream. It was far different from anything she had ever experienced before. Anything. It brought tremors to her limbs and a swirling tempest within her belly; it singed her breasts and weakened her knees.

And worst of all, perhaps, she felt no remorse, no shame. She allowed herself to fall into his arms, to feel his strength support her, the rippling muscles of his chest and thighs . . .

Then his mouth pulled away from hers. She inhaled raggedly and lifted her eyes to meet his. It had been a game; she hadn't been expecting this, and she was suddenly very afraid that her eyes betrayed the depths of her innocence, of her shock, of the staggering sensations that had taken place within her. His eyes were heavily shadowed, and he didn't look at all like a man about to laugh with the pleasure of an easy conquest, but rather like one consumed with some blinding fury or emotion. But he didn't speak. She wanted to reach up and touch the sandy tendrils of his hair, fallen rakishly over his forehead, but she didn't dare move, she didn't dare touch him again, for there seemed to be something explosive about him.

"There she is!"

The accusing cry seemed to awaken them both. Jamie stepped back, surprised, frowning, looking around.

A plump woman was coming out on the porch. She was small and seemed exceedingly broad. Her hair was snow-white and swept up beneath a little cap, and her dress was old-fashioned, her petticoats as wide as they might have been during the war, her dark fringed stole from an earlier period.

She wasn't alone. People were spilling out behind her.

"Clara," Jamie said softly, still frowning. "Clara, what on earth is wrong?"

Clara seemed not to hear him. She pointed a finger at Tess. "You! You—you harlot! You hussy! You whore! Attacked by Indians, and crying out that white men fell upon you! How dare you! You should have been killed! God will smite you down with an arrow for lying! You trash, you white trash!"

"Clara!" Jamie shouted.

Tess, stunned by the violence of the attack, stared in silence.

"Clara, you're overwrought, but you owe this lady an apology, you can't know—"

"No!" Clara shrieked. "She's the devil's spawn!" Tess realized then that the porch was full of people.

The young soldiers who had been ready to die for her looked as if they'd gladly nail her to the wall.

"How many of us have lost our dear loved ones to the bloody savages? You, Lydia, the Pawnee took your only daughter! Charlie, the Comanche cost you your arm, and Jimmie, your boy Jim went down in that fight with the Apache. Heathens, bloody heathens, all of them! And now she's lying about what happened to her little wagon train. She won't let the men go after the real culprits, she wants a war with the white men! She wants us all at one another's throats so the bloody savages can move right in. She—"

"No!" Tess shouted furiously. "You don't understand, you weren't there, and don't you dare—"

"She ought to be tarred and feathered and thrown right out of here naked as a jay. Then she can run to her Indian buddies."

There was a startled moment of silence. Tess felt certain they were all about to step forward and tear her into little shreds.

"Yes, yes—" Clara began wildly. But she was interrupted.

The sound of a clinking spur struck loudly and discordantly upon the floor as Jamie stepped firmly between Tess and Clara. "That's enough!" Jamie stated flatly. "Clara, I don't know what got you going tonight, but you've no right to judge this girl, none at all. You owe her an apology, and I damned well mean it." He paused. Tess realized that he was looking across the crowd.

Looking straight at Eliza. And there was something about her eyes that told all, even if she tried to stare at Jamie with a look of pure innocence.

She had stirred up the people. Jamie had left her on the dance floor, and dear Miss Eliza had made the rounds, talking to those most vulnerable.

"But what if it is true, Lieutenant? What if Miss Stuart was seeing things? Then the Comanche or some other tribe is on the warpath, and if so, we've got to start fighting back!"

"I'll find out," Jamie said. "I promise you, I'll find out."

There was a gasp from the crowd. The sound had come from Eliza, Tess realized. Her plan had backfired.

Tess wasn't sure what victory she felt. Whatever move Jamie made, he made because he had been forced into it, a gentleman caught by circumstance into defending a lady's honor.

"I'm going to escort Miss Stuart to her home, and I'll look into things there. And I will find out the truth."

By then Jon Red Feather had come to stand next to his friend. It was a casual but defensive gesture. They were shoulder to shoulder. If any fighting had erupted, the handsome half-breed would have been ready. But maybe he had come for more than that. He edged forward, taking Clara's hands. "Give Jamie time," he told her.

The little woman looked up at Jon. "Oh, Jon! I didn't mean you."

"I know," he said, grinning. "I'm only half savage and heathen and barbarian."

She flushed brilliantly. "Jon..."

"It's all right, Clara. Heaven help us, if the Sioux Nation went to war now, I'm not at all sure where I would be at times." He raised his voice. "Every single one of you has, at one time or another, seen some savage injustice done to the Indians! You've been with commanders who think nothing of the murder of women and infants! How in hell can you possibly doubt this story!"

There were murmurs, then the crowd began to clear. Clara started to cry softly.

"I'll take her home," Jon told Jamie.

Jamie nodded. He and Tess watched as Jon escorted her through the alehouse.

"Well, damn it, it's just exactly what you wanted, isn't it?"

He was a far different man from the one who had kissed her with such staggering heat. She stiffened, wishing she could wash the taste of his lips from her own, trying to wipe the taste away with the back of her hand. "What I wanted! No! I never wanted to be called any of those things, Lieutenant, and I certainly never wanted to see an old woman in pain, nor did I ever particularly want to be threatened with being tarred and feathered!"

"You wanted me to go to war with your von Heusen."

"All right, yes! I wanted someone else to stand up against him."

She was backed against the pillar still. Her hands slipped behind her to reach for it for support. He turned on her, coming closer, leaning his hands upon the beam and bringing his face very close to hers. She was trapped by his arms, by the prison of his body. "And now," he said softly, "it's my battle."

"You're the damned cavalry, aren't you? You spent time enough telling me that the day that you dragged me into the dirt!"

"I dragged you into the dirt! Why, you little hellion! You're the one who came after me like a bat out of hell!"

It was there again, that feeling of something entirely combustible between them, of static charging the air, of lightning on a still night. She had to fight back, and quickly and hard, or she would lose everything.

"I was frightened out of my wits," she retorted, "not that you probably weren't worthy of everything I did!"

"Oh? Is that a fact? And have you taken to judging me, Miss Stuart?"

"Why the hell not? You're determined to judge me."

They were silent for a moment, and in that moment, they both heard a throat being cleared. Jamie swung around again. Sergeant Monahan was standing there, red-faced.

"Excuse me, Lieutenant."

"What is it, Monahan?"

"The, uh, the colonel wants to see you."

"Right after I escort Miss Stuart to her house."

"Er, pardon me, sir, but no, sir. The colonel says that I'm to escort her and that you're to see him immediately. About this business of your going to Wiltshire."

Jamie frowned, started to protest, then sighed. He cast Tess a warning glare, although she wasn't at all sure of what the warning was about. She was still trembling, she realized, still holding hard to the pillar.

Jamie bowed to her. "Good night, Miss Stuart. We'll leave as soon as possible."

He walked away with long, angry strides. Tess looked at Monahan. Monahan was watching Jamie go. "Well, that might be one heck of a confrontation," he muttered.

"Why?" Tess asked.

"What? Oh?" Monahan flushed, as if he had just realized she was there. "Why, nothing, miss . . ."

"Monahan!"

"Well, the colonel may try to stop him from going."

"What do you mean, might try? The colonel outranks him, doesn't he? Or am I missing something?"

"No, no, but Jamie is up for reenlistment. Technically, he could have walked away from the cavalry a month ago. Paperwork gets slow out here sometimes."

"But why would the colonel want to stop him from going?"

"Oh, the colonel probably wouldn't. Not by himself, that is."

"Monahan, you are near to frustrating me to tears! What are you talking about?"

Now Monahan was a brilliant red. He stuttered, then started again. "Miss Eliza is the one who might mind."

"So?"

"Eliza Worthingham."

"Monahan!"

"Oh, you don't know! Why, miss, Eliza is Colonel Worthingham's daughter.'

"Oh!" Tess cried, startled.

"Tarnation, I didn't mean to upset you none. Don't you worry. The lieutenant ain't nobody's fool, and he ain't about to have his life run by a skirt, even if Miss Eliza is a pretty piece of fluff. Ah, hell, not that you're not every bit as pretty—prettier!—but you see my point? He ain't ever gonna have his mind made up by a woman. Not any woman. Oh, dear, this ain't gettin' no better, not one wit! Come on, Miss Stuart, let me do one duty right and get you home for the night!"

"Ah, yes, thank you, I think that I am quite ready to retire," Tess told him.

He walked her through the now empty alehouse and she thought of how disastrously the evening had ended. Then she found that her fingers were fluttering to her lips and that she couldn't forget the way Jamie had kissed her.

She would never forget the way he had kissed her. Not if she never saw him again, not if she lived to be a hundred and two.

He wouldn't ever let himself be run by a woman...That was what Monahan had said. But if he came with her, he would feel he had been trapped into doing it. He had been forced to say he would come with her to calm down Clara.

But if he stayed...

Then it might be worse, because if he stayed after he had stated he would go, it would be because he had been ordered to stay—because of Eliza.

He's torn between the two of us, Tess thought. And which one of us will win?

They had come to the Casey house. Monahan opened her door and lit a lantern for her, then looked around the small building. "Seems clear," he said.

"Why, Lieutenant, this is a cavalry outpost! What would I be afraid of here?"

"Never can be too careful," Monahan said cheerfully. "We learn that out here, ma'am."

"Yes, I'm sure you do," she said softly. "Well, thank you. I do feel quite safe now."

He told her good-night and left. Tess sat down on the foot of the bed and slipped off her black leather dance slippers. Then she paused, feeling as if something in the place wasn't quite right. She stood up and looked around. She hadn't had much brought in from the wagon, but one trunk was shifted away from the wall when she was certain she had left it against the wall. Her brush, which she had set on the small vanity, had fallen to the floor.

She picked up the brush and set it on the vanity. Then she walked over to the trunk and opened it.

It wasn't in wild disarray, but she knew someone had been into it. She always folded her clothing meticulously and kept it in defined piles, her flatiron on the bottom of the chest, her heavy skirts next to it, her light blouses and lingerie on top. Things had been moved.

She sat again. Maybe Monahan was right. You never could be too careful. There was no one in the little house now, but there had been. Who?

Eliza. Tess was certain of it. She smiled. "Eliza," she whispered softly. "I've been dealing with the likes of von Heusen. Fighting you is going to be easy."

She finished undressing, slipped on the borrowed nightgown and crawled beneath the covers. Her eyes wouldn't close, though. She was ready to deal with Eliza...

But what if she had already lost the battle?

There was no way she could know until morning.

It was a horrible night. She kept feeling Jamie's kiss upon her lips again and again...

And no matter how she fought it, she kept imagining that kiss falling against her throat, her palm...and other places.

She slept very late. Despite the bugles and the commotion of a company heading out for a day's scouting, when Tess finally slept, she did so deeply and well.

It was nearly noon when she imagined she heard a sharp rapping on the door. She ignored it. Then she shot up as the door burst open and heavy footsteps fell within the house.

The covers fell away. Her hair was tousled and falling around her shoulders, her gown dislodged from one shoulder and draping precariously low over her breast. Startled and disoriented, she gasped when she saw Jamie Slater in full uniform, his plumed hat low over his eyes, his legs apart and his gloved hands on his hips as he stared at her.

"You," she muttered.

He swept his hat from his head, bowing very low. "Yes, do excuse me, Miss Stuart. I wanted to let you know that we would be leaving at the break of dawn tomorrow. I realize, of course, that dawn might be difficult for you, since you are still abed this midday, but I do intend to leave promptly. Are we understood?"

"Tomorrow! You're still—you're still taking me?"

His eyes narrowed sharply. "I said I was. Why wouldn't I be doing so?"

"No—uh, no reason." She allowed her lashes to fall, shading her eyes. "I was just worried that maybe...that maybe you hadn't meant what you said."

He was silent for a second. "Miss Stuart," he said softly, "I always mean what I say."

"I was just worried that you didn't really want to go—"

"Oh, for God's sake! I'm going. We're going. Tomorrow. That is, if you get up on time."

She smiled, then forgot her animosity toward him, and just about everything else for that matter. She threw back the covers and leaped from the bed and raced toward him, casting herself into his arms. His hands came around her as he held her uptight, his arms wrapping around her.

"Thank you!" she said earnestly. Then she realized what she had done and how she was standing. And that there

asn't much of anything between them. She could feel the
ressure of her breasts against the hardness of his body, and
he knew that the thin cotton gown wasn't hiding anything
f herself.

She backed away, swallowing fiercely. "Thank you," she
epeated. "I really do appreciate it. Very much. I don't
uppose that you could ever understand, but I do." The
own was falling off her shoulder again. She tried to re-
ieve it. Then she realized that she was standing in the
norning sunlight and that every curve and twist of her form,
nd even the shadows of her body, would be completely ev-
lent to him. And her body was warming, and she was cer-
ain that her breasts were swelling, and she was breathing far
oo quickly, and he could probably see the pounding of her
eart.

"Sincerely, thank you." And she was still muttering. A
road grin stretched across his features. She plunged quickly
ito the bed beneath the covers.

"Miss Stuart?"

"Yes?"

"Do me a favor once we're under way, will you?"

"What's that?"

"Please don't chatter away endlessly like that, huh?"

"I never chatter!" she said indignantly.

"Never?" His brow arched.

She flushed. "Almost never. Lieutenant, do you realize
ow very rude you're being? You've disturbed my sleep, and
ow you haven't the decency to leave me alone to dress."

His eyes fell upon her. Lingered over her. He was still
niling. "Do excuse me then, Miss Stuart. But count on
is—for the next few days, I'll disturb your sleep often."

He tipped his hat to her and strode from the room. Tess
ulled the covers close around her, then she smiled and sank
ow into the bed.

It was a busy day for Jamie. Jon Red Feather was going to be accompanying him, but other than that, they would travel alone. Since he didn't know quite what he was going to come up against, he spent a fair amount of time determining what he wanted to pack on the supply horses and what he might bring in Tess Stuart's wagon.

Dealing with Colonel Worthingham hadn't been hard. Eliza had been behind the trouble, he had known that. Worthingham might be blind about his daughter, but he was a good officer. Not that Eliza wasn't careful. She had been with Worthingham when Jamie went to see him. She had spoken of the danger, of how Jamie was needed at the post, and she had been so sweet no one might ever have suspected her of having an evil thought.

Worthingham had suggested that another man might do the job; Jamie had politely reminded him that he wasn't officially in the cavalry anymore, and that had done the trick. He had three months now, three months on his own.

And Jon was his own man. He always had been. Jamie was glad Jon was coming along, even if he was being a thorn in Jamie's side over Tess. As if the minx needed any champions. The girl did know how to fight her own battles.

He didn't want to battle, he thought. He closed his eyes, then remembered the way she had looked that morning, half dressed and completely seductive, the outline of her delineated by the sunlight against the soft white cotton. And she had smiled and thrown herself into his arms. He remembered the taste and feel and texture of her and had known that he had to get out of the room before he took a running leap and fell upon her in the disarray of her gown and covers.

He was a fool. He should be steering as clear of her as he could. Instead, he had given his word to take her to Wiltshire. And he kept his word.

There was just so much he wanted from her in return. And she was desperate enough to give it.

That wasn't the way he wanted her, he told himself. But then he reflected that he wanted her in any way possible, and he wasn't quite sure ethics entered into the question.

And he had to stop thinking about her. He clenched his teeth and set to work.

It took most of the day to requisition the weapons and ammunition he wanted to take. It was dark by the time he was ready to return to his rooms. He wanted a good dinner and a long, hot bath before he started out on the trail.

His orderly would have arranged for his bath. When he opened the door to his office and saw that the lantern had been lit and a steaming hip bath set in the bedroom, he breathed a sigh of relief. He tossed his hat onto a chair, unbuckled his scabbard and holster and set his weapons on his desk. He pulled off his boots and left them where they fell. By the time he reached the doorway to the bedroom, his shirt was unbuttoned and he was flinging it on the floor. He was anxious for the bath.

But then he paused in his trousers, his eyes narrowing. He wasn't alone. Eliza was in the bedroom. And Eliza had been in his bath. She was curled up on his bed, her dark hair damp and forming tiny ringlets to frame her face. She wasn't exactly naked, but her appearance would have been less decadent if she had been. She was wearing a lace corset he could almost see through, and which lifted her cleavage to bold new heights. She wore some kind of silk and lace pantalets, and nothing else.

"I came to say goodbye," she told him huskily.

"Eliza, you're a fool," he told her irritably. "What the devil do you think you're doing in my room?"

"Aren't you glad to see me?"

"Frankly, no."

She curled up on the bed, watching him like a cat. "I'm not letting you go off with that little blond slut."

"Eliza, take a look at yourself and think about what you're saying."

"I'm in love with you!" She stood and walked toward him, swaying, her lips parted and damp. "I'm in love with you, Jamie, why do you think I've made love with you? Do you think a secret rendezvous is all right, but you're afraid of me being here because of my father?"

She had reached him. She started to slip her arms around his neck, but he caught her hands. "Eliza, I'm not afraid of your father. You should be. He'd send you back east in two seconds if he had the least idea about your trysts."

"He'd make you marry me!"

"No one will ever make me marry anyone."

"You owe me!" She pouted. "Jamie, I've lain with you—"

"Hm. And half of Companies C, D and E," he agreed.

She freed a hand, ready to slap him. He caught her hand, and for a moment they were very close. Then he saw her smile. Smile like a wanton, with tremendous pleasure. She was looking over his shoulder.

Tess was standing in the doorway. Chaste and beautiful with her golden ringlets piled atop her head, her pure white blouse buttoned to the throat, her full skirt navy and subdued, her only jewelry a brooch at her throat.

She stood there, very still.

"I was told by a young officer that you wanted to see me here, Lieutenant. I wouldn't have been so careless as to enter myself, but he pushed open the door, and so here I am, to my great embarrassment. Good evening, Miss Worthingham. Lieutenant, did you send for me?"

"I did not!"

"Then I must offer my apologies. Excuse me."

She turned.

"Wait a minute!" Jamie thundered.

Tess ignored him.

Eliza was laughing softly. He caught her and shook her hard. "You did this!"

"Mm. You'll never get beneath her skirts now, Jamie!" Eliza said happily.

Jamie didn't reply. He shoved her from him and walked away. He didn't give a damn that he was barefoot or barechested; he was just glad he still had his trousers on. He didn't know why it was so damned important that he catch Tess, he only knew that it was.

"Tess!"

She was walking away from him, ignoring him. He caught up with her and took hold of her shoulders, swinging her around. "Tess!"

"What?" She wrenched herself from his hold.

He circled her, determined to catch her if she moved. "I called you! Why the hell didn't you stop?"

Tess looked at him, wishing she could be half as calm or serene as she was pretending.

She hadn't suspected a thing. The young soldier had appeared at her door just minutes ago, and he had been very proper, and she had imagined his mission to be a true one. Lieutenant Slater had requested her presence at his office. She hadn't even known that his office and his bedroom were connected.

And she had thought that the summons sounded just like Jamie. He would give her some other trivial order about the next morning. Don't oversleep, don't be late, don't touch anything of mine that I set in your wagon.

And so she had come without a thought. Without a single thought.

She had never imagined what it would feel like to see him in another woman's arms. It had been awful seeing the brunette worse than naked, draped all over him. Her hair curling over his naked flesh. Her breasts cast against him, his arms locked upon her, the fever between them . . .

She inhaled and exhaled. She wondered if she had heard the words right between them. No one can make me marry anyone. That was what he had said to her. Wasn't it?

They had been lovers. He had all but admitted it. And maybe they would be again. Maybe he would take Tess to Wiltshire, and he would come back . . .

Maybe he shouldn't go to Wiltshire. Because if he did, if they were together, they would become lovers. And maybe he would be just as cool to her. Maybe making love meant nothing at all to him, when the desire within her was something that had never happened before. It was special, unique, precious.

But then again, she couldn't allow the brunette to win the game. Not this way. She didn't deserve to win anything this way.

"Damn you, Tess, will you listen to me?"

"I don't see what difference it makes, but go ahead."

He stared at her hard. "That was a setup."

She didn't reply. He caught her shoulders again, pulling her against him. "I'm telling you, it was a setup!"

She still didn't reply, and he looked into his eyes and swore suddenly. "Why the hell am I explaining this to you? Think what you want, Miss Stuart. To hell with you."

He left her standing in the street. She heard his angry stride as he started away.

"Lieutenant!" she called. She didn't turn around until she sensed that he had stopped. Then she turned to meet his eyes. "I'm very aware that what I just saw was a setup. I'm sorry for Miss Worthingham, that she felt it necessary to put on such a show. Perhaps you might want to provide her with a bit more tenderness or care."

He swore and walked away.

Tess smiled and started to her room. But then her smile faded. It had been a setup, but she had sent him right back to the enemy's arms.

When she went to bed that night she lay awake in torture, wondering what had happened next. She had advised him to offer tenderness.

Had he done so? Had he slept with the bewitching brunette in his arms, against his heart?

She tossed and turned in wretched anxiety and she very nearly overslept. If it wasn't for the timely arrival of Dolly Simmons, she would have done so.

"Up, up, now, Tess, dear! This is the cavalry, you know! Things are done by the dawn here. Lieutenant Slater will want to be on his way!"

Dolly had brought coffee. She slipped a tin mug into Tess's hands, then, chatting, picked up things in the room. "What are you wearing, dear, this nice brown cotton? Perfect choice for a hot day on the trail. And just one petticoat—no corset, of course. You'll be much more comfortable that way. Come on, now, Lieutenant Slater and Jon Red Feather are already out by the wagon."

Tess gulped down the coffee and was grateful when Dolly helped her slip into the brown traveling dress she had chosen. Then she frowned, realizing that Dolly was dressed for travel in a mauve suit with a huge, wide-brimmed hat on her head.

"Dolly?"

"I'm coming with you, my dear."

"You are?"

"Yes. You don't mind, do you?"

"No, no, I don't mind. It's just that..." She paused. In the outpost, it had almost been possible to forget that von Heusen offered death.

"Dolly, no one wants to believe me, but it could be very dangerous for you."

"Miss Stuart!" Dolly drew herself up and looked terribly dignified—and menacing. It would take a hearty soul to go to battle against Miss Simmons. "I have met danger all my life. I have lived in places that would make the ordinary woman's skin crawl. I have fought Apache, Comanche, Shoshone, Cheyenne and Sioux. I think that I will hold my own wherever I may go." She was quiet for a minute. "And besides," she added softly. "I've really nothing left here. I'd like to come with you. I'm a wicked good cook, and I can organize any type of household in a matter of hours."

Tess smiled. "Dolly, you're welcome," she assured her.

She finished dressing quickly and stuffed the last of her belongings in a portmanteau. She and Dolly gave the room a last look, then they departed together.

She almost didn't recognize Jamie when they came to the wagon. Instead of a uniform he wore a blue denim work shirt and pants and his knee-high boots. His sandy hair fell over his eyes as he cinched the girth on his huge horse, then cast her a quick stare. "It's about time."

"It's barely dawn."

He didn't reply, but nodded Dolly's way. He must have known that the older woman had determined on coming, because he didn't say a word about her appearance.

"Get up—I want to get started. Jon and I will take turns driving with you—there's no reason for you to completely destroy your hands again. And for God's sake, keep your gloves on."

"I can manage—"

He caught her arm as she was about to crawl up. "And don't tell me that anymore. I know you can manage. It's just that you can manage better if you listen to me. Got it?"

She saluted, gritting her teeth. "Got it, Lieutenant."

She climbed up and took the reins and Dolly got up beside her. The mules were harnessed, Jon was mounted and two packhorses were tethered to the rear of the wagon. All was ready for their departure.

Colonel Worthingham walked up as they were about to leave. "Goodbye, Miss Stuart, good luck."

"Thank you, sir."

"Lieutenant, Red Feather, take care. Remember, we're here if you need us."

"Thank you, sir!" Jamie wasn't in uniform, but he saluted smartly. The colonel stepped back.

"Jamie! Jamie, take care!" Eliza ran dramatically from the shadow of the command post. She raced to Jamie's horse and clutched his hands where they lay casually over the reins.

"Eliza, thank you, I'll be just fine," he said harshly.

"Eliza, come back, darlin'. Lieutenant Slater has ridden out again and again. You know he always makes it back." The colonel set his hands on his daughter's shoulders, drawing her back. Eliza didn't even glance at Tess, but Tess felt the hostility that rose from her.

She wondered again about what had happened after Jamie had left her last night, and she was infuriated that it should bother her so much, that it should hurt and dig into the very center of her being.

Maybe he would turn around now. Eliza was stunning this morning, her hair ebony against a yellow dress, her eyes huge with anguish. Tess held her breath. Then she realized that Jamie had picked up his reins, that he was shouting to her, telling her they were going.

She called out to the mules. The wagon rumbled forward.

She didn't look back. She followed Jamie and Jon Red Feather through the open gates of the compound, and she sighed with a soft sound of relief as she heard the gates closing behind her. They were really on their way. Jamie Slater was coming with her. Eliza hadn't been able to convince him to stay.

About last night...

She didn't know. She just didn't know. She needed a gun, she reminded herself. She needed a gunman.

It didn't matter that she wanted the man...

If rumor was right, he was one of the fastest guns in the west.

Maybe fortune was beginning to smile upon her just a little.

And maybe, just maybe, she was setting herself up for the heartbreak of a lifetime.

She couldn't think, and she couldn't worry. He was with her, and they were on their way, and for now, that just had to be enough.

Chapter Five

Jamie Slater didn't seem to do anything by half measures. When he set out to move, he moved.

They pushed hard throughout the morning, either Jamie or Jon riding ahead to scout out the road, the other riding with Dolly and Tess. Jamie was true to his word—somewhere around midmorning he called a halt, and Jon came up to take over the reins of the wagon. Dolly and Jon were comfortable together, old friends who knew one another well and respected what they knew. And both of them seemed genuinely fond of Tess, which was nice.

Dolly was full of stories. She didn't chatter, but she kept Tess amused with tales of Texas in times before Tess had been born. "Why, Will and I came out here long before Texas was a state. Before there was a Republic of Texas! And long, long before the Alamo. Why, I remember some of those boys, and it was a privilege to know them. Mountain men, they were good men. They were the stuff that Texans were made of. Will missed being at the Alamo by just a hairbreadth. He'd been sent out to deal with Cheyenne. By the time he came back, the boys were dead. They say that Davey Crockett was killed there, but that ain't true. The Mexicans took him prisoner, and they tortured him to death, that was what the boys said. He was a fiery old cuss.

They never broke him. You can't break a mountain man. You can kill him, but you can't break him. Kind of like a Blackfoot, eh?"

"A Blackfoot—or an Englishwoman, eh, Dolly?" Jon agreed, grinning.

Dolly chuckled gleefully and agreed.

Tess found herself studying Jon's handsome features. There was no denying that the man had Indian blood, proud blood. His cheekbones were wide and broad, his flesh was dark bronze. And his hair, too, was Indian, black as ink and straight as an arrow. But his eyes were a deep, startling green.

He caught her studying him, and she blushed. "I'm sorry. I didn't mean to be rude."

"It's all right. You're welcome to wonder about me. I'll tell you, because I like you. My father was a Blackfoot chief. My mother was the daughter of an English baronet."

"A baronet?"

"Um. Sir Roger Bennington. Actually, he's a very decent old fellow." He smiled.

"What does that make you?"

Jon laughed softly. "A half-breed Blackfoot. Sir Roger did not marry his daughter to an Indian. She was kidnapped, but she discovered that she was in love with my father. She stayed with the Blackfoot until my father was killed. Then she went back to England. She died there."

"I'm sorry."

"Don't be. They were both happy while they lived."

Tess hesitated. "Did you go to England with her? Is that where you acquired your accent?"

"My accent?" he repeated.

"Well, you don't sound like a Texan or an Indian."

"I'm not a Texan, except by choice for the moment. I was born in the Black Hills. And my father was still alive when

I went to England. My mother convinced him that a half-breed needed every advantage. My mother knew that the Indian's day was dying. That the buffalo were being slaughtered. That the white men were going to push west, and push us west, until we were pushed right into the sea or given desert land as our reservations. Our prisons.''

He spoke hard words, but he spoke them softly. "You don't seem very bitter," Tess commented.

"Bitter? I'm not. Bitterness is a wasted emotion. I ride with Jamie now because I choose to be with him. Some time this year, I'll go back to my father's people. And if the whim takes me, I'll go visit my grandfather in London. I enjoy the theater and opera there, and Grandfather is a hardy old cuss. I think he's actually damned pleased when people stare at his Indian grandson. Actually, I wear formal clothing rather well." He grinned ruefully, but then his grin faded as he studied her. "I love the west, too. I love horses, and the feel of a good one racing beneath me. I love my tribe, and I love this harsh, dry land. And I've stayed with Jamie because he knows people. He's spent most of his life fighting, but he still knows people. He goes to war with men, but he never attacks children."

He gazed at her curiously, looking her up and down, studying her. "Jamie believes you. He's come into Indian villages and seen what certain white men are capable of leaving behind. There are many men in the cavalry who think that an infant Indian is still an Indian, and that it will grow to put an arrow in someone's back. There was a lieutenant who liked to order his soldiers to shoot the women, then bash the infants' heads together to save bullets."

"God, how awful."

"Jamie knows about things like that. God knows, he saw enough of it during the war."

"There was nothing like that during the war—"

"Jamie came from the Kansas and Missouri border. There was all kinds of stuff like that."

"Yes, but the war's over now," Dolly interrupted matter-of-factly. "We need to put it behind us. Bless us and save us! It's been five years! And Mr. Grant is president now—"

"Mr. Grant could use some help out here in the west," Jon said dryly. He smiled again at Tess. "Ever been to London?"

She shook her head. "I've never been out of Texas."

"Now that is a great loss. A girl like you ought to see the world." Jamie was heading toward them. "Miss Stuart, you are welcome to travel with me at any time, in fact, I'd consider it quite an honor."

Jamie was scowling. Tess lowered her lashes, knowing that Jon had said the words strictly for Jamie's benefit.

Jamie's great roan stallion was prancing around. "We seem to be clear for quite a while ahead. Jon, want to ride again? I'll take over the reins for a while."

"Sure thing." Jon pulled in on the reins. He started to hop down while Jamie dismounted from his horse. Tess looked at Jamie. "I do appreciate your concern, but I've scarcely taken the reins myself—"

"Miss Stuart, I'll drive the wagon for a while now. After all, we wouldn't want to ruin the hands of a newspaper woman."

Dolly slapped her on the knee. "You let him drive!" she said, then she yawned. "I think I'll ride in back for a while." She smiled at Tess like a self-satisfied cat and crawled into the back of the wagon. Tess watched her stretch out on Uncle Joe's bunk. Jamie climbed up beside her and took the reins. Jon had untied his pinto from the back of the wagon. "I'll ride on ahead," he said.

Jamie nodded. Tess was left alone beside Jamie, very aware of the heat of his thigh despite the heat of the day.

They rode in silence, and the silence seemed to stretch on and on. Finally Jamie drawled out, "You made it on time this morning. Did you manage to have a good night's sleep?"

"Yes, I did," she lied pleasantly. She turned to him with her eyes innocently wide. "What about you, Lieutenant? Did you manage to have any sleep at all?"

He studied her eyes, then smiled slowly. "Yes, I slept." He didn't elaborate and Tess was infuriated. She wanted some kind of an answer on this subject, and he was determined not to give her one.

"You seem to have been having a darned nice morning," he commented.

"Have I?"

"I've known Jon Red Feather a long time now. I've never known him to talk so much."

"He's charming."

Jamie grunted. He flashed her a quick gaze and gave his attention to the road once again. "And I'm not?"

"No. You're impudent, insolent and a royal pain, Lieutenant Slater."

"Oh, is that so? Then why were you so anxious for my company?"

She inhaled sharply, staring at him. "Because you can shoot," she said flatly.

"Why, thank you, Miss Stuart! Thank you kindly. And you threw yourself right into my arms the other morning, half naked and all, just because I shoot."

"Right. Wrong! I was not half naked—"

"You felt as if you were."

"Lieutenant, you are a scurvy, low-down, no-good rodent—"

"But a no-good rodent who can shoot, right?"

"Precisely, Lieutenant," she said with a touch of silk. He nodded, looking ahead.

"You are awfully determined to stay in Wiltshire, Miss Stuart. Couldn't you run a newspaper somewhere else?"

"I could. But I wouldn't own the good cattle land that Joe—" She paused. "Well, it's all mine now."

"Is your life worth the land?"

"You don't understand. It's not just the land. Somebody needs to stand against this man."

"You do want it desperately."

He was watching her curiously, the hint of a curve to his lips. She frowned, wondering what he was up to.

"Yes. I do want it desperately. He killed Joe. He might not have ridden with the men, but he killed Joe. And I'm going to bring him down."

"With the help of a scurvy rodent who can shoot."

"With whatever help I can get. And you do believe me about the attack, I know you do."

He shrugged. "Maybe. I've still got my reservations, but I do intend to go into Wiltshire with you."

"And that's all?" she asked, horrified.

He smiled. "Just what, Miss Stuart, do you want out of me? Spell it out. We might need to come to a few terms here."

"But, but—" she sputtered. "But you said you'd find out the truth! You told Clara—"

"I told Clara I'd find out the truth. I didn't tell her that I'd go to war on your behalf."

"Bastard!" Tess spat out the epithet.

"Calm down, Miss Stuart! Such language from a very proper and genteel young Southern woman! I told you, say what you want, and we'll take it from there."

"What I want? Well, I . . . I want you to stay! Then when he sends his guns, I'll have my guns!"

"Jon Red Feather and I against a horde of hired gunmen. Mm. I should stand tall and let this man pump me full of bullets for the benefit of having you call me a scurvy rodent?"

Tess caught her breath and tried to control her temper. She lowered her lashes and counted to ten, then kept going to twenty, then started all over again because he was laughing at her. She moved suddenly, and he must have thought that she meant to strike him because he cast an imprisoning arm around her. She stiffened in his hold. "Lieutenant, this is completely unnecessary."

"Is it? I can't help but feel cautious around you, Miss Stuart."

She swore softly.

He laughed.

"Go ahead! Laugh!" she said angrily. "And just run like a cur with its tail between its legs when we get to Wiltshire."

"A cur? I thought I was a rodent."

"I can't find words for what you are, Lieutenant."

"Pity," he drawled. His eyes were on her, smoke and fire. His arm was warm and strong around her. The heat of the sun bore down on them, and she felt as if it touched her and brought a liquid rush throughout her. She could not draw her eyes from his, nor could she dispel the sudden, brilliant memory of his lips upon hers.

"We could bargain, Miss Stuart."

"Bargain?"

"Yes. If I'm going to die, I'd like it to be for a little more than a smile."

She stared at him. She felt a heat like that of the sun suffuse throughout her body, bringing a rampant beat to her heart, a flood of burning red to her cheeks and a tremor deep inside her. He could only mean one thing, she was certain. If he was going to stay, he wanted her.

She should have been outraged. She should have been able to say that he could be damned, that her honor was worth far more than her life.

Except that...

There was something that washed over the outrage like the deep, rich waves of the ocean. It was the same thing that caused the pulse to beat ever more fervently in the column of her throat, the thing that held her speechless. He watched her, that wry smile twisted so tauntingly into his features. He was horrid. He was awful.

He was exciting, sensual, masculine. The scent of him beguiled her, just as his arms beckoned and just as his kiss evoked feelings inside that she would never be able to forget.

She couldn't just stare at him. She moistened her lips and swallowed quickly, vowing that she would never let him know just how deeply he did affect her.

"Did you bargain with Miss Eliza, Lieutenant?"

"Is she still on your mind?"

"Is she on yours?"

He cast back his head and laughed.

"The situation is not at all amusing, Lieutenant."

"Oh, but it is, Miss Stuart, it's very rich. As you might have noticed, I didn't really need to bargain with Miss Worthingham. If that's what you were inferring. And yet, I didn't happen to mention yet what our bargain should be. Alas, I could see it in those huge, innocent, violet eyes! He wants to sully my honor, this cavalry man. For the price of a pair of spitting Colts! Her heart beats, and she wonders—my cause! This is my cause! Shouldn't I lay down my honor and my pride, and give all to this wretched rodent—all for my cause?''

''Someone should shoot you,'' Tess warned him.

''Well, you're trying to make me into a target, aren't you? Ah, but then maybe, just maybe, I could die with the exquisite Miss Stuart's kiss still damp upon my lips . . .''

She squirmed. She did intend to slap him.

''Whoa, Miss Stuart!'' He laughed, and his arm wound even tighter against her. They were sitting like newlyweds, she thought disgustedly. She was halfway atop his lap and she could barely move.

''Lieutenant, you're squashing me!''

''I'm trying to save my jaw, Miss Stuart! Now calm down. You are desperate, aren't you?'' His eyes looked into hers, and a hard note crept into his voice. ''You would do anything—anything at all that I asked. How very intriguing.''

''Jamie Slater—''

''Jamie!''

A sharp call from Jon caught their attention. Jamie's arm fell from around her shoulder, and he leaned forward, reining in. Jon was riding hard toward them.

''What is it?''

''Company,'' Jon said.

''Comanche?''

''Yep.''

''How many?''

''Fifty at least. They're covering the hill over the next dune.''

''Is it a war party?''

''They're out in feathers and paint, but I think it's a show. I'm pretty sure it's Running River.''

Tess watched as Jamie climbed from the wagon. She wondered if she should be frightened, and she wondered with greater exasperation if he should be walking away from her without a thought. He disappeared behind the wagon, then reappeared on his roan.

"Let's go see Running River," he told Jon.

"Wait a minute—" Tess began.

"You wanted to drive the wagon," Jamie called. "Pick up the reins. Drive."

Then he turned, and he and Jon raced forward. Swearing beneath her breath, Tess picked up the reins and called to the mules. They started plodding along.

Dolly crawled into the seat, puffing. "Comanche! Never did trust 'em."

The mules pulled the wagon over the dune. Tess felt as if her heart stopped, as if it caught in her throat.

The Comanche seemed to stretch as far as the eye could see. Bare-chested, in buckskin pants, with various types of feathers banded around their heads, they sat as still as ghosts. Many carried spears and shields, others wore quivers at their backs and held their bows proudly.

Not one moved.

They just sat on their horses, looking down at the small party that approached.

Tess wondered dismally if she was about to become the victim of a real Indian. Her heart thundered, and she dropped the reins. Jon and Jamie had pulled in before them, and they sat on their horses on the dune, watching the Comanche.

The sky seemed afire with the morning light. Earth and horizon seemed to stretch together in shades of dusty coral and crimson and gold. The quiet was eerie; not even the wind whispered in the sagebrush.

Then Jamie lifted his hand in some kind of greeting. A loud, shrieking cry sounded from atop the hill.

And then the Comanche were coming.

Tess screamed as the Indians started toward them in a blazing cloud of dust, their whoops and cries loud. No one could ride like a Comanche. The men lay braced against their ponies' necks, they swung beneath them, they righted themselves again. They came closer and closer. Their cries sounded ever louder.

Ever more deadly.

"My God, we're going to be butchered!" Tess breathed.

"No, no, I don't think so," Dolly told her calmly. Astonished, Tess stared at the woman. "Well, it's Running River. He and Jamie are blood brothers."

"Blood brothers," Tess repeated.

"Yes. The Comanche are warlike, of course. But not this tribe. Running River has been peaceful since Jamie came out here. He always deals with the lieutenant, and though there have been Comanche attacks, they've never been perpetrated by Gray Lake Comanche."

Tess was still unconvinced. There had never been a Comanche attack on Wiltshire—in fact some Comanche even came to town for work now and then—but she had heard about the things that could happen, and watching the extraordinary horsemen bear down upon them did nothing to ease her spirit.

"My God..." she breathed, sitting very still.

The riders were circling the wagon, shaking their spears and bows in the air. Now that they were closer, she could see that their faces and chests were painted in brilliant colors. She didn't move, although she didn't know if it was courage or pure terror that kept her still. She could see Jon and Jamie, still mounted, as they watched the thundering horses and their riders. Neither reached for a weapon.

It would be suicide, she thought. They were drastically outnumbered.

The Indians raced by them. The whoops and the cries were suddenly stilled, and there was silence. Only the dust remained to settle.

The Comanche were motionless again, surrounding the wagon and Jamie and Jon.

As Tess watched, Jamie lifted his hand again.

One of the Indians, his ink-black hair falling down the length of his naked back, wearing a band with a single dark feather, urged his mount closer. He walked his horse straight over to Jamie. Then he reached out his hand, and Jamie clasped it.

The Indian began to speak. Tess didn't recognize a word, but Jamie and Jon paid rapt attention.

Then Jamie responded in the Indian's own tongue, easily, effortlessly. Jon spoke, too, then the Comanche again.

"See," Dolly whispered. "It was a show. It was a performance. There never was any danger."

Tess exhaled silently. One question had been answered for her. She'd seen something like this before, but there had been differences. She'd seen the riders—but with saddled horses, in wigs and feathers and paint. They hadn't ridden like these Comanche. And they hadn't let out the terrible cries. They had been absolutely mute, carrying out their silent executions.

But she had a right to be afraid of this show.

"What's going on?" she asked Dolly.

"How should I know, dear? I don't speak that heathen gibberish!"

Tess stiffened, realizing that Jamie was gesturing to her.

The Indian he was talking to urged his pony toward her, followed closely by Jamie. Reining to a halt in front of her, the Comanche stared at her. He started to speak. Tess swallowed. He was lean, wiry, menacing in his paint, and yet when he spoke he smiled, and his teeth were good and strong, and the smile gave some strange appeal to his face.

Tess smiled in return. "What did he say?" she asked Jamie, between her teeth.

"He said that he did not kill your uncle."

"Tell him I know that."

Jamie spoke, then the chief broke into a barrage of words again. Lost, Tess kept nodding and smiling.

"What did he say now?"

"Oh. Well, I told him we were traveling to Wiltshire, and that I was going to try to prove that the white man had been guilty. If you made it worth my while, that is. The chief is suggesting that you make it worth my while. He thinks that you should bargain with me."

"Oh!" Tess gasped furiously. As she frowned, the Comanche chief frowned, too.

"Oh, my, my!" Dolly murmured beneath her breath.

"Smile, Tess!" Jamie suggested casually.

She smiled. She locked her teeth, and she smiled. The chief spoke again, quietly.

"What did he say?" Tess demanded.

Jamie didn't answer her.

Jon did. "He said that you were very beautiful, and that Jamie should take good care of you."

The chief took Jamie's outstretched hand again, then lifted his spear high and cast back his head. A loud, startling cry rent the air. Then the riders were kicking up tremendous clouds of dust again, and racing across the plain. Moving like quicksilver, they touched the landscape and were gone. They disappeared over the hill from which they had come.

Then, slowly, the dust settled again.

Jamie turned to the wagon. "Come on, ladies. Let's make a little time here, shall we?"

Tess caught hold of the reins, called out to the mules and snapped the leather in a smart crack. The animals started off with a jolt.

A little while later, Jon rode by the wagon. He smiled to Tess and Dolly. "Ladies, are you both all right?"

"Just fine, Jon," Dolly told him.

"Tess?"

She nodded gravely. "Jon, was Jamie telling the truth?" She flushed slightly. "Did he tell me the truth about all the chief's words?"

Jon hedged slightly. "More or less. Running River went a little bit further than Jamie told you."

"Oh?"

Jon shrugged. "He said that it might have been Apache that attacked you. The Apache have refused any treaties, they are constantly warlike, and stray bands have been known to travel in this area frequently. The Comanche and the Apache have often been enemies."

"Does Jamie know the Apache as well as he knows this Running River?"

"No. The Apache do not want to be known."

Tess shivered, and Jon quickly amended his statement. "He does know a few of the warriors and chiefs. They will at least talk to him. He speaks the Apache language as well as he does the Comanche."

"It's all heathen gibberish to me!" Dolly announced.

Jon grinned at Tess, and Tess felt somewhat better. There was something very reassuring about Jamie's abilities. Maybe it could be proven that the Apache were no more guilty of the attack than the Comanche.

Jon waved and rode on ahead.

"I'll take the reins for a bit now," Dolly told her.

"You don't need to—"

"I'll be bored as tears if I don't put in my part, dear. Now hand them over."

Tess grinned and complied.

They rode until sunset, then until the first cooling rays of the night touched them. Jamie and Jon knew the terrain. Again, they knew where to find water.

Tess climbed from the wagon the minute they stopped, stretching, trying to ease the discomfort in her back. Jamie pointed out the path through the trees to the little brook, and she started out in silence, aware that Dolly followed her.

The water moved over rock and along the earth, barely three inches of it, but she cupped her hands into it and drank thirstily, then splashed in huge handfuls over her face and throat, heedless that she soaked her gown. Beside her, Dolly dipped her handkerchief in the water and soaked her face and throat and arms with it. "Ah, the good lord doth deliver!" she said cheerfully. "Jamie! Come on in, the water's fine, Lieutenant!"

Tess froze, aware only then that Jamie was standing silently behind her. Dolly hefted up her bulk. "Guess I'll head back and see if Jon's got a cooking fire started yet."

She stepped by. Jamie knelt in Dolly's place. He doffed his hat and untied the kerchief from his throat, then soaked it as Dolly had. He leaned low and plunged in his whole head, then rubbed the kerchief over his throat and shoulders. Tess stared at him, unaware that she did so.

He smiled, watching her. She jumped slightly when he touched her cotton-clad shoulder.

"You're soaked," he told her.

"I suppose so."

He grinned, recalling memories of a different brook, a different time. "I rather like you wet."

"You—"

"Ah, now, please, Miss Stuart!"

She fell silent, but his smile faded and he sat on his haunches, folding his hands idly over his knees.

"We've got to talk, Tess."

She didn't intend to blush, but color rose swiftly to her cheeks. Damn him!

"What?" she said harshly.

"Well, I'm waiting to find out if you're going to bargain with me or not."

She was silent, feeling her body burn.

"Well?"

"You are a bastard."

"Come, come, now, Miss Stuart, will you bargain?"

She leaped to her feet. "Yes!" she spat at him. "Yes—and you were right, you knew damned well that I would do so. I am desperate. You can have anything. Anything that you want."

She swung around in what she hoped was indignant fury. She was suddenly blinded. She nearly tripped as she started forward. She reached for a branch to steady herself.

"Miss Stuart!" he called to her lightly.

"Oh, for God's sake! What now?" she demanded.

"Well, pardon me, but you didn't wait to hear just what it was that I wanted."

"What?" she gasped.

"I said—"

"But, but . . ."

She stared at him. He was still seated so comfortably on the ground, casual now, idly chewing upon a long blade of grass. "But, but, but, Miss Stuart! Where is your mind, dear lady, but deep, deep down in the gutter?"

He stood. Warily she backed away from him. "Listen, Lieutenant, I'm not sure that you do shoot well enough for all this! What do you want now?"

She backed straight into a tree. He was right in front of her, smiling. He stroked her cheek lightly with his knuckle and laughed softly as she indignantly twisted her face to the side.

"Still waters do run deep, eh, Miss Stuart? You ready to listen?"

"What—"

"Land."

"What?" she repeated, dazed.

"Land. I want some acreage. Some of your prime acreage, and maybe a few cattle. If I'm going to go out and die for this land, I'd like to have a bit of it in my own name."

"That's—that's what you want?"

"That's it."

"Land?"

"Land, Miss Stuart. I know you've heard the word."

She pressed against the tree, slipping her hands behind her to hold furtively to keep herself from falling. Then a crimson blush surged to her cheeks again, and she raged out in a tempest. "You! You made me think that—oh, God! You are the lowest, most horrid, most terrible—"

"Disappointed?" he interrupted pleasantly.

She shrieked something unintelligible and swung at him. He caught her hand before she could strike him, but she continued to pit herself against him. He pulled her against him, lacing his arms around her.

"Don't be angry—"

"Angry! I could gouge out your eyes—"

"Ouch! It would be hard as hell for me to aim at this von Heusen of yours if you did that."

"I could shoot off both your knee caps!"

"Then how could I get places to find out the truth?"

"All right! All right! You fight von Heusen, *then* I'll gouge out your eyes and shoot your knee caps. Now let go of me!"

"No, not yet, I'd be risking my eyesight, I'm afraid. Or my—ouch!" he said as she stamped on his foot. Her feet were dangerous. And her knees.

"Don't even think about it!" he warned her, pressing her so close against the tree trunk that she could barely breath. Nor could she kick him—his thigh was pressed close to hers. Her breasts heaved with agitation; her heart was thundering. His lips were close. So close to hers. He was going to kiss her again, she thought. And if he did, she'd probably let him get away with it, despite all he had done to her.

"Did you know that you have a really beautiful mouth, Miss Stuart?" he asked, his own nearly touching it.

"Ah! Not nearly so beautiful as my cattle!" she retorted.

He laughed softly again. "You are disappointed."

"Don't deceive yourself, Lieutenant. I am vastly relieved."

"Why don't I believe you?"

"Because you're an egotist and a scurvy rat."

"Why is it that you just beguile me so, Tess Stuart? Is it that you taste like wine and smell of roses, even in the most god-awful heat of the day. Is it that fall of golden hair, or your eyes, like wild violets? No . . . it must be the tender words you're always whispering so gently to me. Words like . . . scurvy rat."

"Lieutenant, will you please—"

"I do want you."

"What?" she cried.

"Very much. But I don't want to bargain about it. When you decide to be with me, you'll do so because you want to. You might have to think it through and weigh all the factors, or you might just wake up one night and come to realize that it's going to be, that there's just something there. I feel it when I touch you, when I'm near you."

"You're a fool!"

"Am I?"

He leaned closer. He was going to kiss her again.

"Don't!" she cried out.

He ignored the warning, taking her lips with his own, and though she mumbled a second protest, her mouth was already parting to his. And his tongue was deep, deep within her, and it touched her in places it could not possibly reach. She knew that he was right, and she hated him for it, but she needed him still, and she wanted him still. She trembled against the sweet savagery of his touch, and she felt the pressure of his body, of his thigh against hers, of more than his thigh. His hands were in her hair, stroking her face, rounding over the full rise of her breast, and she was still braced against him, unable to do anything other than feel.

Then he released her. She gasped raggedly and fell back. His lips lightly brushed first her forehead, then her cheeks. He smiled. "Egotist, eh?"

He was off guard. She slammed her knee against him. She didn't quite hit home, but she must have given him a good bruise in the thigh. He groaned at the pain, gritting his teeth, flashing her a lethal glare.

"Miss Stuart, if I didn't have some vague memory of being a gentleman—"

"If you have any memory at all, sir, it must be vague!"

"Miss Stuart, I should tan—"

"Do excuse me, Lieutenant," she said, attempting to step past him. "It's not that you haven't got decent lips, it's just that it's impossible to know where they've been before."

"Decent lips!"

"Decent, yes," she said sweetly, still walking.

He caught her arm and pulled her into his arms. "I could just—" he began, but then he laughed. "Impossible to know where they've been before! Why, honest to God! I do believe that you're jealous!"

"Not on your life, Lieutenant!" she protested.

But he touched his lips to hers again, sweeping her swiftly into realms she was just beginning to discover, then righting her just as quickly and dropping his arms. He cast his arm out, indicating the trail. "After you, Miss Stuart. I will always wait."

"You'll wait until you're old and gray!" she snapped. She was jealous, she thought. Anguished. It was painful to care like this, so deeply and so quickly.

He smiled serenely. "Will I?"

She managed to return the smile. "Not all women are like Miss Eliza, Lieutenant."

"No? I had rather thought that they were—at heart."

"You're mistaken."

"Maybe you're mistaken. Maybe most women are hypocrites."

"Oh, you are impossible!" Tess cried. She swung around and began to stride angrily toward the wagon.

But before she could reach the break in the bushes, he had pulled her back. She started to snap something to him, but the words caught in her throat when his smoky gaze fell upon her.

"Tess, you are different."

"Different from what?"

He smiled. "From any other woman I have met," he said softly.

Then he stepped past her and preceded her to the camp fire Jon had burning with a welcoming warmth and light.

Chapter Six

The delicious aroma of cooking was already filling the air as Tess stepped toward the fire. She inhaled deeply as she tried to dispel her immediate memories of Lieutenant Slater.

The fire had been set in the center of the clearing. A small animal roasted on a spit atop it. Jon, on his haunches, turned the spit. On a bed of hot rocks surrounding the fire sat a coffeepot.

Dolly was coming from the wagon with tin plates, and with mugs for the coffee. She smiled at Tess. "Rabbit! A nice, plump brown rabbit. Jon caught and skinned that thing in minutes flat. I do declare, he's a fine provider!"

"Yes, he is," Tess said, smiling at Jon. She strode past him and daintily swept her skirts beneath her to sink upon the ground. Jamie was coming across the clearing toward them, too. He sat beside her.

"You caught a big one," Jamie acknowledged. "Good."

"We need some water for this coffeepot," Dolly said.

"I'll get it," Jamie and Tess volunteered simultaneously.

"Fine, you get it," Tess said.

"No, you can go."

"But, Lieutenant—"

"Jon, give me the damned pot, will you?" Jamie said. He started toward the brook, then paused, looking back. "How's our supply in the barrels?"

"Good," Jon said. "Later we can fill the canteens."

Jamie nodded and started toward the water. Tess hesitated a minute, then started after him.

"Tess!" Dolly called.

"I'll be right back!"

"We'll never have coffee!" Dolly said dolefully.

Tess ignored her. She was panting and breathless, and wondering what in hell had made her rush into the den with the lion. She caught up with Jamie at the brook. When he wanted to, he could move quickly.

He stared at her as he filled the coffeepot, arching one brow.

"You want acreage," she said. "How much?"

"Well, now, I don't know. I haven't seen the property, have I?"

"Give me an idea."

He shrugged. His eyes were hard as he stared at her. "Half. Half of what you own."

She gasped, stunned. "You're insane!"

"I can ride back to the fort."

"But you don't even know what I own!"

"That's right. You're the one pushing the point here."

"A quarter."

"Half."

"Never!"

"Half. And that will be it. I won't ask another thing of you, Miss Stuart."

"Not on your life."

"We can ride right back." He stood and walked toward her. He didn't touch her, but he was smiling still. "Miss

Stuart, normally I don't barter at all, not without seeing what it is I'm willing to risk my life for."

"You're in the cavalry. You risk your life daily."

"They pay me. And you—"

"I'll pay you wages."

He shook his head slowly. "You know what I want."

Tremors swept through her. She did know what he wanted—and he kept saying it was property. He kept smiling, and his eyes roamed up and down the length of her. "Like I said, I usually like to see what I'm buying with my time and my Colt. Since I trust you so, I'm willing to take a chance in this circumstance."

"A quarter," Tess said firmly.

"Half."

He walked by her quickly. She stumbled to keep up with him, but he moved too fast. She was still stumbling when he walked into the clearing. She slammed into him and he turned, lifting her chin.

"Half!" he whispered.

She pulled quickly away from him. "We'll discuss it later. I think you're insane. I think you're just as crooked as von Heusen. Just another Yankee carpetbagger."

He stiffened, dropped her chin and turned in harsh, military fashion, then took the coffeepot to the fire. He sank down across from Jon.

"Well, the coffee will taste much better once we've eaten that sizzlin' sweet rabbit all up!" Dolly said cheerfully.

"It's cooked enough for me," Jon said, leaning over and ripping off a leg. He winced as the meat burned his fingers, then he smiled. "Dig in!"

They all ate hungrily, and in silence. Jamie rose and brought a loaf of hard bread from the supply pack. It didn't matter that it was hard—it was delicious. And when they were finished eating, the coffee was done. It did taste wonderful after all the food, just as Dolly had so cheerfully suggested.

It grew dark as they sipped it. Velvet dark. The moon was a bare sliver in the sky, but there were hundreds of stars out, dotting the heavens.

"It's beautiful, isn't it?" Dolly said.

"Very nice," Tess agreed. She yawned. "We should take the dishes to the water and wash them now."

"Don't be absurd. It's dark as Hades," Jamie said harshly. His eyes were smoke when they touched her. He was furious, she realized. And it wasn't their arguing over the payment in acreage, it couldn't be. He liked to taunt her and anger her, the silver light of challenge was always in his eyes then.

But he wasn't feeling fondly toward her at all at the moment, she was certain. Her heart beat too hard as his eyes touched her, and she thought she saw something lethal in him, something that made her shiver, something that made her think she did not want him to be her enemy.

He was coming to fight her battle, she reminded herself. But then why did he look as if he wanted to strangle her?

"I—I can bring a lantern," she heard herself saying.

"Dammit, you can just wait until morning!" Jamie said irritably. He stood, tossing the last of his coffee into a bush. Then he strode away, disappearing into the darkness.

Tess cast a quick glance toward Jon. "What's the matter with him?"

Jon shrugged. "I don't know. You'll have to find out yourself." He stood and stretched. "Ladies, I suggest an early night."

"He's gone off on his own!" Tess said indignantly.

"He's taking first guard," Jon said softly.

"I'm going to bed," Dolly announced. "Tess, now you come, too."

Jon was dragging his saddle and blanket to the fire. He stretched out and closed his eyes, setting his hat over his face. Dolly headed for the wagon. Tess hesitated, then decided to go after Jamie.

She heard Jon rise as she moved into the bushes, and she swore softly, certain that he would follow her. He did. But before he could reach her, a hand snaked out for her, catching her arm, swinging her around. She tossed back her head and met Jamie's angry eyes. She wrenched free from his grasp. For safety's sake, she took a step backward.

"What are you doing?" he demanded.

"Looking for you."

"I told you not to run around in the dark!"

"But you—"

"Miss Stuart, from now on, you're taking orders from me. And from now on, you listen. And if I hear one more crack out of you about my being a Yank just like von Heusen, I'll tan your backside until it's the color of a Comanche. Are we understood?"

"No!" she snapped indignantly.

He took a single step toward her. In the near darkness, his eyes seemed to glitter with a menacing light.

She decided that she wasn't going to tempt fate any further that evening. She didn't think he made idle threats.

She turned and fled.

Jon was standing not far from the camp fire. He had seen her reach Jamie. She slowed her pace as she saw him. She smiled pleasantly and wished him good night.

"Good night, Tess," he told her.

She crawled into the wagon. Dolly was already softly snoring. Tess unhooked her shoes. Closing the cover of the wagon, she stripped down to her chemise and pantalets. She crawled into her bunk, closed her eyes and made every effort to sleep. Her heart was still pounding, and she didn't know if it was with vexation or excitement. He wanted her property, not her person, she reminded herself.

Then how could he seem to insinuate so much that seemed sensual when they talked about dry land? And then, of course, he could change so quickly. Lose his temper over simple words when he could tease so long himself...

She didn't understand, but he was occupying more and more of her mind. And more and more of her heart.

It was light when she awoke. Dolly was already up.

Tess quickly slipped into her dusty brown dress for the second day on the trail. She tied her shoes and slipped from the wagon. She could smell coffee brewing already, and something was cooking in a frying pan.

She could hear voices by the fire. Jon and Dolly, she determined. She started around the wagon then held still. Jamie, bare-chested, in only his boots and jeans, was shaving. His mirror was leaning against the steps at the front of the wagon, his shaving mug was on the second step, and he was wielding a straight razor against his cheeks. Apparently he caught sight of her in the mirror. He nicked himself and scowled deeply at her. She should have walked by. She could not. She smiled, enjoying the sight of him so. He had wonderful shoulders, broad and very bronze. He was nearly as dark as Jon, with powerfully bunched muscles in his arms and chest, and hard, unyielding ones at his lean waist. She swallowed suddenly. She'd seen lots of men bare-chested. The hands often stripped off their shirts after a long day and doused themselves with water at the troughs.

Jamie Slater's chest was different. She couldn't look at him and wonder if the herd was doing well. She looked at him and wondered what his flesh would feel like beneath her fingers.

Maybe he read her mind. Maybe her thoughts were obvious in her eyes. They were still locked with his in the mirror.

Her smile faded and she felt a crimson blush rising to her cheeks. She prayed for motion then and she managed to move her feet and hurry past him to the fire.

"Fish!" she said delightedly.

"Freshwater fish, just wonderful," Dolly supplied happily.

"Jon, you're wonderful!" Tess claimed.

"Oh, I didn't catch these. Jamie did," he told her casually.

Dolly passed Tess a plate. "I'm taking a walk to the brook with a few of the utensils. I'll be right back."

"Thanks, Dolly," Tess said. Dolly winked. Jon smiled at Tess as she hungrily ate her fish.

"Coffee?" he asked her.

"Please."

He handed her a mug, then said something about finishing the harness. She was left alone with a beautiful, early morning sun and the delicious food and coffee.

She set down her plate and took a long swallow of coffee. She closed her eyes, inhaled the aroma and felt the heat. When she opened her eyes, Jamie was standing before her.

"Miss Stuart, you might want to hurry along a little. The rest of us have been up a while now, and I'm ready to ride. We can make Wiltshire by tomorrow if we keep moving."

She gazed up at his newly shaven face. All the planes and angles were handsome, smooth and rugged all at once—masculine . . . and still belligerent. It was war, she thought.

She sighed softly. "Why, Lieutenant, I, at least, am fully clothed. And I do promise that I can finish this coffee and the fish before you can be dressed and ready to ride."

"Then let's see it, huh?"

He started to walk by her. "Oh, Lieutenant," she called.
"What?"

"You're bleeding, sir. There seems to be a—a gash right
at the tip of your chin. Have you been shaving long, sir?"

"Longer than you've been wearing a corset, Miss Stuart.
A whole lot longer," he told her pleasantly. That time, when
he stepped by, she quickly leaped to her feet, finished her
coffee and, as quickly and delicately as possible, peeled the
last of her fish from the bone. She glanced over her shoulder. He was buttoning the last button of his shirt.

She cast the last drop of coffee and bit of food into the
ashes of the camp fire and raced for the steps to the driver's
seat of the wagon.

She made it just as he rode up on his roan.

"I won," she told him.

"At best—and that's if I'm in the mood to be cavalier—
it was a tie, Miss Stuart."

"At best for you, Lieutenant."

He smiled. "Half of your acreage, Tess."

"A quarter."

"That remains to be seen," he told her, riding close. "But
then, a lot of things remain to be seen, don't they?" He
nudged Lucifer and rode to the rear of the wagon. "Jon,
you ready? Where's Dolly?"

"Here, here, I am coming, I do declare, the rush you boys
get yourselves into! I was just down at the brook, cleaning
up the pans, and there you are, riding off without me."

"Dolly! We'd never ride off without you!" Jamie promised her solemnly.

"Never," Jon echoed.

"But times awastin', Dolly," Jamie said. "And suddenly, I'm just darned eager to reach Wiltshire."

Dolly climbed onto the wagon. Tess lifted the reins
against the mules, and they were under way again.

By late afternoon of the following day they had reached the outskirts of Wiltshire. Then Tess gave the directions to her home, a large ranch outside of town.

Tess held the reins. As the house came into view, she saw Jamie pull in on his big roan and stare. He glanced her way.

"That's it? That's your—ranch?"

"That's it."

He started to laugh suddenly, looking at Jon. Then he spurred the roan and raced toward the house. Tess flicked the reins and hurried after him with the rumbling wagon.

The house was magnificent. Joe had put years and years of work into the sprawling, two-story ranch house. There were two large barns to the left and a large red carriage house to the right. The vegetable garden, lush with summer, could be seen behind the house. The paddocks, stretching before and behind, seemed to go on forever. Horses, her uncle's prize thoroughbreds, roamed in the paddocks, the year's foals seeming to dance alongside their mothers.

Tess knew about the weathered paint on the fine old house, however. Since the war, nothing much had been done. They had considered themselves lucky to hang on to the property once the battles had ended and the dust had died down. There were floorboards on the blue-gray porch that needed to be mended, and Tess thought that if Jamie Slater looked long and hard at the velvet drapes in the parlor, he would see the material was old and fraying.

In the past few years, all their efforts had gone into their battles with von Heusen.

She drove the wagon between the paddocks toward the house. Jamie and Jon were far ahead of her. They'd reached the clearing before the house, and Jamie was turning around on the huge roan, looking at everything around him. He was still amused—and pleased.

He must have thought I was a potato farmer and that he bartered himself for a few dusty acres! Tess decided. Well, he should be pleased.

The front door burst open as the wagon reached the clearing. Hank Riley, Joe's foreman, came hurrying down the steps, followed by Janey Holloway, who had worked for them since Tess had begun to work at the paper. Hank was as tall and skinny as a young oak sapling, with a weathered face so browned and crinkled that he sometimes looked like an Indian. Janey was young and plump and pretty, with sandy hair and soft gray eyes.

Jane stared from Jamie to the wagon, then screamed with joy, clutching her heart when she saw Tess. Hank didn't make a sound. He came hurrying down the steps of the porch and over to the wagon and reached right up, catching hold of Tess and swinging her down. He lifted her up and swung her around again, a smile crinkling his face to even greater depths. "Tess! The Lord be praised, but that man told us you were dead!"

"I'm not dead, Hank, I'm fine." Hank had set her down. Jane was crying softly. "Jane!" Tess took the young woman in her arms to comfort her. "It's all right! I'm here. I'm alive, I'm well!"

"Oh, Miss Tess! Miss Tess, it's just so wonderful to see you! He said he was coming back tonight, and at first we thought that you were him coming back a little early. He had the sheriff with him, you see, and he said as how everyone had heard that both you and your uncle had been killed in an Indian raid, and that the land would go up for public auction. Hank and me and the hands were to clear out. Well, the hands could stay on until the actual auction, but—" She paused, gasping for breath.

Hank, casting a curious glance toward Jamie and Jon, continued the story indignantly. "He said that since Jane and I might think ourselves too close to the family, we'd have to get out before we started stealing property from the deceased!''

''He—who the hell is he?'' Jamie demanded, dismounting.

Hank frowned, not about to answer the question until he had a signal from Tess. ''Well, Miss Tess, I'll answer him about who the hell he is—once this fellow tells me who the hell he is himself!''

Jamie's eyes narrowed, and his face started to look like thunder.

''Hank,'' Tess said quickly. ''This is Lieutenant Jamie Slater, he's with the cavalry. And Mr. Jon Red Feather. Hank, they've been gracious enough to see me home—''

''Then Joe really is dead,'' Hank said miserably.

She nodded.

He swallowed hard, looking into the distance. ''I'd kinda hoped, seeing you and all . . . Then he really did get it from the Indians.''

''No. From von Heusen.''

''Him again,'' Hank muttered.

''He—him,'' Jamie interjected. ''Are we, or are we not, talking about von Heusen all the way around here?''

''Of course!'' Tess stated firmly.

''You mean to tell me,'' Jamie said, striding toward Hank, ''that this von Heusen has already been here, telling you that the property is going to go up for public auction in lieu of being granted to legitimate heirs?''

''Yep, something like that.''

''Just like a vulture,'' Jon commented.

''Well, he'll be back,'' Hank promised. ''Soon enough. You'll get to meet him.''

Dolly, still on the wagon, cleared her throat. ''Oh, Dolly!'' Jamie exclaimed apologetically. He hurried around to help her down. Dolly smiled and took Hank's hand firmly.

"I'm Dolly Simmons, Hank. Nice to make your acquaintance. And you, too, young lady. Jane, isn't it?"

"Yes, ma'am."

"A fine name, a fine name. And I'm mighty parched. Perhaps we could go inside and have ourselves a sip of something."

"Yes, let's!" Tess said.

She started for the house. Jon dismounted and looped his pinto's reins around the hitching post in front of the house. Tess was halfway up the stairs before she realized that Jamie hadn't moved. He was still standing with the roan's reins in his hands.

"Jamie, come in, please," she said politely. A bit distantly perhaps—they were still involved in their fierce, personal battle. "We'll see to the wagon later. Hank and the boys will help."

He shook his head, looking at Hank, not her. "That the trail to follow into town?" he asked, pointing toward the road.

"Yep, that's it."

"Where's the action congregate around here?"

Hank was smiling but curious. "Why, the Bennington saloon. The best card games in town go on there, the best whiskey flows there, and the best girls—" He paused, glancing quickly toward the ladies. "Well, Lieutenant, the best entertainment in town can be found there, too."

Jamie nodded. Smiling at Tess, he told her, "I think that I'll take a ride in."

"Now?" she demanded. The best entertainment in town! Von Heusen was expected at the house, and he was about to ride off to enjoy himself with a dance-hall girl!

"No time like the present."

"But von Heusen is going to come here!"

"I don't want to meet Mr. von Heusen. Not just yet." He swung up on his horse and glanced at Jon. Tess tried hard to follow his gaze. Something passed between them, like eons of words, and yet it all happened in a few seconds.

Jon was staying with her. And still, she was furious. Jamie was demanding half her land and he wouldn't even stay around to meet his adversary.

"Lieutenant, if you head into town, perhaps you should stay there for the night," she snapped. They all stared at her. She had to control her temper. She had to quit caring.

He grinned. "Why, Miss Stuart, do you think there'll be enough there to keep me occupied all night?"

"I imagine, Lieutenant, that that is entirely up to you. Do what you feel you must."

She turned her back on him as quickly as she could. He was a free man, she thought furiously. He could do whatever he wanted to do, drink himself silly, consort with whores, gamble his life away. He sure as hell wasn't going to do it on her property, though!

He was going to do it, though. He didn't even enter the house, but turned and rode away. Tess tried very hard to look back, not to let anyone see that her eyes had misted with her ire and frustration.

Damned Yank. Damned Yank.

"It's a nice place you've got here," Jon complimented as they entered the house.

"Beautiful!" Dolly exclaimed.

It wasn't exactly beautiful, Tess thought. But it was nice, and it was livable, too. The parlor into which they entered was vast, and it was combined with a big dining room that held a heavy carved Mexican table that could seat fourteen for dinner. To the left of the dining area, against the rear wall, was the broad staircase that led to the second floor.

Nearer the door was Joe's desk, on a dais, perched on a cow skin. His large wing-chair was behind it, and two heavy leather chairs were situated before it. There was a spittoon in the corner for those who felt they absolutely must chew tobacco. In the center of the room, on a beautiful hooked rug, was a large, soft, brown leather sofa. It sat next to the fire, with matching chairs across from it and occasional tables beside it. There were bright Indian flower vases on the tables. There were flowers in the vases, and Tess smiled. Hank and Jane had kept up, no matter what.

"Well!" Dolly said. "Now this is nice! Tess, where would you like us to stay?"

"Oh!" She had forgotten that even though Jamie Slater had ridden away the moment they arrived, she had other guests to attend to. "I'm sorry. Upstairs, Dolly. Hank, we can wait a while on the other things, but let's bring up Dolly's trunks. Come up, please!" She urged Dolly and Jon forward. When they reached the second-story landing, they looked down a long hallway with doors on either side and a big-paned window with velvet draperies at the end. "There are eight rooms up here," she murmured. "We shouldn't be wanting."

Jane, who had followed her up the stairs, cleared her throat softly. "Tess, your room is aired, and Joe's room is aired, and I just happened to air the back two, but I haven't touched the others yet. I was getting around to them, but then when we heard . . . When we heard that both you and Joe . . . Nothing seemed to make much sense anymore."

"That's all right," Tess said. "But we'll need linens and all for Mrs. Simmons and Mr. Red Feather. Can you see to that? We'll put them in those two rooms you aired."

"What about the lieutenant?"

"I believe he's staying in town. And should he wander back, well, he can wander into the barn."

Jon made a choking sound, then laughed. Dolly gave a little gasp. Tess didn't care. She walked grandly down the hall. "Dolly, this room here is more appropriate for a lady, I think. There's a big dressing table in here, and the light is wonderful in the morning."

"It is just wonderful!" Dolly said delightedly. "I love it!" She caught Tess's cheeks between her plump hands and gave her a kiss on the cheek. "I am so glad I came. And don't you dare wait on me. I'm here to help. Jane, you run along and get linens, and I'll get this bed made up, and then you show me around the house and tell me what I can do!"

"Dolly, you don't have to do anything but rest. It's been a long trip—"

"You hush, dear. I'm going to get to know my room!" She stepped inside, closing the door. Jane hurried down the hall to the little linen-storage room.

Tess smiled wryly at Jon. "She's wonderful, isn't she?"

"Dolly? Yes, she's a wonder."

"I didn't really give her the best room, Jon, both these rooms are big and have beautiful views. I think you'll be just as happy over here. The bed is large and firm, and it's very airy."

"I'll be quite comfortable wherever you put me," he assured her. Smiling, he looked into the room, then backed out again. "I'll go help Hank with the trunks."

"If you're tired—"

"Tess, do I look tired? If von Heusen is coming back tonight, we want to look settled in, don't we?"

"It's interesting that you should feel that way. Apparently the lieutenant wasn't very worried."

"Don't underestimate him, Tess. He knows what he's doing."

"You would defend him no matter what, wouldn't you?"

"Because I know him," Jon said quietly, and he stepped past her, down the hall and down the stairs.

She'd best get moving herself, Tess decided. She turned and hurried down the hallway in Jon's wake. While the men unloaded the wagon, she could see to the horses and the mules.

Then she'd have to find out how many of the ranch hands had stayed around once they'd heard that von Heusen would be taking over.

And then she'd have to wait . . . for von Heusen himself.

The town of Wiltshire was not a little hole-in-the-wall, Jamie decided as he rode down the main street. It was really quite sophisticated, with rows and rows of Victorian houses with their cupolas and gingerbread lining the roads that ran off the main street. Along the main street were any number of businesses—two different mercantiles, a barbershop, a corset shop, a men's wear shop, a cooper, a photographer, a mortician, a pharmacy, a doctor, two lawyers, a boardinghouse for young ladies and an inn that boasted a sign, "Perry McCarthy's Shady Rest Hotel—Stop Here and Dine! We've a Restaurant for Any Respectable Traveler, Gentleman, Lady or Child."

He wondered how well Perry McCarthy was doing. The streets were very quiet.

In front of the barbershop a few men sat around and puffed on pipes. One was missing an arm, another was minus his left foot. A pair of crutches leaned against the wall behind him. The men looked at Jamie as he rode by. The war, Jamie thought. These men had fought in the war. Southerners, like he'd been. Even if Miss Stuart was insisting upon calling him a Yank. Well, he was a Yank. Hell, they were all Yanks now. Because the damn Yanks had won the war.

"Howdy," he called out to the group.

The fellow with the stump for an arm nodded. "Stranger in these parts, aren't you, mister?"

"Yes, sir, I am. But it seems to be a nice enough place."

"Used to be," the man minus the foot said, spitting on the ground. "Used to be. But then the varmints started coming in and taking over. You know how that is. You don't hail from these parts, but I don't think that's any Chicago accent you got on you, boy. Where you from?"

"Missouri," Jamie said.

"Missouri," the footless man repeated. He stroked his graying beard with a smile and settled back. "Well, now, I hope you stay a while."

"I was planning on it. I thought I'd buy some land."

"Don't think you're going to be able to, not good land. Oh, there's some land up to the north for sale, but it's pure desert. You don't want that, boy."

"Well, I'll look around. I heard that Joe Stuart was killed. Maybe I can get my hands on some of his land."

The man without the arm was up in a minute. "Don't you go looking around to be a vulture after Joe's place. You'll wind up dead yourself, young man."

"Maybe you'd better shut up, Carter," the other fellow muttered.

Jamie leaned down, smiling. "Fellows, Joe's niece is alive and well and kicking, I can tell you."

"Miss Tess!" The one named Carter gasped with pleasure. "Why, that's the best news I've heard since '61! You telling the truth there, boy?"

"Sir, I'm over thirty," Jamie politely told him. "And I think I count double time for the war, my friends, so that makes me pretty darned old, and nobody's boy."

"Sorry there, Carter and me, we didn't mean to offend."

"No offense taken. My name is Jamie Slater. I'm looking to buy land. You hear of anything, you let me know."

"We'll do that. But you aren't going to get the Stuart ranch. Von Heusen wants that. He wants it bad."

"But he doesn't want that other land. That's interesting," Jamie mused.

"Hope you stay a while," Carter said.

"Thanks. I intend to."

"My name's Jeremiah Miller, you need any more information, bo—young man, you look me up. Hell, anybody younger'n me is a boy, son!"

Jamie laughed and urged his mount on. He could see the saloon ahead. He reined in before it, tossed his reins over the tethering bar and entered through the swinging doors.

He paused for a minute, letting his eyes adjust to the dimness and the smoke. There was a piano player in the rear. A singer with a short mauve shirt that barely covered rich black petticoats and stockings perched on the piano. Her voice was as smoky as the atmosphere.

There was a bar to his right, running the length of the establishment. Two heavyset bartenders in white aprons leaned against the mahogany bar talking to customers. There were a number of patrons at the twenty or so tables in the place. Some were well-dressed small-town merchants, others were ranch men, wearing denim pants and spurs and tall, dusty hats. Their spurred boots were sometimes up on chairs or tables. It was a lazy crowd, it seemed, an interesting one.

The crowd went silent the minute Jamie entered the room. The singer forgot the lyrics to her song. The piano player swung around and stared, too.

"Howdy," Jamie said casually.

People stared. Then the brunette hopped off the piano and walked forward. "Hello, there," she said, frowning at he others, offering Jamie a broad smile. "What's the matter with you all! We've a stranger in town. Let's not make him think we haven't a single wit of manners between the lot of us!"

"Sure thing, Sherry, honey!" one of the cowboys called out. He let his feet fall to the floor. "Howdy, there, stranger. Welcome to Wiltshire. We ain't rude. We're just surprised. Strangers just don't come here very often very more."

"Why is that?" Jamie asked.

The cowboy shrugged, but not before looking around the room. In one corner, a few men in suits were playing cards. "It ain't a good gamble, that's why," a tall, thin man with heavy iron-gray whiskers called out. "But you're here now, so come on in. Hardy!" He called to the bartender. "Give the stranger a whiskey, on me."

"Thank you kindly," Jamie said. He strode into the room. Sherry brought his whiskey. He sat across from the man who had invited him, next to a small, nervous man with wire-rimmed spectacles.

"My name's Edward Clancy," the bewhiskered man said, offering Jamie a hand. "I'm the editor of the *Wiltshire Sun*."

Jamie nearly betrayed his surprise. He kept a firm smile plastered to his face. "The *Sun*, huh? The newspaper?"

"The gossip rag," the man said flatly. "That's all I dare print, and I'm careful about that. Oh, well, I write up some articles about President Grant and about the Indians. But not much else."

"Why?"

"'Cause I like living," Edward Clancy said flatly. "We're playing poker. You in?"

Jamie pushed back his hair and reached into his pocket for money. "Sure, I'm in. I like to gamble."

"Then you're in the right town, mister. You're surely in the right town. What's your name?"

"Jamie. Jamie Slater."

Clancy smiled slowly. "I've heard of you. You're one of the Slater brothers. Why, I heard that you can hit a fly in the clouds with that—"

"Rumor," Jamie interrupted him. "Rumor, that's something I'd just as soon keep quiet for the time being."

"It's quiet. It's quiet." Clancy stared at him hard, then grinned again. "That's Doc Martin. He was one of Joe Stuart's best friends. We'll keep things quiet. Whatever you say."

"Thanks."

"We'll help you any way that we can," Doc volunteered.

"Information is what I need now," Jamie said, leaning closer. "Why does this von Heusen want the Stuart property so damn bad?"

"You know, we haven't figured that one out yet. We just haven't figured it out. But he does want it badly."

"Badly enough to kill?"

"Hell, yes, I think so. Why, if the Indians hadn't gotten old Joe…" His voice trailed away as he stared at Jamie. "It wasn't a tribe of Indians that came after him, was it?"

"Not according to Tess."

"Tess! She's alive!"

Jamie nodded. The look of pure, unadulterated joy on the man's face was somewhat irritating. The sun-honey blond seemed to be a golden angel around these parts.

Edward Clancy leaned so far across the table that he was nearly on top of it. His voice was soft; his features were knotted up and tense. "If Tess says it was von Heusen, it was von Heusen all right. Are you—are you going to stay around and fight him?"

"Yeah. Yeah, I guess so."

He didn't guess so. He was committed, and he knew it. He had been committed since he'd first seen Tess's face.

He just hadn't known it right away.

"Hell! Don't look now," Doc muttered suddenly.

"What?" Jamie demanded.

"Some of von Heusen's boys. The four fellows who just came in. The mean-looking ones."

They were a mean-looking group, Jamie decided. Lanky-haired, glitter-eyed. Two were light, two were dark-haired. One chewed tobacco incessantly.

The dark-haired man who chewed tobacco seemed to be the spokesman for the group. He slammed his fist on the bar, rattling all the glasses on it. He shouted to the bartender, who couldn't seem to move swiftly enough to the end of the bar.

"Hardy! What's the matter with you, ya gettin' old?" one of the men demanded. "Whiskey. And not the rotgut you serve the local swine. Give us the best in the house."

Hardy set a bottle on the bar. The man grasped him by the shirt collar and nearly pulled him over the bar. Hardy was starting to turn purple, and his attacker was laughing like a hyena.

"That's enough."

Jamie was on his feet. Once again, everyone went silent.

Von Heusen's men were silent, too. The four of them stared at him with astonishment. Then they began to smile.

"Who the hell are you?" asked the dark-haired brute.

"That doesn't matter. Let Hardy alone."

"Why, son, you don't know anything about this town at all, now, do you?"

"Let him go," Jamie repeated.

"He needs to be taught a lesson," one of the light-haired men said with a nasty snarl.

"Yeah. A fatal lesson."

In a flash, the man released the bartender. He drew his gun.

He was fast, but not fast enough. Before he could aim he had dropped the gun, howling in pain. His friends tried to draw.

Rapid shots sizzled from Jamie's Colts. The second man was on the floor, clutching his leg. The third grasped an arm. The fourth was on the floor. He might have been dead. Jamie didn't know or care.

He looked at Edward Clancy. "Thanks for the drink, friend," he said quietly.

Then he left the bar, walking over his fallen enemies.

Chapter Seven

By nightfall the wagon had been unloaded except for the printing press, which would be taken into town in the morning. Tess had even managed to fill the hip bath in the kitchen with steaming water and soak for a long time, washing away the dust and dirt from the trail. She kept reminding herself that von Heusen was coming back, but she felt strangely calm, despite the fact that Jamie had deserted them. Von Heusen wasn't going to come right up to the house and murder her. He hadn't the guts for that.

She dressed in a soft summer-green cotton and set about making dinner with Jane and Dolly to help her. She was accustomed to Jane, but it was really nice to have Dolly with her. Dolly kept up a steady stream of conversation, mostly about her husband, Will, and their days in the military. Her stories were spicy and fun, and Tess enjoyed them thoroughly.

They cooked a huge wild turkey on a spit and summer squash and green beans and apple turnovers. When the table was set and everything was ready, Tess went out to find Jon.

He was leaning against a pillar, a band tied around his dark hair and forehead, a repeating carbine held casually in his hand. He looked over the landscape.

"Dinner's on, Jon."

He glanced her way, smiling. "Thanks, Tess, but I think I'll wait out here a while longer, keep an eye on things."

"It's turkey and all kinds of good things. I'd like to repay you for the trip."

"I'll eat soon," he promised. She nodded and left him. Halfway inside the house she paused, wondering if he was looking for von Heusen or Jamie.

She hoped Jamie was eating stale, weevil-riddled bread somewhere. She had a feeling, though, that he was not.

She walked into the house and to the dining-room table. Hank had come in, and he was smiling. "The boys are out at the bunkhouse and they're pleased as peaches that you're home, Miss Tess. Well, them that's left. We've still got Roddy Morris, Sandy Harrison and Bill McDowell. They won't be going anywhere."

"Wonderful!" Tess told him. "Bring the boys in for dinner, will you, Hank?"

"They're already fixin' their suppers in the bunkhouse, Tess. We'll have a big Sunday dinner for them all, that's what we'll do."

"Fine. That sounds good, Hank. Now, let's all sit."

Dolly offered to say grace. She thanked God for His bounty, for their being alive and being together, then she asked God to take a good look at their enemies and see if He couldn't do something to put bad men in their proper place. "Amen," she finished.

"Amen," they all chorused.

Tess was about to take her first bite of dinner when she heard the sounds of horses' hooves. She set down her fork. How many of them had come with von Heusen? It sounded like five, no more.

"Excuse me," she said primly, setting her napkin carefully on the table and rising casually. It didn't matter. Dolly,

Hank and Jane all catapulted to their feet, and they attached themselves to her like shadows as she walked to the door. She could hear voices before she reached it. Jon's first.

"That's close enough, fellows. Close enough."

"It's an Injun!"

"I said close enough."

Someone must have moved. A barrage of shots went off, followed by a startled silence.

Then von Heusen started to talk.

"Hold it, boys, hold your fire! I've just come to talk to Hank and Jane about removing themselves from the property—"

"There's no need for them to remove themselves from the property," Jon said. "This is private property, and the owner seems to want them here. One step nearer, boy," he warned someone, "and there'll be a hole in your chest where your heart used to be."

"Who in the blazes are you!" von Heusen thundered, losing his control.

"A friend."

"A friend! Well, listen here, you red-faced monkey. The Stuarts are dead. They were attacked by Comanche or Apache—"

"Apache?" Jon interrupted. She could hear something cold and dangerous in his voice. "Tell me, which Apache? Which Apache do you think did it? Or don't you know? I'll tell you, I'm damned sure it wasn't any Apache. Apache, any Apache, make war, or they go raiding. They make war to 'take death from their enemies.' They raid to fill their bellies. I haven't met an Apache yet who would leave dead cattle scattered with the corpses of men."

"Who the hell knows or cares what Apache!" von Heusen thundered. "It doesn't matter. Maybe it was Comanche—"

"Running River denies it."

"There are more tribes of Comanche!"

"Yes, there are," Jon said softly. "But the Comanche usually know what they're doing, too. When it comes to scalping a man.

"Of course, the whites have been scalping for a long time now. I read somewhere that they started scalping way back in the east in the sixteen hundreds. But still. White men in a hurry do a sloppy job. Neither a Comanche nor an Apache would do a sloppy job. No matter what his hurry."

"Takes an Injun to know!" someone muttered.

"Maybe we ought to string him up. Who knows? Maybe he's some renegade in charge of the party that did it himself!" von Heusen said.

"Let's hang him!"

"Let's see you try!" Jon said very softly.

"Hold it! Hold it!" von Heusen said. "Now listen, Joe Stuart and his family are dead. And this property is going to go up for public auction. Now I have—"

Tess had taken his statement as her cue. She threw open the door and stepped onto the porch behind Jon. "Correction, von Heusen. I am not dead."

Even in the dusky light that sifted down from the moon and the stars, Tess could see the startled look that flashed briefly across von Heusen's features.

He was a lean man, tall, spare. His features were almost cadaverous, his cheekbones sucked in, his chin very long and pointed. His eyes were coal black, and they seemed to burn from his skull. He sat atop his horse well, though. Jon had his repeating rifle aimed right at his heart, and von Heusen still sat casually, his hands draped over the pommel.

Around him were four of his men. He had about twenty hired guns on his place. Only four of them were with him.

Tess didn't like it. He usually paid his visits with an escort of at least eight to ten.

It made her wonder where the rest of his men might be.

Von Heusen found his voice at last. "Why, Miss Stuart. I am delighted to see you alive and well."

"Like hell you are, von Heusen."

"That's uncalled for, ma'am."

"Be damned, you carpetbagging riffraff, but it is."

"Someone ought to wash your mouth out with a little soap, lady. I just came by—"

"You just came by to rob Joe of everything he ever had, now that you've murdered him!"

"You watch your accusation there, Miss Stuart."

"It's the truth. You know it, and I know it. And somehow, I'm going to prove it!"

Von Heusen was smiling. "I don't think so, little lady. No, I don't think so. You want to know what I do think?" He leaned toward her. It was just a fraction of an inch and he was still far away, but the gesture made her tremble inside. "I think that this ranch was meant to be mine, Miss Stuart. Now I've offered you good money for it. Real good money. And you still don't want to sell. Miss Stuart, I want you out of town."

"I'm not leaving."

"I wouldn't be so adamant, little lady. You may find that you leave in one way or another."

"You threatening her, von Heusen?" Jon asked.

"She seems to think that I'm guilty of something," von Heusen said. "The whole damned town can tell you that I was in the saloon playing cards the day the Indians attacked the Stuart train. The whole damned town can tell you that. But still, if the lady is so worried and so certain, well then, maybe she ought to plan on riding out of town. What do you think?"

"I think that you should give reasonable thought to the idea of riding out of town yourself, von Heusen," Jon warned quietly.

Von Heusen started to laugh. "On the word of a half-breed Indian?"

He started to urge his mount closer to the porch. Jon fired a shot that must have sizzled a hairbreadth from the man's cheek. Von Heusen went as pale as the clouds.

"Hey, boss—" one of his men began nervously.

Von Heusen lifted a hand. "Calm down now, boys. Just because Miss Stuart's resorting to violence is no reason that we should. We'll be riding off now. But you remember what I said, Miss Stuart. I'd hate to see you leaving town other than all dressed up right pretty and in a comfortable stagecoach!" He smiled at her. "It is good to see you alive and well. Such a pretty, pretty woman. And all that blond hair. Blond hair alone is worth a pretty penny in certain places, did you know that?"

He stared at Tess. As he did so, she suddenly realized that she could smell smoke.

Suddenly she knew where the rest of von Heusen's men were. The smoke was coming from the direction of the carriage house. The printing press was in the wagon still, and the wagon was next to the buckboard and the chaise in the carriage house.

And so far, it had been a dry summer. If the carriage house went up in flames, the blaze could quickly spread to the house, to the barn, even to the stables.

Von Heusen was smiling.

"You bastard!" she hissed at him. Jon hadn't moved; he didn't dare. If he moved the rifle a hair von Heusen just might decide to take advantage and shoot them all down.

They stood there, locked in the moment, von Heusen staring at Tess with a smile, Tess staring at him, hating him so fiercely that she should have been able to have willed him dead. It was lost now. All lost. The house, Joe's house. The press. It didn't even seem to bother von Heusen that he would slaughter all the horses.

Then suddenly, in the midst of von Heusen's triumph and her own despair, a commotion sounded from the direction of the carriage house. There was still smoke issuing from it—no sign of fire yet.

But men suddenly spilled out of it. Four of them, their hands held high above their heads. They nearly tripped as they walked, for someone had apparently ordered them to lower their breeches, and their pants were tight around their ankles. Three of them wore long johns; the fourth must have been buck naked. Tess only caught a glimpse of his bare legs, as he managed to stay behind the other three.

"Tarnation!" von Heusen swore. "You fools! What in bloody hell is going on—"

He broke off and never finished his question. From the smoke of the carriage house, another man appeared.

Tess felt her heart catch.

It was Jamie. He had a single gun trained on the men and he followed them out with the casual air von Heusen had had.

The men kept walking forward. The half-naked one paused, and Jamie nudged him forward.

"Ladies, do excuse me," Jamie apologized, "but they seemed to be a little more docile and trustworthy in this fashion."

"I'll kill you yet!" one of them muttered.

"Well, I don't doubt that you intend to try," Jamie assured him. Then he stared at the men still mounted upon their horses. "Which one of you is von Heusen?"

"I am Richard von Heusen. Who the hell are you?"

"Jamie Slater. But that doesn't matter. What does matter is that I own part of this spread now. And I'll thank you kindly to keep yourself and your half-sawed ruffians off my property, is that understood?"

"Your property—" von Heusen began.

"My property, yes. Now, take your arsonist friends here and move."

"You must be mistaken. Why would my men set fire to anything here?"

"Who knows why? But that was what they were doing. Ordinarily, of course, I'd want to get to know my new neighbors. But since you and the Stuarts don't seem to be very good friends, I really don't think you should stay. I bet dinner is on. Tess, is dinner on?"

"Yes!"

"Something good?"

His eyes touched hers across the dusky night. She nodded, fighting for speech. "Turkey. Dressing. Squash. All sorts of things."

"And getting cold. I do declare. Gentlemen, good night," Jamie said firmly. He prodded the men. "Move 'em, now, von Heusen; or they'll start turning into corpses."

"We're nine to one, you fool—"

"Nine to two. See my friend there? He could hit the hair in a man's nose at a thousand yards, and he's faster than greased lightning. You're outmanned, and outnumbered, you just don't know it yet."

"We'll see about that," von Heusen said angrily. "Get those half-naked idiots up on your horses!" he ordered his mounted men. He jerked his mount around to face Tess and pointed a long finger at her. "You'll pay for this, Miss Stuart. You'll pay dearly. I promise you."

He swung around again, and his men followed. They raced off into the darkness, the horses' hooves pounding on the dry earth.

Silence and stillness fell over the small group on the porch. Jon Red Feather slowly lowered his rifle. He stared at Jamie. "What the hell took you so long?"

"Well, there were four of them in the carriage house!" Jamie announced indignantly. He strode up the stairs. Tess was still staring at him blankly when he tweaked her cheek and walked past her.

She managed to turn and follow him. He walked over to the table and sat, then pulled off a turkey leg and bit into it hungrily. Looking up, he saw Tess staring at him, Dolly and Jane on either side of her, and Jon and Hank on either side of the women. He paused in midbite.

"Do you all mind?"

Tess stood in front of him. "Where did you go? How did you happen to come back right then?"

He chewed before answering her. "I left the saloon as soon as I met a few friendly people—and a few not so friendly people. I knew he was coming out here. I didn't know he intended to burn you out." He paused, looking past Tess to Jon. "Seems strange, doesn't it? The man wants this property, but he doesn't seem to care if he destroys it. Makes you think, doesn't it?"

"Sure does."

"Makes you think what?" Tess asked irritably.

"Tess, think about it. It needs a little paint, a little shoring up here and there—but this is a darned nice house. Solid, sound, big. Then you've got the outbuildings, the carriages—and the horses. I haven't seen enough to really make an estimate on the value of the stock, but I imagine that we're talking hundreds and hundreds of dollars in horseflesh alone. And von Heusen doesn't care. He wants the property, but he doesn't care if he burns it to the ground.''

"He's a vile son of a bitch, that's why!" Tess stated.

"Well, yes," Jamie acknowledged with a wry grin. "But there's more to it than that, I think."

Dolly took a seat at the table again and spooned up a mouthful of squash. "Vile, certainly! Why, our dinner has gone quite cold!"

"That's the spirit, Dolly," Jamie told her. "Jon, sit. The turkey may be cold, but it's delicious."

"That's it?" Tess demanded heatedly.

"What do you mean, that's it?"

"Where did you go? What were you doing? You were supposed to be here!"

"Jon was here," Jamie said evenly.

"But—"

Jamie was buttering a roll. Jane and Hank and Jon sat and picked up their forks. Jamie's butter knife went still and his eyes were slightly narrowed as he stared at her. "Miss Stuart, I don't like the tone of this conversation. I came back in time to save your hide."

"You wouldn't have had to rush back if you'd been here—where you should have been! You want to be paid so highly, and you can't even stick around!"

He stood suddenly. His knife clattered against a dish. "I don't argue like this in front of others, Miss Stuart."

"There is no argument!" she snapped.

"No, there isn't. I'll make it simple. Wherever I choose to go is my own business, Miss Stuart. You are not my keeper. And as to payment, hell, yes. Tomorrow we'll go into town and you'll turn over half interest in this place to me."

She gasped aloud, stunned.

"Jamie, she doesn't understand what you're doing," Jon said, ignoring the rising tensions and reaching for a roll himself. "If you just explained—"

"Explained! Hell, I feel as if I'm up before the judge and jury!"

"Judge and jury! I really don't give a damn what you do with your time, but—"

"You begged me to come here, Tess."

"Begged!"

"Begged!"

"Oh!" she cried. Then she wound her fingers tightly together. "I don't argue in public either, Lieutenant!" she snapped. She was shaking, she realized. She'd been so damned amazed and grateful to see him, but she'd also been scared, and now she was furious and shaking and she wasn't even sure what she did want. She turned, having no taste left for dinner. Angrily she began to stride for the door.

"Tess!" He was on his feet, calling to her. He really expected her to stop because he had commanded her to.

She didn't stop, she didn't turn, she didn't even pause. She sailed straight for the front door. She would go to the carriage house to make sure the fire von Heusen's men had started had been stamped out.

"Jamie, give her a minute," Dolly suggested.

"The hell I will!" Jamie snapped.

Before Tess heard the door slam in her wake, she thought she heard Jamie's chair hit the floor as he pushed it over.

She started running toward the carriage house, anxious to reach it before he could see her. She was at the side door when she heard the front door to the house slam.

She slipped into the carriage house. She inhaled and exhaled, but couldn't smell any smoke. All she could smell was the fresh scent of the alfalfa hay that was being stored behind the chaise.

She fumbled in the darkness to light the gas lamp by the door. When the glow filled the carriage house, she went to check the wagon and the printing press. She crawled into the wagon and gave a soft sigh of relief as she saw that the printing press was fine. She sank down on one of the bunks.

"Tess! Where are you!"

Jamie was obviously angry. She clenched her teeth and tried to ignore him. She stepped from the wagon and went to the buckboard. No flames had lapped against it. The chaise, too, seemed untouched. Walking around, she discovered a half burned bale of hay. It had been dragged into the center of the room and lit. Von Heusen had meant it to be a slow fire. He had really meant to be long gone when the place burned.

She moved away from the hay and from the faint, acrid smell of fire that remained.

"Tess!"

He was still calling her, like a drill sergeant. With a sigh she determined that she would have to open the door, but she hesitated with her hand upon it. Where had he been? He'd been gone for hours. Had he really enjoyed the saloon so much? What part of the saloon?

And why was she torturing herself so thoroughly over him? She couldn't change the man.

The door slammed open before she could twist the knob. With a startled yelp she leaped back. Jamie was there, hatless, his shirt open at the neck, his hands on his hips, his sandy hair tousled casually over a brow, but his manner anything but casual.

"Why didn't you answer me?" he demanded.

"Because I didn't want to speak to you."

"It didn't occur to you that I might have been worried?"

"I could have been in and out of the carriage house all evening, and you wouldn't have known. What, I'm supposed to be on a ball and chain if you're around? But if you're not, it doesn't matter?''

She saw his jaw twist and a pulse tick hard against his throat. ''That's about it, yes. Think you can live with the rules?''

''No!''

''Then I'm leaving.''

''What?''

''You heard me.''

''But—'' In astonishment she stared at him. She inhaled sharply. She couldn't let him leave her. She couldn't!

But she thought he wouldn't go. He just wanted to see her beg.

''Leave,'' she told him. She'd call his bluff, she determined.

He turned and reached for the door. She thought quickly and desperately, then said, ''I thought you liked the property. And the house, and the horses. And I thought you wanted half of everything. If you want it, you have to earn it.''

He swung around. A smile curled his lip as he leaned against the door. ''You just can't say please, can you?''

''It isn't that! My God, this isn't fair! You want thousands of dollars worth of property—''

''If von Heusen has his way, there won't be any property.''

''But you're unfair!''

''Because I went to the saloon?''

''Because you weren't here!''

''But I was here. I was here exactly when you needed me.'' He walked toward her. She took a step back and tripped over the pile of half burned hay. He kept coming, and she reached out a hand, expecting he would help her up. He didn't.

He dropped down, half on top of her and half beside her, his arms braced over her chest so that she couldn't move. Gray eyes looked into hers. He'd had a shave in town, she thought. His cheeks were clean, and he smelled slightly of a cologne. He smelled good all over, like good clean soap and like a man. He'd had a bath, too, she realized, and her temper soared again. He had stayed at the saloon. He'd had a drink and a bath and maybe a meal and...

Maybe a woman.

"Get off of me, Yank!" she said angrily.

The smoke left his eyes. He stared at her with a gaze of cold steel. He leaned closer. So close that their faces nearly touched. The heat of his body was all around her, and she forgot everything, afraid, excited, wanting to escape him and run...

And wanting to know more of him.

"You're hurting me," she began.

"No, I'm not," he corrected her flatly. "And I'm not moving a hair, because I really want your attention. Now listen. I can go, or I can stay. The choice is yours. But if I stay, we do things my way. I'll try to explain. I'm not desperate for land, cattle, a house or money. I've done all right myself, thanks, despite the war, despite everything. But tomorrow, you're going to turn over half of this place to me on legal papers. That way you may have a chance of keeping it. Pay attention. You're a smart girl, Tess. Von Heusen thought that all he had to do was kill you and your uncle and he could have this place. You have no next of kin. But darlin', I've got plenty. I've got brothers, nieces and nephews. It would take von Heusen years to find them all if he did manage to kill both of us. That might give him some serious pause. Do you understand?"

Staring at him, Tess simply nodded. He was right, and every word he was saying made such perfect sense. And she wanted to be sensible. She wanted to be dignified, grateful, strong. She wanted to be able to fight her battles, but she could not fight alone.

If only she didn't want him as a man, if only she didn't grow jealous and angry so quickly. And yet...he still had that haunting aroma. His flesh would be slick and clean, and she wanted to know how the warmth would feel beneath her tongue.

The way he lay against her, she felt the thunder of his heart, and her own, and the beats seemed to rise together, and fall away, and rise together again, quick, wild, rampant. She felt his breath against her cheeks, and the iron lock of his thigh upon her own. She wanted to reach out and run her fingers through the sandy tendrils of hair that fell so hauntingly over his forehead, and so often shadowed and shaded his eyes, and hid his innermost thoughts.

"Yes? You do understand?"

"Yes!" she cried out.

"And it all makes sense to you? You'll do what I'm asking you to do?"

"Yes. We'll go into town. As soon as I've stopped by the paper—"

"Before."

"What difference does it make?"

"Maybe none. But the sooner von Heusen hears about this, the better things are going to be."

"Fine!" She was nearly screaming again. She was close to tears because she was desperate to escape him and the sensual blanketing of his body upon hers. "Please, let me up!"

He rolled to his side, and she was free. "You do sound more like him every day, though," she muttered heedlessly, rolling from him to rise and dust the hay from her gown. "Carpetbagging Yanks, all of—"

"That's another thing we're going to get straight here once and for all!" he stated. Before she could flee as she had intended, his arm snaked around her, and she was tumbling into the hay again. He straddled her, and his hands pinned her down. "I'm not a Yank. I'm a U.S. Cavalry officer now, Miss Stuart, but I was born and bred in Missouri and I fought with Morgan for many long years in the war. As a *Reb*, Tess. Got that straight? Don't you ever go calling me a carpetbagging Yank again, and so help me God, I mean that! Understand?"

She stared at him blankly. She had called him a Yank a dozen times, and only now was he telling her the truth.

"Tess!"

"Yes!" she cried. She tore at her wrists and freed them from his grasp, then shoved him as hard as she could. He didn't move. "Either Jon or I should know where you are at all times. All right?"

"Yes!"

"No hiding in barns or carriage houses."

"I wasn't hiding! I was trying to make sure the fire was really out."

"I wouldn't have walked out of here without making sure the fire was out."

"Maybe I needed to see for myself. The printing press is in here."

"That damned press! It's everything to you."

"Yes! The paper does mean everything! It's the only means I have to tell the truth!"

He was silent for a moment. Then he moved slowly to his feet and reached down for her. She tried to ignore his helping hands, but they were quickly upon her. He stood her up, but he wasn't ready to release her yet.

"I know what I'm doing."

She inhaled the scent of him. "I do imagine that you do, Lieutenant."

"What does that mean?"

"You've had a nice bath, so it seems."

"And a shave."

"May I go now?"

He was smiling again. "Jealous little thing, aren't you?"

"Why should I be? I had a wonderfully pleasant afternoon with Mr. Red Feather. He's extremely well read and well traveled."

Jamie's eyes darkened and narrowed. For an instant she hated herself; she had no right to want to cause trouble between the friends. But she seemed driven to try and make Jamie angry.

And then it hit her like a bolt from the blue. She was falling in love with Jamie!

No! I am not in love with him, she thought in dismay.

But maybe she was. She wanted him. In ways she had never imagined a woman would ever want a man.

"It's important," Jamie repeated softly, "that Jon or I know where you are at all times. Did we get that one down yet?"

"Yes, thank you, I think we did. But since I do seem to get along much better with Jon, don't you think I should report to him, Lieutenant?" She twisted free and saluted stiffly.

He caught her shoulders and pulled her back. "You're a minx, Tess. A tart-mouthed little minx with siren's eyes and the longest claws this side of the Mississippi."

"Lieutenant, you're—"

"I'm not a Yank, or a carpetbagger, Tess, and so help me—"

"You're about to crush my shoulder blades, Lieutenant," she said as regally as she could manage.

"Oh." He released her. "Do excuse me."

"I try, Lieutenant. Daily. Hourly." She started for the door.

"Tess?"

She didn't turn.

"I could have made you beg, you know?"

She spun around. He was laughing. She raced forward in a sudden surge of energy and butted him in the stomach. Taken off guard, he fell into the singed hay.

She didn't stay to hear anything else he might have to say. She raced from the carriage house and back to the house, not pausing until she was inside. She leaned against the door, gasping for breath.

The dining table was clean. Jane came from the kitchen and paused when she saw Tess. "They've all gone to bed, Tess. Hank just went to the bunkhouse. Mr. Red Feather suggested that the hands take a few hours apiece on a kind of a guard duty. Roddy called in that big guard dog of his and he's going to have the dog on the porch, once he sees the lieutenant and tells the dog that the lieutenant is a friend. I was going to go to bed. It's been a big day for me, Miss Stuart. A real big day."

Her eyes rolled and Tess laughed. Impulsively she gave Jane a big hug. It was a mistake. Jane looked as if she was going to start crying all over again. "I'm just so happy that you're alive!" she said.

"Thanks. And I'm happy to be home. Come on, let's go up."

They walked up the stairs together. Jane hugged Tess quickly and fiercely again and headed toward her own room. Wearily Tess pushed open the door to her bedroom and walked in. Lighting the lamp at her bedside, she shed her clothing and dressed in a soft blue flannel nightgown. She sat in front of her dressing table and picked up the silver-embossed brush that had belonged to her mother. It was good to be home.

She pulled all the pins out of her hair—and then all the little pieces of hay that had stuck into it—and began to brush it. It fell down her shoulders, long and free. She brushed it mechanically for several minutes, staring at her reflection and not seeing a thing.

Jane had been right. It had been a big day.

But von Heusen had been beaten back. Between Jamie and Jon, he had been beaten back. She never had told Jamie that she was grateful. Truly grateful.

He never seemed to give her a chance to say thank you. He was on her side, but it seemed that she was always fighting him. At first, she had been fighting him to make him believe her. Now she was certain he believed her. He had met von Heusen. He couldn't have any doubt that von Heusen had been responsible for the attack on the wagon train.

And now...

Maybe she wasn't fighting him. Maybe she was fighting herself.

First it had been that darned Eliza. Tess had managed to walk away from Eliza with her dignity intact, but she had heard Jamie speaking to the woman. *No one can make me marry anyone. No one can make me marry anyone...*

So he wasn't the marrying kind.

She was. She wanted a man, a good man. She hadn't had much time to think about it, what with the war and then everything that had happened since. But when she thought for a moment, she knew. She didn't want to be a spinster. The paper was important to her, and she wasn't just copublisher and a reporter anymore, she was the only publisher. She had to keep it alive. But she wanted more, too. She wanted a husband, one she really loved, and one who loved her. And she wanted children, and she wanted to give them a world that wasn't forever tainted with the memories of conflict and death.

And she wanted Jamie Slater...

She wasn't at all sure how the two things intertwined—they didn't intertwine at all, she admitted. She sighed.

She had to get by the present for the moment. She had to survive von Heusen.

She shivered suddenly, violently, remembering the way von Heusen had threatened her. She would be getting out of town, he had told her. If not by stagecoach, then by some other means.

What could he do to her? She wasn't alone. She had help now.

But to pay for it she was about to turn over half her property—half of Uncle Joe's legacy to her—to Jamie Slater. If he chose, he could be her neighbor all her life. She could watch him, and torture herself day after day, wondering who he rode away to see, wondering what it was like when he took a woman into his arms.

She groaned and pushed away from the table. She couldn't solve a thing tonight. She needed some sleep. She needed some sleep very badly.

She doused the light and crawled beneath the covers. It felt so good to be in her own bed again. The sheets were cool and clean and fresh-smelling, and her mattress was soft and firm, and it seemed to caress her deliciously. A faint glow from the stars and the moon entered the room gently. It kept everything in dark shadows, and yet she could see the familiar shapes of her dressing table and her drawers and her little mahogany secretary desk.

The breeze wafted her curtains. She closed her eyes.

Perhaps she dozed for a moment. Not much time could have passed, and yet she suddenly became aware that something was different. Her door had been thrust open.

She wasn't alone.   •

Jamie was standing in the doorway, his hands on his hips, his body a silhouette in the soft hazy moonbeams. There was nothing soft or gentle about his stance, however. She could feel the anger that radiated from him.

"All right, Tess, where's my room?"

His room? "Oh!" she murmured. "Your room . . . well, I didn't think you were going to stay here."

Long strides brought him quickly across the room. She scrambled to a sitting position as he towered over her. "I just spent two days riding with you to get here. I spent two nights sleeping on the hard ground beneath the wagon."

"The hay in the barn is very soft."

"The hay in the barn is very soft," he repeated, staring at her. He leaned closer. "The hay in the barn is very soft? Is that what you said?" She felt his closeness in the shadows even as she inhaled his clean, fascinating, masculine scent. His eyes seemed silver in the darkness, satanic. She was riddled with trembling, so keenly aware of him that it was astonishing.

"You don't have a room for me?" he demanded.

"All right, I am sorry. But you were gone, and we were all exhausted. And you did have a bath somewhere . . . I just believed that you meant to sleep where you had bathed."

He was still for a moment—dead still. Then he smiled. "Miss Stuart, move over."

"What?"

"Move over. If there's no room for me, then I'll sleep here."

"Of all the nerve!"

"Hush! We share this bed, or we sleep in the hay together," he warned her.

He meant it! she thought, still incredulous. She started to rise, trying to escape from the bed. He caught her arm and pulled her gently back.

"Where are you going?" he whispered.

"Where else! You're bigger than I am—I can't throw you out! I'm going to the barn!"

"Wait."

"For what?" she demanded.

For what? Every pulse within her was alive and crying out. She felt him with the length of her body, with her heart, with her soul, with her womb. He did not hold her against him. He caressed her. He was warm, and his smile and the white flash of his teeth in the night were compelling and hypnotic.

"I said that we'd go together," he told her. He swept her up, cocooned in a tangle of sheet and quilt. He held her tightly against his body and started for the door.

Her arms wound around his neck. She stared at the planes of his face and felt as if the soft magic of the moonbeams had wrapped around her. She should have been screaming, protesting, bringing down the house. But she was not. Her fingers grazed his nape, and she felt absurdly comfortable in his arms. He was dragging her out to the hay, she thought, and she did not care.

Nor was there anything secretive or furtive about his action. He moved with long strides and went down the stairway with little effort to be quiet. He opened the front door, bracing her weight with one arm, then let it close behind him. He stood on the porch and looked out into the night. Then he stared at her, and she knew that she was smiling.

"Where am I heading?"

"I don't know."

"Where do the hands sleep?"

"In the bunkhouse, by the far barn."

"Then I want the first barn?" he demanded softly.

She couldn't answer him. She wasn't sure what the question was. All she could think was that he meant her to sleep in the hay. She wasn't sure what else he meant for her to do there, but though she was in his arms now, and though he carried her with a certain force, she suddenly knew that what happened would be her choice. Still, he had caught hold of something deep within her, and she wasn't angry.

She smiled again as she looked at him and told him primly, "You, sir, are completely audacious."

"Maybe," he said, and smiled in return. Then it seemed they were locked there in the night, their eyes touching, and something else touching maybe, with the tenderness of the laughter they shared. Then the laughter faded.

He pulled her more tightly against him, higher within his arms. And as she watched him, fascinated, in the glow of the moonbeams, his lips parted upon hers, and the world seemed to explode as his kiss entered into her.

Darkness swirled around her, and sensation took flight.

She had to get away from him . . . and quickly.

No . . . she had to stay. She was where she wanted to be. Exactly where she wanted to be.

Chapter Eight

He carried her, in the moonlit night, to the barn. He entered it and laid her, in her cocoon of covers, in the rear of the building, where soft alfalfa lay freed from its bales, ready to be tossed to the horses. The smell of the hay was sweet, almost intoxicating.

He lay down beside her and brought the back of his hand against her cheek, touching the length of it, as if he studied just her cheek and found the form and texture both beautiful and fascinating. Then his finger roamed over the damp fullness of her lip. He watched the movement as he touched her, then his eyes met hers. She could still feel, in her memory, in the pulse that seemed to beat throughout her, the touch of his lips against hers. And yet when he kissed her again, though the feel was poignant, she knew that he would move away when he did.

He lay back against the hay, staring at the rafters and the ceiling. He groaned softly, then rolled suddenly, violently, to face her again. He didn't touch her, but leaned on an elbow to stare at her reproachfully.

"You couldn't have just arranged a room, for me, huh?"

"You couldn't have just stuck around for a while, huh?" she retorted. He was ruining it, dissolving the moonbeams, destroying the moment she had imagined and waited for.

He rolled on his back again. "Go to your room," he told her. "I had no right to drag you out here."

Tess leaped to her feet, her cheeks flaming, her body and soul in torment. She stared at him furiously. "You have no right to do what you're doing now! To ruin everything!"

"To ruin everything?" He scowled. "Tess! I'm trying damned hard to do the decent thing!" And she would never know what an effort it was taking. He felt on fire, as if he burned in a thousand hells. It had been all right before he touched her, before he felt her lips parting beneath his. Before he sensed her innocence and the sweet wildness beneath it, the passion, the sensuality that simmered and swept beneath it all, that promised heaven. She was different. He wasn't sure if he dared take her all the way, because he knew it would mean fragile ties that might bind him forever. He couldn't find a simple fascination in her beauty; it would be more, and though he couldn't begin to define it, it was there. He already slept with dreams of her haunting his mind; he never forgot for a moment the way she had looked upon the rock, as naked as Eve, as tempting as original sin.

"Tess, don't you see? I'm trying to let you go!"

She paused, and it seemed that she waited upon her toes, as if she would go or stay according to the way the breeze came. There was a curiously soft smile on her face, almost wistful, a look he had seldom seen. "What if I don't want to be let go?" she asked him very quietly, with a breathless, melodic whisper. He wasn't sure he had really heard the words. Real or not, they ignited embers within him. He came to his feet and looked at her across the small, shadowed distance that separated them. He could almost reach out and touch her. If he did, he would be lost. If he put his hands upon her now, he would never let her go.

"You have to make up your mind." He almost growled the words. "No strings, no promises, no guarantees. You should run. You should run from me just as fast as one of those thoroughbreds of yours."

"Why?"

She didn't move; she hadn't taken a step. There was a note of amusement and challenge in her voice. Her chin was raised high; her eyes were brilliant, nearly coal-black in the shadows. He forced himself to walk around her, but that was a mistake. The moon was filtering through the windows, and the light played havoc with the flannel gown she wore. Light touched fabric, molded it, saw through it. He felt again the softness of the woman he had held, and his hands itched to touch her again. A hunger took root inside him, one that made him long to caress and taste and know.

"Why?" He repeated her question.

The reasons were swiftly leaving his mind. If she was willing, he was more than anxious to drown in the sweet depths of her fascinating waters. He clenched his fingers and kept moving casually. "Because we're in a barn, because I've the distinct feeling you don't know what you're doing, because you're young and because you're probably the type of woman who ought to fall in love, deeply in love, with the right man, and have a band of gold, and all the rest. Because I'm the hardened refuse of an ill-fated war, and though I don't mind a fight, I wouldn't be looking for more than a lover."

She smiled. "Lieutenant, what makes you think I'd be looking for anything more than a lover?"

He almost groaned aloud. If she didn't leave soon...

"Tess, I don't think you know—"

"I'm twenty-four, Lieutenant. And just as much the refuse of an ill-fated war as you are. That war taught me a great deal. You can't always wait to seize what you want. Life is too short, too quickly severed."

She was smiling still, and there was something poignant about her words that caught hold of his heart. He had never seen her more beautiful, more feminine, more arresting. Her eyes were wide; her smile was gentle; her still form was compelling in the flannel that was draped over her shoulders, nearly falling from them, that conformed to the rise of her breasts, then fell to the floor. Her hair was a river of dazzling, honeyed light that caressed and embraced her, waving around her shoulders and falling almost to her waist. Her eyes... When he came close, he saw that they were not coal-black at all, but so deeply colored in the near darkness that they appeared to be a rich and hypnotic purple.

He held still. He watched her and tried to find the right words, the words that would get her to leave. She would hate him for humiliating and rejecting her, but maybe that would be better than what he wanted. To own her, to have all of her, to teach her everything she wanted to know so thoroughly that she would forget everything but the feel of him beside her...

"Come here then," he said hoarsely.

She still seemed to pause. Like a sprite, like a night witch or angel, he knew not which. A rueful curve came to her lips, and she said softly, "Jamie?"

"What?"

"Where did you take your bath?"

He smiled, too. "At the livery stables. Not at the saloon."

"Thank you," she murmured, then she took a step toward him, and another step, and she was in his arms.

His mouth closed upon hers, and he let his hands wander where they would. He had tried to do the decent thing. And it hadn't worked. So now...

She was fragrant, like a drug. He breathed in the scent of her hair and the scent of her flesh. He kissed her lips and her earlobe, and he pressed his tongue against the surge of her pulse at her throat, and he took her lips again, savoring the caress of her tongue, feeling the rise of heat and need and the rampant beat in his loins as the thrusts of their tongues became ever more erotic and telling. He stroked her body through the flannel, caressing her breast, finding the peak and massaging it to a hard pebble with his thumb and fingers. Then he cried out and lowered his mouth upon her, his teeth grazing the fullness of her breast and the hard peak through the fabric, the dampness of his mouth pervading it and bringing whispers and whimpers to her lips. She braced herself upon his shoulders, and cried out, falling against him. Trembling, he lifted her and set her on the cocoon of sheet and quilt in the hay. Then he stood over her, watching her. He ripped away the kerchief at his throat and slowly undid the buttons of his shirt. He watched her all the while, but her eyes did not close. He threw his shirt upon the hay, and pulled off his boots and socks, unbuckled his gun belt and then his pants belt and finally peeled away the last of his clothing. Her eyes closed at last, but not before her cheeks had taken on a dusky hue.

"You can still run," he told her harshly.

She shook her head. Her hair lay spread across the quilt and sheet and dangled into the hay around them. He knelt before her and set his hand upon the hem of her gown, pushing it up. She had beautiful feet. Small, the toenails neatly manicured. Her ankles were trim. Her calves were shapely.

He paused to press kisses against her kneecaps, then he continued, thrusting the gown up to her hips where he paused because his breath had caught. The entire length of her legs was fine and beautiful, and her hips were seductively flared. Her waist was very narrow, and she was endowed with the same touch of honey hair to add even greater purity and innocence to her beauty. That very touch of purity seemed to be driving him insane. A ragged pulse beat at his groin, and in his mind, and raged throughout his fingers and his limbs and all of his body. He buried his face against her belly, and a harsh sound escaped him, a cry of longing, of need, of desperate desire. Some soft sound escaped her, and she gasped when his lips moved upon her flesh, when he turned his head against her, his hair teasing the flesh of her abdomen, then his kiss and lips caressing it again.

As he kissed her he continued to push the gown up. The flannel raked over her breasts, over her hardened nipples. He rose and knelt over her again, taking each breast fully into his mouth. She was alabaster, as perfect as marble with the dusky, rose-tipped peaks, so hard, so compelling, drawing his body into a tighter, harder knot all the while, exciting him to an ungodly high with the mere whisper of her breath, the tiny gasps that escaped her, the sultry, sensual way her body moved against him. Such little movements, as if she was afraid, as if she discovered the haunting rhythms of making love.

He paused, meeting her eyes. Half-closed eyes—dazed, damp, luminous and honest—meeting his. Her gaze fell upon his naked and aroused body, and her eyes widened again. They met his again, and the beautiful flush of rose came to her cheeks. He reached for her gown and pulled it over her shoulders, and they knelt facing each other. She threw her arms shyly around him, but that served to press them together, all their nakedness, and he felt her breasts upon his chest as thoroughly as he knew that she felt the ripple of his muscle and the blinding heat that led him now.

He pressed her into the quilt, down, down, into the hay. He crawled over her again, seizing hold of her lips, kissing her until her breath came raggedly, until her breasts rose and fell heatedly in his hands, until she trembled wherever he touched her. Then he kissed her breasts again, fascinated by the shape and texture and by the perfect marble beauty. He lowered himself against her, near blinded by his own need yet driven to see that she felt no pain, that she savored this time between them as he did, that she remember the passion, the desperation, the aching, longing need.

He kissed her between her breasts, then strayed down the length of her breastbone. He touched her ribs with the tip of his tongue and delved deeply into her navel the same way. And then he dropped his head still lower. He felt her legs quiver and a quickening within her and heard the soft, shocked protest on her lips. But he ignored her and made love completely to her, delving into the very femininity of her. She cried out, this time not so softly. He laced his fingers with hers and touched and delved ever deeper. He brought the searing, damp heat of his kiss and caress to the very bud of her desire. Her fingers tightened painfully around his, but he wedged himself firmly between her thighs and tenderly caressed her. She whimpered, tossing her head so her hair spread out like a burst of sunrise. And still he drank ever more deeply of her sweet scent and taste, until he could feel the pulse of desire rising within her.

He crawled atop her then, discovering her eyes closed, her face ashen. And yet her fingers dug into his shoulders, and when he carefully lowered himself over her and pushed slowly within her, he found her damp and welcoming. He watched her face even as he thrust past the portals of her innocence, and she never cried out or murmured a single protest or whimper. He sheathed himself slowly inside her, then he held and caught hold of her chin.

Her eyes flew open, so large and dark, then they fluttered closed again as he took her lips and caressed her with long, slow, leisurely kisses—taking all of her mouth, exploring, tasting, savoring. And as he kissed her he began to move within her, strokes as soft as velvet, slow and evocative, coercive...

He felt something give within her when the pain had faded and the new pleasure began. There was an easing of her arms around him, and her long, enchanting legs wound tightly around him. Her fingertips grazed his shoulders, the nails lightly stroking. Soft sounds of passion began to escape her.

He thrust hard then, unleashing the passion that had grown and simmered and become explosive within him. He moved like the wind and like the earth, and he whispered to her, words that meant nothing, words that barely found syllables, and yet words that meant everything. Their lips met again and again, parted, fused and sealed together, as did their bodies. He felt himself grow slick with the heat they ignited in the night, and he knew that he could not hold on much longer. And still he fought the climax that clamored in his loins, in his heart, in his mind. He fought it, driving her ever upward, leaving her shivering in moonbeams, taking her ever higher. Then he felt it. A wild stiffening in her body, a stark moment in which she seemed to fight him, then she was trembling beneath him in great shudders.

He cast back his head. He felt a groan rumbling in his throat just as the heat and fever and excitement within him drew to a massive pitch. The sound escaped him, the life and energy and heat of his body shot from him, filling her. Again and again, shudders seized him, and he filled her again and again. Then he wrapped his arms around her and held her very tightly. He eased to her side, taking his weight from her but keeping his arms around her so that she fell atop him. She sighed softly. Damp tendrils of her hair curled

over him. He touched it and remembered wondering how i
would feel against him.

Like silk . . . it felt like silk. And it looked like the sun, so
blond against the bronze of his skin. And she felt like silk
her body so slick with all that had been between then, cov
ering him.

Her face lay against his chest. She didn't say a word, and
she didn't seem to want to look at him.

"Are you all right?" he asked her, softly smoothing back
a tendril of her hair.

She nodded against him.

"Did I—hurt you?"

She shook her head, but still she didn't say a word.

"You're not crying, are you?" he asked her.

"No!" she said in muffled, indignant protest.

"Women do, you know."

"Women do!" she repeated, speaking at last. She sat up
and her eyes met his. "How many women do you—did
you . . . Oh, never mind!" She started to pull away. He
breasts swung heavy and fascinating before him, and he
quickly laughed, pulling her back. His voice was husky
when he spoke.

"I've never, never, been in a—er, circumstance like thi
one before."

"Like—"

"With a virgin," he said flatly.

She flushed crimson. He pulled her close to him. She wa
wiggling and squirming, ready to retreat now that it was al
over, despite the way she had played the seductress so
boldly. He didn't want to lose her.

"Tess!"

"What? Will you please—"

"I didn't go back to Eliza that night, either. The whole
thing was a show—"

''Eliza is in love with you.''

''Eliza is in love with a lot of people.''

She paused, tossing her hair, studying him with her enormous eyes. ''And what about you?''

''I'm not in love with anyone,'' he said. Again, he felt her pulling away. He tightened his hold around her. ''But I am in love with your eyes. And I love the way you fight until the bitter end, though I could also strangle you for that same quality. I love the way you think, and I love the way you take care of the people around you, and I even love the way your eyes flash when you're jealous.''

''I'm not jealous—''

''Then you're nosy. You were damned determined to know where I had taken my bath.''

''Because—'' She broke off, staring at him.

He grinned. ''Because you weren't about to come near me if I had been near another woman, was that it?''

''Yes!''

He laughed again, hugged her close and rolled her over in the hay. ''Never fear, my feisty little love. When I am near you, I will never find the need for another.''

His lips closed over hers. He stroked his hand down the length of her, touching her openly and intimately. A sound rumbled in her throat against his kiss. He ignored her.

All the fires of hell were burning inside him again, and this time he need not be so slow, so careful. She had learned about tenderness. She was ready to learn about the tempest.

Later, when dawn neared, she slept. Jamie stared at the rafters as the first pale light of day appeared, impressed by the eagerness and complete abandon with which she had approached lovemaking. He had never known a feeling of such relaxation, of physical bliss as her sleeping body against his. She had learned many things this night . . .

She slept with her knee slightly curved upon him, her hair tangled around his shoulders and chest. He touched a strand lightly, and it was almost as if the gold and honey touched him back, as if it gave him warmth. He looked at her face, so beautiful, so perfect, her lips just slightly parted, cherry red in the first rays of light, tempting. He stroked her shoulder and her back. She moved against him, and he felt the warmth of her breath upon him as she sighed softly.

She had learned so much . . .

But he had learned a great deal that night, too. He had learned that he'd never really made love before. He'd had women, but he had never really, truly made love.

He'd never wanted anyone like he'd wanted her.

Wanted her still . . .

Who had taught whom? he wondered.

He kissed the soft skin of her back and wondered again at the ripple of longing that went through him. Then he sighed. He had to wake her up and let her go back to the house before the morning began, before the ranch came alive.

By nine that morning they arrived in town. Jamie drove the wagon with Tess sitting primly by his side.

Morning had changed things amazingly, he thought. Since he had awakened her, she had been distant. She had donned her flannel gown, and with it a peculiar silence. She hadn't seemed remorseful about anything; she had been cool and quiet. She hadn't sneaked back to the house; she had walked very calmly. She had promised him she would be ready in thirty minutes. When he had pressed his lips to hers on first awakening, she had responded with warmth, but already there had been that widening within her eyes, as if she thought that something very grave had gone on, something she hadn't quite realized at the time. He'd almost braced himself, waiting, but she hadn't anything to say to him at all. She had dressed quickly and walked to the house. Her chin was high, and she wasn't about to hide anything, but then again, Jamie thought, maybe she wasn't about to do anything again, either.

I never wanted to rush it! he reminded himself in silence. But he still hadn't found the right words to say to her, and she sat by him quietly as they rode into town. They didn't exchange five words.

It was early, and the streets were nearly still. Only a passerby or two walked the plank sidewalks in front of the bank and the barbershop and the offices of the *Wiltshire Sun*. Tess bit her lip and looked at the newspaper office, but she remained silent on that point. "Mr. Barrymore's office is right ahead. He was always Joe's solicitor."

"Well, then, fine, we're going to go see Mr. Barrymore."

He helped her from the wagon. She was dressed for spring, in light-blue-and-white checked muslin, with a matching wide-brimmed bonnet.

The touch of her fingers against his seemed electric. She met his eyes and flushed.

"We need to talk," he told her.

"I need to get to the newspaper," she retorted. "So hurry along now, will you?"

"Eager to turn it all over to me, eh?"

"I shall resent it to my dying day," she said sweetly, "but then, you *are* better than von Heusen."

"Such a compliment!" he teased, bowing low as he opened the door to the lawyer's office.

Tess started to reply, but instead smiled at the tall, lean man behind the desk. "Mr. Barrymore, how are you?" she inquired, walking forward, reaching out her hand.

The man rose instantly to his feet. He reached out for Tess's hand, but his eyes were on Jamie. Jamie winced inwardly, realizing this man had been in the saloon the other night when he had met von Heusen's boys.

Tess didn't see the recognition in his eyes. "Mr. Barrymore, this is Lieutenant Slater. Lieutenant, Mr. Barrymore, who has helped my family for years."

Mr. Barrymore was still staring at Jamie.

"Mr. Barrymore!" Tess said more sharply.

"Oh, my dear, my dear, I am so glad to see you! Of course, you know that Joe left everything in your name—"

"That's why I'm here," Tess said.

"Of course, of course—"

"No, you don't understand. I want to turn over half my holdings to Lieutenant Slater."

"Half your holdings?"

"Half."

At last, Mr. Barrymore looked at Tess. The pen he held in his hands nearly snapped as he stared at her. "Half?"

"Half."

He cleared his throat and stared at Jamie. "That will make you a very rich young man."

"I intend to pay the lady, but the money is going to be due to her in payments over the next few years. Can we draw up a schedule?" Jamie said.

Tess stared at him then. "You're going to pay me?"

"Of course. You didn't think I was just going to whisk away your property."

"Yes, but—"

"Tess," he said softly. "You're—I mean, the land is worth it."

He thought she was going to leap to her feet and scream. She managed not to. She leaned over the desk and smiled at

Mr. Barrymore. "Make sure he pays the premium price then, will you?"

"Well, yes," Mr. Barrymore said nervously. He looked at Jamie, then he looked at Tess, then he cleared his throat. "You're sure this is what you want, Tess?"

"Yes."

"And Mister—er—Lieutenant Slater, would you, uh, like to explain how you want these payments to be made?"

"Certainly," Jamie said. He rattled off sums and amounts, and Mr. Barrymore began to write quickly. "And when we're done with this," Jamie said, "I need to make out a will, and Miss Stuart is going to do so, too. In the case of both our deaths, the property is to be equally divided in ownership between my two brothers, Cole Slater and Malachi Slater, and in case of *their* deaths, to their heirs."

He smiled at Tess reassuringly. "Oh, yeah, and Mr. Barrymore, I want you to make sure you talk about this. I want the whole town to know that there's just no way, no way at all, the Stuart spread is ever going to be up for sale. Do you understand me?"

Barrymore stayed silent for a long moment, then he began to smile. "You've got it, Lieutenant Slater. Damn, but you've got it! Oh, excuse me, Tess. I plumb forgot you were sitting there!"

"How amusing," Tess said with a stiff smile.

"They'll know, all right, they'll know...." Mr. Barrymore was writing quickly. "I must hand it to you, Lieutenant, you do seem to know what you're doing with property and the law. Though it ain't surprising, not one bit. You sure do know what you're doing with those Colts of yours. Why, in all my life, I've never seen anything like the shootin' you did in the saloon the other night—"

"Shooting?" Tess interrupted, sitting straight.

"Oh, my, yes, you should have seen him! Some of those hooligans of Mr. von Heusen's come in and they were giving Hardy a bad time, but the Lieutenant here, he stood right up to them." Mr. Barrymore slapped his hand hard on his desk and hooted with laughter. "It was a joy to these weary eyes, Tess, it was! Didn't you tell Miss Stuart about it, Lieutenant? Hell—heck, boy, if it had been me, I'd have told the whole damned—darned—world about it!"

"I didn't seem to have the chance, Mr. Barrymore. When I got home, a few more of Mr. von Heusen's boys were at the ranch. And someone needed to tell those fellows that it wasn't a good thing to play with matches."

"You shot von Heusen's men in the saloon?" Tess asked, staring at him.

"Sure," Mr. Barrymore said cheerfully. "Why, you would have heard about it if you'd gone into the paper, Tess. The lieutenant was sitting with Ed Clancy and Doc."

Tess stood and stared at Jamie. "I think I'll take a little walk over to the *Wiltshire Sun* right now. I'm sure, Lieutenant Slater, that you know exactly how you want everything worded. Then Mr. Barrymore can draw up the papers and I will come back and sign them. Excuse me, will you?"

Jamie and Mr. Barrymore both stood quickly, but Tess was already at the door. She stormed out, feeling her face red, wondering if she should be furious with the man or if she should run back and kiss him. She wasn't going to do either—she was going to see Ed and find out exactly what had happened.

She walked into the *Wiltshire Sun* office as if she were a battleship. Harry, the printer, looked up from his plates. Edward, at work at his desk, also looked up. The naked joy in his eyes as he saw her made her first questions flee. He leaped up to hug her, nearly breaking every bone in her body. "I knew you were all right, Tess, because I saw Slater. But, girl, it does an old body good to see you!"

"Thank you, Edward, thank you!" she told him.

Harry, toothless and shy, was standing behind him. "And you, too, Harry, come here. Let me give you a big, sloppy kiss right on that jaw of yours!"

He flushed a bright red from his throat to his white, tufted hair, but he accepted a kiss and hugged her tightly in return. "We just kept doing the paper, Miss Tess. Even when they tried to tell us that you weren't coming back, we just kept the *Sun* going out on schedule. Every Tuesday, Thursday and Saturday, we had a *Wiltshire Sun* out on the street!"

"And I'm so grateful and so proud of both of you!" Tess assured him.

Edward cleared his throat. "Well, I didn't exactly have the news of the nation going out," he admitted. "Ah, hell, Tess! I didn't really have the balls to print too much. Von Heusen was breathing down my neck, and I—"

"You kept it going," Tess said. "And I'm grateful." She pulled off her gloves and headed for her desk. "Am I in time to get in a story for the Tuesday edition?"

"Yes, yes, Miss Stuart! I'll clean out the presses, I'll—"

"I've just got one story," Tess assured him. "But it's an important one. I want it on the front page."

She smiled at Edward and inserted paper into the new-fangled typewriter she had insisted they buy. She closed her eyes, pausing for a moment, smelling the ink on Harry's plates. Then she smiled and started to type. She described the small wagon train, then she described the attack. She described the attackers, who had looked like white men painted up to look like Comanche. She wrote about being saved by the cavalry, then she wrote about Chief Running River and how he had sworn his people had not had anything to do with the attack. Then she wrote that she knew she was an eyewitness...and a survivor. She ended the piece with a bold accusation.

"Certain tyrants in this town will stoop to any means to bring about their chosen results. This town has been mercilessly seized upon. We've seen our friends and neighbors disappear. Some say it was the war, but the war has ended, and all good men are trying to repair broken fences and lend a helping hand. In this town, however, we have been met by evil. Yes, my friends, evil lives in man. The evil that killed a man like Joe Stuart. Joe Stuart's death must not be in vain. We must band together and fight the evil. It does not come from the war. It comes from a man, and no matter how he threatens, we can beat him—if we stand together."

She left it at that. She hesitated for a moment, searching for better words, then shrugged. She had said what she wanted to say. She pulled the sheet of paper from the machine and handed it to Edward. "Read this over for me, will you, Ed?"

His eyes were already racing over the piece. He was a swift proofreader, and he quickly came to her final paragraph. His fingers trembled, and the paper wavered within them. "Tess—"

"I want it out tomorrow," she said.

"Tess, he'll come after you lock, stock and barrel—"

"He already left me for dead once," she said.

"But, Tess—"

"Print it, please. And now tell me—what happened at the saloon the other night?"

Edward stared, trying to change his train of thought as quickly as she was changing the conversation. "The other night? Why, Miss Tess, I was just in a little need of companionship—"

"Not that, Clancy, not that! I want to hear about the lieutenant."

"The lieutenant?"

"Slater, Edward Clancy! Jamie Slater and the von Heusen men and the blazing guns."

"Oh, it was something, Tess. Honest to God, but it was something!"

"Something? Fine. What? Tell me about it, please!"

"Why, he just come into the bar, and we all kind of greeted him—"

"Everyone in the place stared at him, wondering if he was dangerous or not?"

"Right, right. Doc and I were playing cards and we invited him over for a whiskey. He started asking questions right away, then von Heusen's guns came in. One of them had Hardy the bartender by the throat when Jamie Slater asked him to stop. The man laughed. Then they were all threatening to shoot up Slater, but that Slater, he had their number! Before you know it—one, two, three, four! All of them were lying on the floor and choking and crying and carrying on like babes. And Slater just stepped over them, cool as a cucumber, and walked over to the barber and got himself a shave and a bath.

"Well, of course, von Heusen's fellers, they were threatening him right and left, but those boys lit out of town as soon as Doc patched them up, lit straight out of town, they did. Don't know if they went back to von Heusen or if they rode away for good. I ain't seen a one of them since. Of course, one young feller, he ain't gonna be ridin' anywhere for a while, he kind of took his shot in the posterior section, if you know what I mean."

"I think I know what you mean," Tess said. She gave Ed another kiss on the cheek. "You take care now. I'll be in tomorrow morning. You make sure my piece goes on the front page.''

''Yes, ma'am!''

Tess left the office and walked slowly down the street toward Mr. Barrymore's office.

What had she gotten?

She'd wanted a hired gun. And she'd gotten one. She railed against Jamie for leaving the ranch when he'd been finding out what he could—and shooting it out with some of von Heusen's toughs at the same time.

And gaining quite a reputation as he did so. She shivered suddenly. She'd seen him shoot the snake. She'd known that he was fast and good. She shouldn't have been surprised to hear that he had knocked down four of von Heusen's men in a matter of seconds. Then he'd humiliated von Heusen at the ranch . . .

Von Heusen was going to be mad, and he was going to be thirsting for blood. Her blood.

But she'd known she had to fight him. And she had Jamie. She'd wanted the gun.

And she'd wanted the man.

And now she had both.

She tightened her fingers around the drawstring of her little purse and stopped walking to lean against a wooden wall as a fierce trembling swelled within her. She swallowed hard and inhaled deeply as she remembered the previous night. She couldn't have been so brazen.

Or so wanton . . . or so decadent . . . or so searingly intimate. But she had been. He had warned her away. He had given her every opportunity. He had told her that she should be with a man who cared. He implied that he didn't care.

Surely that wasn't true. He liked her. There were things about her he loved.

But it didn't mean anything. That was the rub. It didn't mean anything at all. She was just a woman, a warm, willing body. Just like Eliza. She had thrown herself at him . . .

And one day he'd turn away from her, just as he had turned from Eliza.

She inhaled, exhaled, then forced herself to walk. She must not let it happen again. Even if it had been more than she had ever dreamed. She'd never imagined that making love could be so erotic, so wonderful. She'd never imagined that it was possible to feel so excited, so cherished, so explosive and so sated. She'd never imagined that a man's hands could do what his had done, or that a man's kiss could awaken everything in her body, or that a man could join with a woman so completely and bring about such splendor.

It could quickly become addictive . . .

But he didn't intend to stay. Even if he bought her land and settled down, he had made it clear that he didn't intend to stay with her.

She had taken care to sound independent, too. And now . . .

Now she wanted to lie down beside him again. She wanted to laugh and feel his touch and explore his shoulders and his chest and his long, muscled legs and . . . everything. Everything. Even the parts of the body that she couldn't quite bring herself to name aloud. She had wanted him. She'd never deny that. But now she was afraid of the longings that seemed to have escalated since she had known his touch. Having him hadn't quenched the desire at all.

It had set it all afire . . .

She was in front of the lawyer's office. She set her hand on the knob and twisted it and walked in. Mr. Barrymore was just finishing copying out a second set of papers. Jamie had obviously directed him as to what he should write.

"Good timing," Jamie said, applauding her. "We need your signature."

"Shouldn't I read the documents?"

"Be my guest."

Tess took the papers from Mr. Barrymore, but she couldn't quite manage to read. She pretended to, skimming the words. They all swam before her.

"We need a witness," Mr. Barrymore said.

"No problem," Jamie told him.

He stepped outside. A moment later, he was back with Doc. He signed one set of papers, then Mr. Barrymore and Doc signed as witnesses. Then Tess signed, not having the least idea of what was really on the papers, and her signature was witnessed, too.

"That's that, then!" Jamie said, pleased. He counted out gold coins to Mr. Barrymore, who seemed very pleased. So much was being done in paper currency lately.

"Let's go, Tess," Jamie said.

"Good day, Mr. Barrymore, Doc. Thank you," she told the lawyer. But Barrymore and Doc were hardly able to respond before Jamie had his hand on her elbow and was leading her out.

When they reached the wooden sidewalk, she wrenched her hand free. "Jamie, I just might not be ready to head home."

"We're not heading home," he told her.

"Then—"

"We're going to talk."

"What if I had something to do?" she demanded.

"It would have to wait."

"It wouldn't!"

"Today, Tess," he insisted, "it would."

The brim of his hat was pulled low over his eyes, and his hands were firmly on his hips.

"Now, listen—"

"You listen," he told her, wagging a finger beneath her nose. "I'm not going to live like this. We're going to straighten out the relationship."

"There is no—"

"The hell there isn't. Now get in the wagon, or I'll put you in it."

"You wouldn't—"

He took a step toward her. Before she knew it she was off her feet, then she was sitting in the wagon. She swung around, but he was beside her in an instant, and the reins were in his hands, and he was clucking to the thoroughbred that pulled the small conveyance.

Tess crossed her arms over her chest, staring straight ahead. "You are intolerable!" she told him.

"I just don't like a bunch of bull, that's all."

"Bull—"

"The way you're acting."

"I'm not acting—"

"I hope to hell you are."

"I don't know what you're talking about."

They were already out of town. He was silent for a moment. The horse picked up its gait and it seemed they were flying down the road. Then, suddenly, Jamie reined in. The horse slowed and Jamie hooked the reins around the brake. He jumped down and came around the wagon for Tess.

"What?" she demanded, staring down at him.

He reached up, placed his hands around her waist and lifted her down. When she was on the ground, his hands still stayed upon her. His eyes were like smoke, and his jaw was twisted. She knew that he did, indeed, intend to have things out.

She opened her mouth, wanting to protest again, wanting to deny and denounce him and run away. But she was trembling because that wasn't what she wanted at all. She wanted to trust him. She wanted to lean against him. And, most of all, she wanted to feel his lips upon hers again, as hot as the sun, as rich as the earth. But she didn't want to want him so badly... she didn't want to make a fool of herself, like Eliza.

Because, like Eliza, she was falling in love with him.

"Come on," he told her.

"Where?" she protested.

"Down by the water."

The road ran along the river. He held her hand and led her through the trees until they came to a little copse. They were alone with the sounds of the rippling waters, with the occasional call of a bird, the soft rustle of a tree. He drew her close, and when she stiffened, he drew her even closer.

"What is this?" he demanded.

She moistened her lips, staring at his eyes, then at his mouth. "What is—what?" she asked.

"Miss Stuart, I gave you a chance last night. Hell, I gave you several chances last night. You wanted to stay."

"I—"

"You wanted to make love."

"I... yes," she whispered.

"And now you're running. Why?"

"I'm not!" she protested. "It's just that—"

"I can't do it, Tess. I can't live with it if you think you can blow hot and cold in a matter of hours."

"I'm not!"

"Then what?"

"I'm just trying to give you... space!"

She lowered her head. She desperately wanted to put her shoulder against his shirt. She breathed in, smelling the clean male scent of him, and she felt a furious pulse take flight at her throat, in her heart, in her veins. He slid his fingers into her hair at the sides of her head and lifted her face. He stared, and she tried to return his gaze without faltering. But then his hand came to her breast. She murmured something softly, then she did lean against him. The sky seemed dazzling, but not so dazzling as the man.

"Tess, Tess!" he whispered to her, holding her close. "It's frightening, it's damned terrifying. You're coming to mean so much to me . . ."

His arms were around her. She parted her lips and moistened them with her tongue again. His parted and moved upon hers, and they melded and tasted until finally he drew his lips away. Then they sank down together upon a bed of leaves, with the river just beyond them. Their arms locked together and they kept kissing, tasting one another, and it seemed that the sound of the rushing water grew louder and louder.

Tess found that she was pressed into the leaves. His hands were upon her. She set her palms against his cheek, and desire took flight within her as she felt the planes and textures of his face. She thought confusedly that she loved the way he looked with his smoke-dark eyes and sandy, disheveled hair, with the rough touch and the rugged angles and lines of his face, the twist of his jaw. She wrapped her arms around him, sliding her fingers through the hair at his nape, drawing him to her for another kiss. The earth beneath her began to heat. She ran her fingers over the opening of his shirt. She felt the ripple of muscle with her fingertips. She teased at his buttons until his shirt opened, until she could reach her hands inside and slide her nails over his naked flesh and feel the trembling that she evoked.

She heard him groan and she felt his touch upon the tiny buttons of her dress, then she felt herself being freed from her gown. Her slip and her chemise remained, but they were no barrier to the feel of his searing kiss upon her body and breast. Soon her slip was wound beneath her, and she felt the earth with her bare flesh. His hard and driving manhood teased her for a split second, then drove within her with a startling, shattering thrust that swept her breath away.

The sun was above him. She heard curious cries, then realized that they came from her and that she was clinging to him, arching, writhing...meeting him, welcoming him, wanting him. She felt the slap of his body against hers, and it was earthy and real. She felt the sun upon his naked flesh, and that, too, was real. And she felt more...the certain heat, the glow of the sun, which heightened every swift pleasure, a touch of the blue, cloudy sky...

She was damp, and so aware of him within her, and aware of the rising ecstasy inside her body. Coiling tighter and tighter until she was crying out again, then gasping in a soft shriek as something came upon her so strong and sweet and volatile that it rent the whole of her with shivers, while something like hot nectar seemed to swamp her body. She couldn't move. She could scarcely breathe, and it seemed that the world went dark before the sun burst upon her again. And just as it did, he thrust hard within her and stayed and stared at her, the whole of his face tense and haunting and taut with passion. Then he exploded within her, and thrust and thrust again...and lay down beside her, wrapping her in his arms.

The sun was still above them.

"I'm afraid of you," Tess admitted.

He had been flat on the earth. He rose up on an elbow. "What?"

"I'm afraid of caring too much."

He touched her cheek. "We're all afraid of caring too much."

"I don't believe you're afraid of anything."

He smiled, a crooked, rueful smile. "Yes, I am. I'm afraid of losing you right now."

"Right now," she repeated. "But what...what about tomorrow, Jamie? That's what frightens me."

"What do you mean?"

She shook her head. She rolled away from him, rising to her feet, straightening her slip and dusting bits of leaf and dirt and grass from it. She smiled at him, then hurried toward the water.

He must have stripped off the remnants of his clothing, for when he came up behind her, he was stark naked. He placed his hands around her waist and kissed her nape. Then he whispered in her ear, so softly that she wasn't sure she heard him. "Tomorrow? I'm not sure. But I think that I'm falling in love with you, Tess."

He left her, walking into the river, then ducking beneath the surface and swimming into the center of it. He rose, let out a cry and shivered. "It's damned cold for summer!" he called out to her.

Tess stooped and threw water over her face. She watched as Jamie dove beneath the surface again.

A twig snapped suddenly behind her. She leaped up, spinning around.

There were four of them. The so-called Indians. They were clothed in bronze paint and breechclouts. "Jamie!" she whispered.

But of course there was nothing he could do. The men were armed with bows and arrows, rifles, even a few tomahawks. They were going to kill her, she thought, and Jamie would never have time to reach the surface. And it would be her fault, because if she had talked to him this morning, he would never have brought her here, and he would never have become so involved with her that he forgot danger...

"Jamie!" she screamed as one of the men lunged toward her. She fought. She kicked, she scratched, she screamed and struggled, but a second man came up, grasping her legs, and between them, she was tossed over a shoulder. She still fought, clawing, screaming, pounding.

Bronze coloring came off in her hands...

"Tess!" Jamie was charging, naked and unarmed, out of the water. She saw his eyes. They met across the distance and locked with hers; the pain and the horror of the moment was mirrored between them.

"Tess!" He screamed her name again in a loud, long cry of anguish, and he was speeding furiously toward the embankment.

The man carrying Tess began to run with her. She craned her neck, straining to see Jamie. She saw him reaching the shallows, and she saw him running, running to the shore. He rammed one of the armed attackers with such violence and force that the man fell. He spun and kicked his next opponent, then thrust his fists against him in a fury.

But then Tess saw that another man was behind Jamie as he fought. She saw the second man raise a battle club and bring it down upon Jamie's head with all his strength.

She heard the cracking sound...

And she screamed as she saw Jamie crumple to the ground, and then she saw no more, for blackness descended over the sun.

Chapter Nine

Tess didn't know how much time passed before she regained consciousness. When she did, she was hanging facedown over the flanks of a sweating horse in front of the pseudo-Indian who had grabbed her. She was acutely uncomfortable. Although the sun was setting, it was still ferociously hot. The sticky, wet hair of the horse irritated her flesh, and the continual and monotonous thump-thump-thump of its gait was bringing a ferocious pain to her head. Her arms hurt, her back hurt, and her neck burned like blue blazes. She was a great mass of pain, and at first that was all she could think of.

After a while she remembered. She'd been kidnapped. The bronze paint worn by the "warrior" behind her was coming off on her flesh and chemise where the man's thighs and knees rubbed against her.

And Jamie Slater was by the river with his head bashed in. He couldn't be alive. He had fought for her, and he had been killed in the attempt.

Scalding tears stung her eyes. She fought back the urge to scream aloud. Jamie could perhaps have survived. Maybe he had just been knocked unconscious. They had left her for dead once, and she had survived. Jamie was tough. He had survived the war, he had . . .

She had seen the club come against his skull.

Still, she couldn't accept it. She had to believe that he was alive because if she didn't she wouldn't care if she lived or died.

Maybe there wasn't much chance of her surviving, anyway. Von Heusen didn't know yet that there was now no way he was going to get his hands on the Stuart holdings. She wondered briefly about the other Slater brothers and their wives. Would they come to Wiltshire to accept an inheritance? When they saw what had been happening, would they pick up her fight? Why should they?

Because they were probably close. Because Jamie wouldn't have taken the time and the care to see that things were done the way they were if his brothers weren't willing to fight. To fight for him. To avenge his death. No, no, he couldn't be dead. Please! God in heaven! she prayed silently. Don't let him be dead, don't let him be dead, don't let him be ...

"Let's hold up here!" someone called out.

The horse she was thrown over ceased plodding. A second animal trotted up beside it. The man spoke again. "We've come far enough. Even if someone manages to find Slater's body, they won't be able to track us. Not across the river. And we left plenty of Comanche arrows behind. She still out, David?"

"Seems to be, Jeremiah."

"Well, that's good. Still, let's stop here for the night. By tomorrow afternoon we'll meet up with the Comancheros and turn the girl over to them."

Comancheros? Despite herself Tess felt a sizzle of terror sweep through her. They weren't exactly Mexicans, and they weren't exactly Indians; they were a wild grouping of both who savagely lived off the land. They raided, pillaged, murdered and raped without thought, and they made much of their income by selling arms illegally to the Apache.

Von Heusen meant to have his revenge this time. He hadn't planned a quick, easy death for her. He had consigned her to a living hell.

She couldn't let them give her to the Comancheros. Somehow, she was going to get the best of these men. And if they had killed Jamie, she had to see that they were brought to justice.

"Come on, let's get started setting up a camp for the night," the man David said. He started to dismount. "Boy, that did feel good, swinging that club against that bastard Slater. After everything he did to us out at the Stuart place the other night, I just wish I'd had time to gouge out his eyes."

"Or take a scalp?" Jeremiah suggested with laughter.

"Yeah—or take a scalp."

"Do you think Hubert and Smitty have made it back with the good word for von Heusen yet?"

"Probably. I told them to head straight back. Someone will find Slater's body soon enough. We want to make sure we can't be blamed for it. Come on, now, let's get her down and tied up before she comes to."

Jeremiah hopped off the horse. The one named David reached for her. The one whose hands would be forever stained with the blood of Jamie Slater.

Tess let out a wild scream when those hands touched her. She was ready. He wanted to gouge out eyes? Her fingers were flying madly for his. She caught him completely by surprise. He howled like an infant when her nails swiped his face, missing his eyes but digging deeply into the flesh of his cheek. He stumbled, and she tried to right herself upon the horse.

The animal, panicked by the screams, reared high, its forelegs kicking and flailing. Desperate as she was, Tess couldn't quite gain her balance. The horse came down on four legs, kicking up great clouds of dust, then rose, pawing the sunset-hued air once again. Tess went flying into the bushes.

She lost her breath and lay stunned for several seconds. David and Jeremiah were shouting at one another, David giving the orders. "Get the horse! Get the fool horse! I'm going for the girl."

Fear spurred her aching and bruised limbs into action. She managed to rise to her bare feet and race down a narrow trail between rows of dry bush. Her feet encountered rocks and stickers, and she gasped out and tried to pray. Despite the pain she kept running. She felt as if her lungs would burst, as if her calves would buckle, but she kept going, desperate to be free.

But arms suddenly swept around her legs, and she plunged forward into the dirt. Mouthfuls of it seemed to choke her and fill her nose. She gasped and choked and wheezed and finally managed to open her eyes.

David sat atop her, straddling her. He was still wearing a breechclout and streaked theatrical paint, but he had discarded his black braided wig. His own reddish hair looked strange against the melted bronze paint, but matched the blood-red welts she had drawn across his face. He wasn't much past his early twenties, and might even have been halfway attractive if his way of life had not done things to his face and his eyes. Both were cold, and there was a permanent twist of dissatisfaction about his jaw. He smiled as he looked at her, enjoying her situation, reveling in his power and in her misery.

She swung out again and managed to connect her fist against his cheek. He swore and secured her wrists, then started laughing as he stared at her. "My, my, Miss Stuart, it is a pleasure to see you this way!"

She was barely clad, she realized. Her chemise was dusty and pulled high, leaving her midriff bare. And her cotton petticoat was rucked up against her knees; her legs were bare beneath it. As he stared at her she felt sick. She could see his intentions in his eyes, and she wanted to die.

Not long ago Jamie had whispered on the breeze that he thought he was falling in love with her. And not long ago, he had taught her what it was to feel feminine beyond belief, to know the beauty of a mutual yearning, a soaring passion, all the sweet and fascinating things that should be shared between a man and a woman. Not long ago.

And now this horrible man with blood on his hands was looking at her and laughing.

"I always did want to get to know you better, Tess!" he assured her.

He lowered himself against her. She twisted wildly, hating the feel of his greased flesh, despising him. He tried to find her lips. She twisted and thrashed and screamed, and still she felt him touching her.

"That's all right!" he hissed against her cheek. "It's all right. You'll come to like it soon enough. I'm real good. I'm real, real good. I'll have you screaming in a way you just ain't imagined yet, honey. And later on, you'll be grateful. 'Cause you're going to Nalte, one of the chiefs of the Mescalero Apache. He's wanted a blond woman like you for a long time. They say he tried a few raids to acquire one, but he kept coming up with brunettes. Our Comanchero friends promised him a beautiful young blond white woman. Nalte is tough, Miss Stuart. You'll be real glad that I initiated you into this . . ."

He tried to secure both her wrists with one hand while he spoke. Tess fought him like a wildcat, delaying his purpose but losing her strength quickly. Nalte? An Apache?

Then the Comancheros were the delivery men. Von Heusen was dealing with the Comancheros, and the Comancheros were dealing with the Apache. She would be safe from the Comancheros . . .

Because she was meant for the Apache!

But she wasn't safe from David. She sobbed as she fought to free her wrists. She threw his weight from her hips, but he seemed to enjoy feeling her move against him. She twisted and sank her teeth into his fingers.

He shouted out in pain and sat hard on her, plunging his fingers into his mouth and staring at her murderously. Then his palm connected sharply with her cheek, and the world seemed to spin. His hands were upon her, upon her breasts, tugging at her petticoats.

"No!" she screamed in desperation and horror. But there was no one to help her out here. Jamie was by the river, dead. The vultures might well find his body before anyone else could. David's hands were upon her, and he was tugging on her clothes. He was about to violate the only beauty she had ever really dared to reach out and hold.

"Get off her!" someone suddenly roared. And David was plucked away from her.

Tess crawled quickly backward on her elbows. Her heart soared as she saw that David and Jeremiah were involved in a fistfight with one another. David was swinging and screaming at the same time.

"What the hell's the matter with you, Jeremiah? You can have your damned turn when I'm done—"

"No! Von Heusen said no! He promised the chief an innocent woman—"

"What do you think she was doing by the river with Slater?"

"I don't know anything! I saw the girl washing her face, and I saw Slater going for a swim. That's all I saw. Von Heusen promised the Comancheros an innocent. And he made us swear not to touch her. I'm not getting my balls shot off for your entertainment, and that's a damned fact."

"I give the orders here—"

"Von Heusen gives the orders here!"

Tess realized that she was just staring at them. They were fighting like madmen and not paying the least bit of attention to her, and she was just staring at them. She rolled over and stumbled to her feet. It was time to start running again, before David convinced Jeremiah that she was no innocent and that no one would ever know if the two of them used her, too.

She hadn't gone three steps before fingers laced into her hair, dragging her back. She gasped and sobbed, swinging and flailing out, but she was so exhausted, and in so much pain, that she knew that no matter what her will, she could not fight much longer.

"Stop it! Stop it! Come on, Miss Stuart, calm down, and make the night easier on all of us! I won't touch you, and he won't touch you, you understand? Just calm down."

It was Jeremiah who held her. He was as young as David, she decided. He had lanky blond hair and colorless blue eyes, but they didn't yet hold that absolute cold, cruel streak that touched David's. He almost smiled. "I'm going to get you something to wear. Then I'm going to tie you up. I have to. But I'll get you water, too, and something to eat. We're not going to touch you."

"Speak for yourself!" David snarled from a few steps away.

"We're not going to touch her!" Jeremiah snapped. "We're going to turn her over to the Comancheros, just like we promised von Heusen."

Tess didn't know who would win out. Jeremiah kept a firm grip upon her arm and pulled her along. She saw that there was a third horse on the trail, and that a number of rolled packs were tied on the animal's back. Jeremiah kept one hand and one eye on her as he tugged at the bundles to free them. When they fell to the ground, he pulled her down with him to dig into one.

"Here," he said roughly. "Take this. And get into it. But if you try anything funny, I'll turn my back and close my ears and David can do whatever the hell he wants. Understand?"

She understood. She hadn't the strength to fight them. She needed some sleep. She needed a little time to think and plan.

She snatched the clothing Jeremiah handed her. Apache, she thought. There were fine, soft trousers and a traditional blouse of buckskin with beadwork and tin cone pendants. She slipped into the bushes with the garments.

"You stay where I can hear you!" Jeremiah called.

"I'm here!" she replied.

The buckskin garments concealed much more than the tattered remnants of her clothes had. She couldn't believe she could be grateful to Jeremiah for anything, but she was glad of the clothing. If—not if, when!—she found her opportunity to escape, she would be much better able to weather the elements.

"You still there?" Jeremiah demanded.

Tess tossed her torn undergarments into the bushes and stepped out in the Apache attire.

"She should have had a skirt. No warrior trousers," David commented.

"She couldn't ride in a skirt," Jeremiah retorted.

Tess stood quietly. Jeremiah was the one to work on, she thought. He seemed to have a few human qualities left. She lowered her eyes and stood still.

"Miss Stuart, you come over here and let me tie your hands," he said.

She didn't move. "Please..." she murmured softly.

"Well..." Jeremiah began.

"Well, nothing! She's taking you strictly for a fool, that's what she's doing!" David strode over angrily and snatched the rope from Jeremiah's hands. He walked roughly toward Tess. Seeing his face, she almost panicked. She almost ran.

"Try it. I'd love it if you did!" he told her, his eyes narrowing. He meant it. He liked the chase, he liked the fight and he even liked the smell of blood.

She held out her hands mutely. David looped the rope around them tightly, tugging hard on the knot. Then he caught her arm and dragged her past the horses to the center of the little clearing where they had paused. He shoved her down to her knees and warned her, "Sit! Just sit!" He looked over to Jeremiah. "There's a creek down past the scrub bush over there. Nothing much. But you can go get rid of that paint. Then I'll decide if I trust you to keep an eye on her so I can do the same!"

Jeremiah hesitated. "Don't you go gettin' no ideas, now, David Birch."

"I ain't going to get any ideas! I want to get this blasted paint off, and that's all!"

Jeremiah walked to the bundles and picked up a satchel of clothing. He stared at David, then walked toward the brush.

Tess kept her eyes on David. He smiled as he watched her in turn. "You think you're going to get around Jeremiah, don't you? Well, you're not going to. I'm going to see to that. You're going to reach old Chief Nalte, and then you won't have to worry about writing those rabble-rousing pieces in that newspaper of yours anymore, ever again. You'll have lots of other things to think about." He cackled with laughter. "Lots and lots of other things. Like raising a whole little troop of papooses, yeah."

Tess edged around in the dirt, turning her back on him. He laughed all the harder, then he came forward and jerked her head back so her eyes watered as they met his. "I'm going to enjoy knowing where you are. Just like I enjoyed hearing Slater's skull crush this morning. I really got a kick out of that."

She forced herself to smile. "Maybe his skull didn't crush," she said very softly.

David gritted his teeth and yanked harder on her hair. "He's gone, lady. Dead and gone. And you don't need to worry about that no more, either."

He walked away, leaving her in peace at last. In time, Jeremiah returned, and he became her silent guard.

She hadn't the energy to say anything to him. They sat in silence while the darkness fell upon them. When David returned, the two men made a fire. There was cold chicken to eat and water from canteens, but they wouldn't untie Tess's hands, and the effort to eat suddenly seemed too great. She left the food, sipped some water and lay down in the dirt.

She tried to tell herself that Jamie was alive. Any minute now he would come rushing out from the bushes and kill the two men and take her away.

But he did not come. She closed her eyes in misery and tried to forget the nightmare visions of the day.

Jeremiah came over and tossed a blanket around her shoulders and shoved a pack beneath her head for a pillow. "Don't think about going nowhere," he warned her.

David obviously didn't think the warning was enough. He stood and walked to the piles by the packhorse and came back with a good length of rope. She tried to inch away from him, but he tied one end of the rope around her ankle. Pinching her cheek, he spoke directly into her face. "If you move, I'll feel it. If you run, I'll make you pay for it."

He walked away with the other end of the rope in his hand.

It didn't really matter. If she had been threatened by every demon in hell, she couldn't have run that night. She was too weary. Tears stung her eyes. When she closed them, she saw Jamie again, fighting, then falling. And she heard his whisper. *I think I'm falling in love with you...*

It hurt to close her eyes; it hurt to open them. She prayed for sleep against the nightmare images. She tried to tell herself that he was still alive. But he would have come for her if he was alive. He would have come.

And if he was not alive, well, then, she didn't want to live, either.

Jamie was alive, if only just barely.

Jon found him around midnight, when the moon was full and high. The wagon had come home without Jamie or Tess, but very late. Jon had to try and track them from town in the darkness, and even when he had found signs that the wagon had stopped and the two of them had walked toward the river, it still took him time to find Jamie's still, crumpled body.

He drew off his buckskin jacket and wrapped it around his friend. He touched the wound at Jamie's temple where the blood had dried. Carefully moving his fingers over the skull, he decided that it was not cracked or crushed. He took his kerchief to the river and soaked it and brought it back to

Jamie, cleansing the blood away. Jamie's body was icy cold. He needed warmth, and quickly.

Jon rose carefully and lifted his friend's body into his arms. He called to his pinto and the animal obediently trotted over to him. Bracing Jamie's weight with his hand upon the pommel, he managed to somehow swing up with Jamie in his arms. Then he made a clucking sound and the animal took off at a smooth lope.

At the ranch, Dolly, Hank and Jane were waiting with anxious concern. When Jon burst in with Jamie's half-naked body, Jane gasped and turned white.

"Don't you dare faint on me, young lady!" Dolly ordered her. "Bring him right to the sofa, Jon. Jane, you run upstairs and get blankets, lots of them. And you, Hank, I'm going to need a sewing kit for that wound. Some water and some alcohol to clean him up, and maybe a little for the lieutenant to sip. My, that's a mean and nasty bash!" Hank was on his way out. Jane was still staring in horror. "Move!" Dolly commanded her.

In a moment the young woman was back with blankets. Jon draped them around Jamie and rubbed his feet. Hank returned with water and a sewing kit, and Dolly began to clean the wound. A long gash ran into the left side of Jamie's temple.

"It's amazing he's still breathing!" Dolly murmured.

"He's Missouri tough," Jon told her. "He'll make it, you'll see."

"I intend to do my best to see that he does," Dolly assured Jon. She looked at him anxiously. "What about Tess?"

Jon shook his head. "I don't know. I had to get him back here before he died. I'm going back out to see what I can find." He lifted his hat to Dolly and left. At the door he paused and looked back. "Now, don't you let him die."

"I'm just going to sew him up. And I'm going to pray."

Jon hurried out.

But when he returned to the river, he discovered that whoever had attacked Jamie and Tess had made an escape through the water. He would need daylight to track them. There was nothing he could do that night.

But maybe there was. It was late, but saloons had a tendency to cater to the late crowd. Maybe he could find out more from casual conversation over a poker game than he could from a broken branch.

He turned the pinto toward town.

Jamie's dreams were occasionally dark and occasionally erotic, but always fevered.

He fought giants with buffalo headdresses. Then the battle would fade away, the powder would dissipate, the roar of the guns would cease. He wasn't fighting Yankees anymore, he tried to tell himself in his dream world. He was a Yankee, dressed in blue. He was a specialist in Indian affairs, a linguist...

And he knew Indians. He hadn't needed Jon Red Feather to tell him that the Apache didn't like scalping. It was a contaminating thing to them, and it had to be done with careful ritual. He should have known from the very beginning that the woman hadn't lied.

The woman. Tess...

And the Yankees were gone, and the Indians were gone, and he was lying by still, cool waters, and she was walking toward him. Her hair was like the sun, falling in soft, delicate tendrils over her breasts and down her back, and her smile was at once wistful and innocent and full of the most alluring promise. She knelt beside him and her fingers touched him, raking gently over his naked flesh. He couldn't take his eyes from her. Her eyes were so giving, velvet and deep, deep blue, and startling in their honesty. He had thought that she would run, but she had not. And now, no matter whether he woke or slept, she was with him, the sunray webs of honey-gold hair spinning around him and wrapping him in the sweetest splendor.

Her breath was soft against him. She leaned over him, and her breasts brushed against his chest, and he groaned aloud and waited. He wanted to pull her beneath him. He wanted to see her eyes widen and darken to mauve with the startling strength of passion. He wanted to feel her arms wrap around him.

But the smoke was coming again. The powder. And people were shouting; they were at war again. The war was over, but the fighting hadn't ended. It was the Indians.

It wasn't the Indians. That was it. They could dress up all they chose, but they were not Indians. They had Tess . . . he couldn't remember . . . yes! They had Tess, they had ridden away with her. By God! What they would do with her!

He awoke and jerked up. A staggering pain seized his temple, and he cried out hoarsely, grabbing his head. The pain slowly subsided to a dull thudding, and he opened his eyes.

Jon was sitting in front of him, watching him. Jamie groaned again. "What the hell happened? Where's Tess?"

"Von Heusen's pseudo-Comanche," Jon said calmly, still studying him.

Alarmed, beginning to remember much more clearly everything that had happened, Jamie sat up. He saw that his legs were bare, that he had only been covered with blankets, and he saw that Dolly and Jane and Hank were hovering anxiously behind Jon. He gritted his teeth against the new pain that had come with his movement, frowning. "Tess?"

"She was gone."

"Gone! And you didn't go for her?"

"Wait a minute, my friend," Jon warned him. "You were supposed to have been dead—that's the way they left you. You would have been dead, if I hadn't brought you here. I couldn't trail them in the dark—"

"You can trail anyone!" Jamie savagely reminded him.

"Not when they ran the river, not without some light," Jon said. "But I did find out where they're taking her."

"Where?" Jamie exploded. The sound of the word seemed to reverberate in his skull, and he grabbed it in an effort to ease the savage pain.

"They're taking her to the Comancheros. And the Comancheros are taking her to a renegade Apache chief down in Mexico named Nalte."

Jamie grabbed a blanket and staggered to his feet. Dolly cried out softly then scolded him, "Jamie Slater. What do you think you're doing? You can't go anywhere—"

Jon had risen, too. "Sit down, Jamie. I'll go."

"No! It's my fault they took her. I'm going after her."

"You're in no condition—"

"I'm in damn fine condition!" Jamie roared. The sound of his own voice ravaged his temple. He shook his head. "I need my pants. And if you don't want to be offended, Jane and Dolly, I need you two ladies to disappear. Now!"

"Jamie Slater—" Dolly began. But he was already rising. "Jamie—"

She turned around, pinkening. Jane let out a little gasp and went tearing up the stairs.

"Want to wait until I've got some clothes for you?" Jon asked dryly.

"I'll throw something down the stairs," Dolly said. She let out an indignant little snort. "Although what good you think you're going to do that girl when you can barely hold your head up, I don't know."

"I'll be with him," Jon said.

Dolly was heading up the stairs. "I'll go saddle up your horse," Hank told Jamie, heading out.

Jamie nodded his thanks, then confronted Jon. "You can't come with me. I need you here."

"You can't ride alone. You're in no shape to do so."

"Then I'll let you come as far as the border. Maybe we'll catch up with them before that. If not, you'll have to turn back. Jon, once I go after Tess, you'll be the only one who can stand against von Heusen here. You've got to do it." He shuddered and sat on the sofa. "Comancheros! She could already be dead! And after von Heusen's men—" He broke off, white, panicked. "I'll kill him," he swore. "I'll kill von Heusen with my bare hands, and every other man who came near her. Jesus, Jon, it was my own damned fault—"

"This was going on long before you came into it, Jamie. They meant to kill her on that wagon train. And it's not as bad as you think. Von Heusen's men won't touch her, and the Comancheros won't touch her, because Nalte wants his golden blond for himself, so I learned at the saloon."

"At the saloon?"

"There's a whore there named Rosy who knows von Heusen well—personally, that is. Every once in a while von Heusen sends for her, and she goes out to his ranch. Last time she was there, he was sending out messages and making plans. This Nalte has always wanted a blond woman for a bride. You know the Apache. They usually only take one wife, unless they consider themselves well able to afford more than one. Nalte does very well. He has an Indian bride, but he wants a white woman, too. A blond white woman. And his requirements go a little further. He wants an innocent white woman."

Jamie stared at Jon blankly, then his face began to pale again.

Jon frowned, then slowly sucked in his breath. "She isn't an innocent white woman any more, is that it?"

"Jamie Slater, here are your pants!" Dolly cried, dropping a pair of trousers down the staircase. Jamie wrapped the blanket around his waist and went to retrieve them. His hands were shaking as he stumbled into his pants. Dolly tossed down a shirt, and he shrugged it on also.

"Jamie!" Jon said.

Jamie paused, looking at his friend.

"Maybe they won't know. I doubt it's something that Tess is going to rush around telling them," Jon suggested.

"First, von Heusen's men are going to have to be damned afraid of him not to hurt her," Jamie said. "Then the Comancheros. Who the hell ever trusted a Comanchero?" He strode to the sofa and stared at Jon. "I've got to catch up with them before they get to this Nalte. Or I'll have to try to talk to Nalte himself."

"Yes, you'll very definitely have to talk to him," Jon said gravely. "And carefully, Jamie. Nalte will not be easy to deal with. He's watched wars and treaties go by for years, and he is a law entirely unto himself. He eschews everything white—except for the white men's guns, horses and women. He moved his people into the mountains when the white men took over the plains, rather than have to deal with them.

"He keeps to the old ways. His women do not buy cotton for their dresses, and his scouts do not wear cotton shirts. He moves about in a breechclout as do his braves in summer, in winter he warms himself with hides and furs. He is also intelligent, astute and very dangerous—an Apache to the core."

Hank had come in. "You need the cavalry," he said.

Jamie shook his head. "No, Hank. No. If I do that, they might kill her. If I don't catch up with them before they hand her over to Nalte, I'll have to speak with him personally and convince him to give her back. It's our only chance.

"Listen Hank, von Heusen is going to think that he has both Tess and me out of the picture. If anyone comes around, act as if you haven't seen either of us. That lawyer will let out the information about the will, and that will stall von Heusen for a little while."

He paused, then strode over to the big desk, sat and drew out a piece of paper. He wrote on it quickly. "Now Hank, you make sure that this telegraph gets out today, you understand? It's real important."

"Yes, Lieutenant Slater, I understand."

"Good. Jon will be back soon, and if I've any luck at all, I'll bring Tess home to you again." He paused. "If not, Hank, you hold tight. Help will come. Von Heusen isn't going to win this one." He stood again, gritting his teeth. "I'll be damned in hell a thousand times over before I let von Heusen win this one!" He strode around the desk again in his bare feet. "Hank, I need a pair of boots that will fit me."

"Sure thing, Lieutenant. I'll find you something."

Jamie nodded. "Jon—I need new guns."

In silence, Jon left to fulfill the request. They'd come with plenty of guns, and he would know what Jamie wanted and what he needed.

Twenty minutes later the guns were assembled and Jon and Jamie were ready to ride out. Dolly had made some coffee, and Jamie drank some quickly, wincing as the hot liquid filled him. He felt a twitch at his temple and felt the stitches there for the first time. "You sewed me up, Dolly?"

"As pretty as a young girl's ball gown, Jamie."

"Thanks."

They moved outside. Jamie and Jon mounted with the others looking on.

"You bring Tess home now, you hear?" Hank said.

"Please, please, bring her home!" Jane added, her large doe eyes wide and damp.

Jamie smiled at Jane. "I'll bring her home. I promise, Jane. I'll bring her home, or I'll die trying."

He tugged on the reins, and he and Jon turned their mounts and started off.

The sun was rising already. It was falling in orange and gold splotches across the dry earth. Beyond them, it shimmered upon the mesas.

He'd been out a long time, Jamie reckoned. And von Heusen's men had already had Tess for a long time.

His muscles clenched tight, his jaw locked, he damned himself again and again for what had happened. He should have been more careful. They never should have had the opportunity to sneak up on him. Hell, if he'd been that careless during the war, he'd have been dead half a dozen times over. He'd always been so damned good: he could hear a twig drop in a forest, he could hear the rustle of trees when it wasn't just the wind, he could hear bare footsteps against the dry earth. But when it had mattered, he had failed.

He'd failed Tess . . .

He'd forgotten everything, staring into her violet-hued eyes, feeling her against him, hearing the whisper of her voice, the tremor of her words. He'd just had to prove something. She'd been so aloof, and he'd been so angry, and he hadn't known why . . .

Because she'd tried to draw away, and he hadn't been about to tolerate it. No, he hadn't been about to let it happen. He had just wanted her, and he hadn't wanted her to escape him.

He was falling in love with her.

So what? he mocked himself. He hadn't wanted to do so. He hadn't suggested that she marry him—he'd just wanted to touch her. To sleep with her. To feel her beneath him, her breath coming in a desperate rush, her hips and thighs moving, her eyes, those eyes, so wide and still, sultry upon his . . .

But he hadn't been able to let her walk away from him. He just hadn't been able to give her time.

And so she was gone.

He felt his jaw lock anew. She had infuriated him. No matter how he touched her, she could hold herself aloof. And his anger and determination had brought them both down.

Damn!

He didn't know that he had cast back his head and cried the word aloud with anguish until he saw that Jon was watching him. Until he saw the pity on his friend's bold features.

"It's too late for recriminations, my friend," Jon said quietly.

"Yeah. Too late."

"If you want her back, you'd better forget your feelings. You can't make any more mistakes."

"I won't," Jamie said.

"You should let me go alone."

"A half-breed Blackfoot? The Apache won't like you any better then they're going to like me."

"Nalte isn't going to be fond of either of us."

"I can deal with Nalte," Jamie said. He spurred his horse forward, calling to Jon to follow him.

He would deal with Nalte. One way or another, he would get Tess back.

One way or another.

Chapter Ten

Comancheros.

They lined the dry, dusty hilltop that overlooked the desert, seeming to go on forever, covering the horizon. A hundred of them, at least.

Her hands tied before her, Tess sat in her buckskins in front of Jeremiah on his big horse. She didn't know how long or how far they had ridden that day, but they had finally come to this desert that stretched to the mountains—a beautiful area, with myriad colors, a barren, forbidding area where the vultures sat upon the branches of the few scrawny trees, where cactus eked out an existence, where most life was lived in the cool that settled over the golden landscape by night. Soon, the terrain would change again, as they entered the mountains.

They were already in the land of the Apache. And Tess was realizing how little she knew of this feared tribe. She knew they were fierce, and that they did not go to reservations. She had read that President Grant had initiated a "peace policy" toward the Apache this year, but that meant one thing in Washington, quite another here. Apache... it took an Apache to track an Apache, so they said. Once Cochise had been a captive of the American Army, but the trap had infuriated him. He had drawn his knife, slit apart the tent—and disappeared. An entire cavalry company had been unable to find him.

She shivered. Perhaps more so than any other Indian on the Western frontier, the Apache could strike terror into the hearts of the people.

But nothing could be more fearsome than the Comancheros who faced her now, staring down at their small group of three from the hillside and the horizon.

Tremors tore at her heart. She had ridden with Jeremiah and David for a day and a night and through much of this day as well, and she had done her very best with Jeremiah. She had looked for every possible opportunity to escape, but David had taken great care never to give her a chance. She was never alone. Even when she relieved herself, he was not more than a few steps away, and his promises of what he would do if she even tried to move made her weigh her circumstances very carefully. As long as she was with them, she was safe. Jeremiah wasn't going to let David touch her, and David was frightened enough of von Heusen to listen to Jeremiah.

Hour by hour she had dreamed. Jamie had to come for her. If he was alive, he would have to come for her. His sense of honor would let him do no less. But he had to come while she was still with David and Jeremiah. The odds would have been pretty even then, he could have ridden in with the sun and carried her away into the sunset. But he had not come, and although she could not allow herself to believe that he had been killed, she knew the odds were no longer even. Not even Jamie Slater could come riding into a throng of a hundred Comancheros, guns blazing, and carry her away. She was indeed here, and . . .

The Comancheros were all staring down at her.

Suddenly, wild screams and shrieks filled the air, and the army of Comancheros came galloping toward them. The cries made her heart flutter, and as they came nearer and nearer, Tess felt an even greater terror growing within her. She began to see their faces, and they were frightening. Most were Mexicans, dark, with long, scruffy beards and heavy, dipping mustaches. They wore hats and shirts and trousers and boots; many wore blankets over their shoulders. All were heavily armed, some with shell cases crisscrossed over their chests. They would not run out of bullets in a fight.

There were Indians, too. Renegades of many tribes, Tess thought, Apache, Comanche, Navaho, some in the Mexican regalia of their comrades, others in more traditional buckskin, at least two of them in simple breechclouts, riding nearly naked in the wind, hooting their triumph and their catcalls, racing around and around the three of them again and again.

They meant to terrify her! Tess thought angrily. Well, supposedly she wasn't in danger yet, even if she was so frightened that she wasn't sure if she could talk or move. David had been a nightmare, but this was far worse. Any dreams she had entertained of rescue fell crashing down into a horrible pit of despair. She had never felt more vulnerable in her life.

She swore, though, that she would not cower before these men who were so determined to unnerve her. They wanted to see tears, she thought. Panic and hysteria. She was close to giving them all that they desired, but she locked her jaw against its trembling and raised her chin. And as the Comancheros raced by her one by one, she kept her eyes levelly upon them, and she ignored the dirt that rose to choke her, bringing tears to her eyes. She sat very still, and she waited.

The horsemen rushed by, then doubled back, bringing their horses to a halt behind her. Jeremiah and David swung around to face them. Tess didn't know whether to find pleasure or new anxiety in the fact that her captors seemed as unnerved as she by the rugged Comancheros.

The Comancheros were all lined up again, and silent once more. The leader emerged, edging his horse forward. He was frightening indeed, with coal-dark hair and coal-dark eyes and a dark olive complexion. He had a great, drooping, handlebar mustache, and though he grew no beard, the rest of his face was not clean shaven. A western hat sat atop his head, the brim pulled low. His chest was crisscrossed with ammunition, and a long, lean cigarillo fell in a slash from the corner of his mouth.

He paused before them and reached into his pocket, then struck a match against his boot to light his cigarillo. He stared at Tess, a smile forming on his features.

"So, *amigos*, the goods are delivered, eh?" He smiled, staring at Tess. She returned his gaze. His smile deepened. "She stares at me hard. Maybe she will be just what Nalte desires. Untie her hands."

"Chavez, she is dangerous," Jeremiah warned him.

"Dangerous? One little blond girl is dangerous when there are a hundred men around her? I told you—untie her hands. Send her to me."

Tess felt the movement as Jeremiah reached for his knife. She heard the rasping sound as he severed the ties that bound her hands together. Instinctively she brought her hands before her, massaging her wrists where the rope had burned them.

"Come down here, *niña*," Chavez ordered.

She was ready to defy him; Jeremiah was not. He dismounted quickly from the horse and reached for Tess. He set her hastily on the ground, then moved away from her as if she were a rattler.

"There she is, good as new, just as we promised. Now, where is the gold, Chavez?"

Chavez motioned to one of the men behind him, a half-naked Indian wearing a headband of eagle feathers, a breechclout, twin leather strips of rifle bullets and nothing more. He carried a small leather satchel that he tossed to Jeremiah. Jeremiah instantly opened the bag. He let out a joyous whoop and looked to David.

"Gold. I mean gold!" He bit the coins, smiling wolfishly. "See, David, it was all worth it!"

"Wait, my friend," Chavez said. He took a step closer to Tess. "These rat piss, they did not touch you?"

Tess narrowed her eyes, then thought of her own safety. "No, they did not touch me."

Chavez nodded. "Nalte, he does not like to be betrayed." He raised his voice, shouting in Spanish. A Mexican rode up leading a small pinto pony. "You," he told Jeremiah and David. "You are done. You go. That is all. And you, woman, you will ride this horse."

She did not move. Jeremiah mounted his horse once again, but Tess made no move. Angry, Chavez urged his mount forward until his large buckskin was nearly stepping upon her. Still, she did not move. *"Niña—"*

"I'm not a girl, Chavez, and I have a name. It's Miss Stuart."

Chavez started to laugh. He laughed so hard that he crunched down on his cigarillo. He nearly swallowed part of it and started to choke.

When he caught his breath, he dismounted from his horse and thundered furiously over to her. He was a short man, she thought. One who looked much better on a horse than standing. She was almost as tall as he. She would be taller. She raised her chin and met his stare.

"Get on the horse," he said. Still, she refused to move. "Eh, *niña*, I am talking to you." He reached out a hard, callused palm and set it against her cheek. Tess slapped him with all the strength in her.

There was silence from every man there.

Then Chavez let loose with a spate of Spanish oaths. Tess thought he would strike her, but he did not. He lifted her, setting her upon the bare back of the pinto. She fought and clawed at him. His hat went flying into the dirt. Her nail imprinted a bright line upon his unshaven cheek.

He swore again, stooping to swoop up his hat.

"Hey, Chavez!" David snickered. "We warned you she was dangerous."

Chavez calmly pulled out his pistol and shot David through the heart.

Tess, who had despised David, nearly gasped aloud. She clenched her chattering teeth, managing to remain immobile and silent as she watched the red stain flare out on David's shirt. His eyes widened, and then glazed over, and he crashed down from his horse.

He had deserved it. He had savagely, heinously attacked Jamie. He had nearly raped her. And yet the cold brutality of his shooting sent waves of shock rippling within her.

"You—you shouldn't have done that," Jeremiah stuttered, shocked. "Mr. von Heusen, he—"

Jeremiah's words broke off in a scream as he saw Chavez lowering the still smoking pistol in his direction. Chavez was not a man of mercy. The pistol barked again.

That time Tess did scream. She catapulted from the pinto horse and threw herself against Chavez, clawing, raking, pummeling him. He swore, dropping the pistol, ducking her blows, trying desperately to seize her wrists. Finally he had her. His heavy arms locked around hers, and she was assailed with the scents of onion and sour breath and unwashed human flesh. A sickness nearly overwhelmed her, and she locked her jaw, standing very still as he stared into her eyes with his own coal-black ones.

"Don't be too dangerous—Miss Stuart. You see how I deal with people who can no longer serve me. You will behave until we have delivered you to Nalte. Do you understand?"

"No, I do not. I do not, because I do not give a damn!"

He swore again, savagely. His arms tightened around her as if he intended to break every rib in her body, but as suddenly he released her, thrusting her into the dirt. The dust rose high around her. Tess started to cough and choke. Chavez wrenched her up and helped her onto the pinto pony. The horse protested, letting out a shrill sound and prancing back and forth.

"You will ride!" Chavez yelled, his eyes black upon her.

Trying to maintain her balance, Tess reached for the reins. She wanted to protest; she wanted to fight.

But she said no more. She held the reins and leveled a glare at Chavez. She didn't want to be bound once again. At least she was not tied, and the pinto pony was sound and sturdy. Her dreams had escaped her, but now they were finding a rebirth. There were a hundred men surrounding her, but feeling the power of the horse beneath her, the determination reawakened within her that she would escape. She would survive.

"Ride!" Chavez roared again. She was going to obey him, and he knew it. He started to laugh. "Miss Stuart. Yes, Miss Stuart, you must ride! Nalte is waiting!"

The Comancheros shrieked again. Men lifted their rifles in the air; some chanted.

Horses pranced around, and their hooves hit the dust.

Then they were off. Tess found herself holding tight to the pinto lest she be thrown and trampled in the stampede.

"Damn!"

High atop a cliff where the mountain range began its craggy rise to the sky, Jamie threw himself against a rock near his perch overlooking the broad, dusty plain below. He closed his eyes in pain, then opened them to stare across at Jon, who was still squatting on the flats of his feet, staring down at the riders who were racing away in a cloud of dust. They had ridden hard and long, and they had nearly caught up with Tess before David and Jeremiah had come upon the Comancheros. Nearly. Not quite. They had come in time to watch the Comanchero kill von Heusen's men in cold blood, and in time to see Tess hit the mustachioed Mexican bandit.

And they had come in time to watch the men ride away with her.

"There was nothing to be done. Not now," Jon said unhappily.

Jamie nodded bitterly. "Tonight. We have to catch up with them tonight." He was silent for a moment, then he pulled off the low-brimmed hat he was wearing and slammed it against the dirt. "What the hell is the matter with that woman? Doesn't she realize that Chavez is a cold-blooded killer? He's going to rip her to shreds if she keeps that up! I could rip her to shreds myself right at this moment."

"She can hardly know that we're sitting up here watching her," Jon reminded him.

Jamie stood up, retrieved his hat and set his hands on his hips as he stared at the sun. Twilight was coming soon enough. He didn't want to follow so closely that they stood a chance of the Comancheros doubling back on them, but he didn't want to be very far behind. "She's getting closer and closer to Nalte's territory. I have to get her back before she winds up in Apache hands." He paused. "Before Nalte discovers that he hasn't been brought..."

"A virgin bride?" Jon suggested.

Jamie scowled. He was staring down where the dust still rose in the wake of the horses. "I met Cochise once," he murmured. "I admired the man. He was willing to meet with me under a flag of truce in spite of the number of times the cavalry betrayed his trust. He is our enemy, he is dangerous, but I would not hesitate to go to him. I wonder if this Nalte is a man like Cochise."

"Nalte is powerful," Jon said. "He is the head of his family, and the chief of many families. He usually makes war with the Mexicans because of the war they have made upon him, but he will deal with the Comancheros because they bring him the arms he needs to fight his battles. He is fiercely against the reservation life, and will battle for his land to the bitter end. But from what I have heard, he is still a man with ethics and honor."

Jamie inhaled and exhaled. "I just don't know. I'm going to try to get her back tonight," he said. "I daren't risk waiting to deal with Nalte."

He turned and started sliding down the cliff toward the small clearing in the rock where they had left the horses. "Coming?" he called to Jon.

"I'm right behind you," Jon assured him.

The Comancheros rode hard alongside the range until the daylight waned and night began to fall upon them. Then they moved into the mountains. The terrain became very rugged, and their pace slowed.

Chavez dropped back to ride beside Tess. "This is Nalte's territory. You will meet your bridegroom very soon." He sneered at her, very pleased with himself. Tess said nothing, but watched the man with as much disdain as possible.

"Wait until you meet Nalte. He is tall and as strong as the rock. He crushes arrogant little girls between his fingers. He is fierce in his paint and breechclouts and he is merciless upon his enemies."

"Chavez, he cannot be anywhere near as repulsive as you," she said pleasantly. So pleasantly that it took several long moments for the smile to fade from his weathered features. He shook a fist in her face. "I have not given you to Nalte yet, little girl! You hold your tongue, or you will pay!"

He rode forward again. Tess shivered but kept her eyes straight ahead in the growing darkness. She could feel the horses and the men bunched around her, could feel their eyes upon her, could smell the sweat of their bodies. But she kept her eyes on the trail, looking neither left nor right, trying desperately not to acknowledge them—or her own fear.

The rocks stopped suddenly. They had come upon a small plateau studded with crude buildings barely discernible in the dusk. An open fire with a huge spit set above it burned in the center of the clearing, and there were women there and a number of armed men awaiting them. Tess figured it had to be a headquarters of sorts for Chavez in the mountains. Perhaps his last stronghold before it became Nalte's territory in full.

She remained on her horse as the men rushed into the clearing, yelling, screaming, calling to their women, cavorting as they dismounted.

Chavez rode over to her. "Welcome to my home, little girl." He laughed. " *Mi casa es su casa*. Always, my house is yours. Tomorrow, Nalte's tepee will be your home!" He roared with laughter, as if he had just said the most amusing thing in the world.

He dismounted from his horse and lifted her down from hers. He pulled her close against him, still roaring. "Maybe I will keep you myself. You have so much to learn about manners. Maybe you are like a very fine horse to be broken, eh? A magnificent mare to be ridden and tamed, eh?"

Tess struggled fiercely against him. He enjoyed her distress and continued to smile. She shouldn't fight him, she thought. He enjoyed it so very much.

But just as she went limp, a sharp female voice called out, "Chavez!"

His features hardened. He did not release Tess, but turned around and stared at the dark-haired, buxom young woman coming toward him. She wore a white peasant blouse and a full, colorful skirt. Her brown feet were bare. She was young and pretty, but her features were wide and her hips showed signs of broadening with age and the birth of children. She scowled furiously at Tess and scolded Chavez in Spanish.

"Woman, shut your mouth!" Chavez roared at her.

She did not stop talking until Chavez turned, his fist raised as if he would hit her. The woman fell silent, but her eyes were eloquent. Her look said that she hated Tess.

"I am Chavez, and I will do as I choose!" he warned the dark-haired woman. He pushed Tess toward her. "Take her. Take her to the house. I will come shortly."

The woman put a hand on Tess's shoulder. Tess shook free from her hand. "Don't touch me!" she warned her sharply.

"What a woman!" Chavez sighed, and Tess did not know if it was with mockery or pleasure. She gritted her teeth and stepped past the woman, striding toward a house she indicated.

The dark-haired woman hurried behind her.

The daylight was almost gone. By the glow of the fire, Tess tried to take measure of where she was. The rocks of the mountains rose all around them, but there were many trails that sprang from the clearing. She had no idea where they led, but if she could escape during the night, she could get some distance from Chavez.

"Stop! You stop, you *gringa* slut!" the woman called out. Tess ignored her. She reached the house and threw open the door.

There were just two rooms there. One was a kitchen with dirty shelves and boxes. Old liquor bottles, chipped and broken, lay upon a dirty, rickety table. Beyond the kitchen was a bedroom.

Tess stared in horror. "This is filthy. I cannot stay here."

Behind them, Chavez laughed sourly.

"Anna, she is right. This is a sty. You will clean it up."

Anna turned and hit out at him. He grabbed her hands. She fought him wildly, then went limp. She pleaded with him in Spanish, her voice catching on a sob. Tess tried to ignore them. She looked around and saw there was a back door in the bedroom. She tried not to stare at it, wondering if it wasn't especially designed as an escape route for Chavez if a stronger force came after him.

She didn't want him to catch her staring at the door so she turned around and sat on one of the crude wooden chairs that surrounded the filthy table.

"Tell her to clean it up!" Anna suddenly said, stamping her foot hard on the floor.

"I will not," Tess said immediately. She crossed her arms over her chest. Chavez was convulsed with laughter once again. He unbuckled his gun belt and tossed it on the table on top of the debris. He sat in a chair opposite Tess and stared at her, still very amused, so it seemed. "She will not clean up your slop, Anna. She is Miss Stuart. She wears an

Apache squaw's buckskins, but she is a lady. You don't know this, Anna, to be a lady. You must watch her. You musn't ask her to pick up swill." He stopped looking at Tess for a moment and slammed his fist against the table. "I am hungry, Anna. You will bring me something to eat. And you will bring something—for the lady."

Anna didn't like that at all. She began to argue again. This time Chavez rose and slapped her hard across the face. Anna stared at him, tears forming in her eyes. But she said no more, choosing to obey him. Chavez looked at Tess sternly. "That is how to handle a woman!" he told her firmly.

"That, Chavez, is not even the proper way to handle a dog," she told him.

But a second later it was all that she could do not to shrink away from him as he jumped to his feet and stood over her, his hand raised, ready to strike. She willed herself not to flinch. Slowly, his hand fell.

He smiled, then he laughed, and returned to his seat, still looking at her. "I would like to keep you here. I would like to see you change your tune. I would like to see you after your eyes had been blackened and your body used by every man here. Then you would not be so proud."

"You could never really touch me, Chavez," she said softly. "You can hurt Anna because she loves you. You cannot hurt a woman who despises you. That is something that you cannot even begin to understand."

He looked at her, puzzled, then the door opened again. Anna was back with a plate of food for Chavez and one for Tess.

Tess didn't want to touch anything in the filthy hovel, but she thought again that she needed strength if she was going to escape, and she hadn't had anything but water all day. She accepted the plate Anna handed her, saying a soft,

"Thank you." Anna looked at her curiously, then went to sit in a chair facing Chavez, her head bowed.

Tess chewed the stringy beef she had been handed, and scooped up the beans with a spoon. She ate quickly but she still had not finished when Chavez let out a loud belch and wiped his face with the back of his sleeve. She glanced at him and felt ill. Knowing she could eat no more, she set her plate on the table.

"You see? She does not eat much, just little, little bites, like a lady," Chavez told Anna. He pushed himself back from the table and rose. Belching again, he growled at Anna to get out of his way. "I will drink with my comrades!" he said. He went to Tess and gripped her chin hard. "I will come back when I have drunk my fill. And I will decide if you get to learn your lessons from me—or the Apache."

Laughing, he released her, collected his guns from the table and strode out of the house. When he was gone, Tess stared at Anna, watching the woman's jealous face. Suddenly she leaped to her feet. "Anna, listen to me. You want Chavez. I do not! Help me. Get me out of here."

"No!" Anna cried in alarm.

"You want him. I hate him! Please—"

"No! No, no, no! He will beat me! He might kill me."

The woman wasn't going to help her, no matter how jealous she was. With a deep sigh of exasperation Tess wandered back to her chair. She closed her eyes for a moment. Lord, she was tired.

Seconds went by, then minutes. Anna stayed where she was, her head lowered. Tess looked longingly at the rear door. If she tried to escape, Anna would sound the alarm. She wouldn't have a chance.

She wondered how long Chavez had been gone. The Comancheros were all outside drinking. Drink might make Chavez think he wanted her more than he wanted the gold the Apache was paying for her. He was a brutally cruel man, she had to remember that. It wasn't difficult. She had only to close her eyes to remember how he had murdered Jeremiah and David in cold blood.

And then an idea came to her. She hurried over to Anna, falling to her knees before the woman in her excitement. "Anna! What if we fought? What if we pretend that I bested you and that I—"

"You could not beat me, *puta*!" Anna claimed.

"Anna! Chavez is your man! This is pretend. I tie you up. I gag you. Then I am gone, and you have Chavez, and he cannot hate you for letting me go. He must love you all the more for what I have done to you." Tess didn't know if that was true or not, but she was certain that Anna would survive Chavez, and equally certain that she might not do so herself. Anna's eyes had narrowed, as if she was giving the idea a great deal of speculation. Tess picked up a lock of her hair. "I am blond! That is what they want. If I stay, Chavez might throw you out."

That decided it. Anna stood and looked around the room. She rushed from the kitchen to the bedroom and found some scarves. "Is this good?"

"Yes, yes."

Anna moved to the hearth where she picked up a heavy cast-iron skillet. She thrust it toward Tess. "Hit me. You must hit me hard on the head. I must have a bruise."

"I—I don't think that I can—"

"You must! If Chavez should beat me, it would be much worse."

"All right," Tess agreed doubtfully. "Let's get in the bedroom. I want you to fall on the bed. I don't want to hurt you."

"You must hurt me some."

They walked into the bedroom. Like the kitchen, it was a mess—with the bed unmade and clothes strewn everywhere.

Anna stood before the bed. "Now hit me."

Tess closed her eyes and bit her lip. Then she raised the iron skillet high and brought it crashing down on Anna's head. The woman fell without a sound. Panicked, Tess checked to see if she had a pulse and if her lungs still rose and fell with her breath. Assured that the woman was alive, she set to tying her wrists and ankles and gagging her with the scarves.

She was just finishing the task when the front door slammed open. Chavez was back!

Tess ran to the rear door. She moved soundlessly and with tremendous speed, and yet it wasn't enough. The door stuck when she tugged upon it.

Chavez was behind her. He grappled her shoulders and spun her around, a rich growl thundering against his throat. Tess stared into his ebony eyes. His fingers closed around her throat. "You are dangerous! The *gringos* were right about you! You are trouble and you need to be taken care of, now!"

He was strangling her. She could barely breathe. In desperate self-defense she brought her knee slamming as hard as she could against his groin. It was a powerful and direct hit, and Chavez screamed out his pain, staggering back.

Tess did not want to stay to see if his condition improved. She grabbed the door again. Gasping, nearly crying, she strained against it.

Then, it opened. She nearly fell against Chavez, it opened so suddenly.

She was about to bolt through it when she gasped. Her heart seemed to stop in her chest, her knees grew weak, her mind went blank of anything other than the man standing in the doorway.

It was Jamie. He had come.

Hands on hips, he stood there, staring. The breadth of his shoulders filled the doorway. He seemed to tower over her and Chavez, and indeed, the entire room. He stared at Tess and at Chavez, swiftly summing up the situation.

He was alive! He had come for her. She had not allowed herself to believe he could be dead, but still he was a dream standing before her, the hero come to sweep her away. She was so stunned to see him she could not move, she could not utter a word, she couldn't even cry out her thrill at seeing him standing there alive, warm blood pulsing in his veins, his chest rising and falling with every breath he took.

She saw nothing but Jamie.

Chavez had not seemed to notice Jamie was there. Chavez was staring at Tess, and there was pure, cold murder in his coal-black eyes.

"Tess!" Jamie hissed to her. "Move!"

She found motion at last as Chavez charged after her. She pitched herself toward Jamie. He caught her shoulders, and his smoke-gray eyes stared sternly into hers.

"Go!" he commanded her. "Go, get out of here, run! Do you hear me? Get the hell out and run!"

Then he thrust her behind him and out the door, into the darkness of the night. Tess heard the sound of the impact as Chavez came thundering against Jamie.

She couldn't run. She paused and turned back.

Chavez had pulled his knife. The steel glistened in the pale moonglow of the night.

"Jamie!" she cried.

But Jamie had seen the knife. She expected him to draw his Colt, but when he didn't she realized he couldn't draw down the entire camp upon them with the sounds of bullets.

He, too, drew a knife.

"Go!" he thundered to Tess.

Still she hesitated, tears forming on her eyes.

"Jamie—"

"Go! I'll deal with you later!"

His furious, high-handed tone finally sent her into motion. She had been kidnapped and abused, and now he was yelling at her.

Yelling at her . . . and facing Chavez with a knife.

She bit her lip, then turned and ran. The trail stretched out in the darkness before her, narrow, twisting, rising higher and higher into the mountains. Gasping for breath, half choking, half sobbing, Tess continued to run. She stumbled into a huge rock, glowing white in the moonlight. She caught hold of it, wincing against the pain in her feet, inhaling deeply and desperately. Then she started to run again, almost blind as the shrub grew thicker and rose higher, adding to the darkness of the night.

Staggering, she kept on running. She grabbed at shrubs, still running, heedless of discomfort or pain.

Then, in the darkness, she slammed against something with such impetus that she fell to the ground, barely catching herself to break the fall, scraping her palms with the rock and dirt beneath her hands. Stunned, she tossed the hair from her eyes and looked up, trying to discern what had happened.

She gasped yet made no noise, and her heart began to thunder with renewed terror.

He stood before her, naked except for a breechclout, his arms crossed over his chest. He was as tall as Jamie, as broad, and very, very dark. His hair was ebony and it streamed straight down his back. He was nearly copper in color, and his features were very strong and hard.

He reached down, grasped her wrists and drew her to her feet. Instinctively she tried to pull away from him. His grip upon her tightened. He smiled very slowly, and though she struggled, he held her tightly.

"Let me go," Tess said. "Jamie—er, Lieutenant Slater is right behind me, and he'll shoot you."

She was losing her mind. She was trying to explain things in English to an Apache savage.

"So you are the blond woman who costs so dearly," he responded in perfect English. "You have escaped the Comancheros. You will not escape me."

She shook her head wildly. "No! You do not understand me! Let me go. I've a friend. He's right behind me. He's killing that Comanchero and he's going to kill you. He—"

"Shut up, Sun-Colored Woman."

"My name is Tess. Or Miss Stuart. It's—"

"Sun-Colored Woman. That is to be your name. I am Nalte, and it will be so."

"Nalte!" she breathed. She had escaped the Comanchero to run into the arms of the very Apache who had ordered her as if she was dry goods for a mercantile store!

"You—you speak English," she said.

"Yes. Now you will come."

"No! Please, listen—"

He wasn't going to listen. He grasped her wrists and drew her over his shoulders. She slammed her fists furiously against him.

"Let me go, you savage! Let me go right now! You can't just buy a blond woman! Please..."

But he wasn't listening to her. He was moving fleetly up the trail. He didn't seem to be running, but the trail was disappearing beneath his feet, and they were moving higher and higher into the mountains. He was ignoring her pleas.

"Bastard!" she cried in furious panic. "Savage! Horrid, horrid savage!"

That brought him to a halt. He lifted her and slammed her down upon her knees. She tried to rise, and he pressed her down with such fury that she went still. He towered over her.

"Savage? You, a white woman, would call me savage? No one knows the meaning of brutality so well as your own kind. Let me tell you, Sun-Colored Woman, what the white man, the white soldier has done to us, to my people." The moon rose high, shimmering down upon him with sudden clarity. Nalte, his bronze shoulders slick and heavily muscled, walked around her.

"In 1862 your General James Carleton sent a dispatch unit through Apache Pass. Cochise and Mangas Coloradas lay in wait. There was a fierce battle, and Mangas Coloradas was seized from his horse. He was taken to Janos, but his followers told the doctors that he must be cured or their town would be destroyed. So he survived.

"Mangas Coloradas survived so that he could come a year later, under a flag of truce, to parlay with the soldiers and miners for peace. He was seized. Your general ordered that he have Mangas Coloradas the next morning, alive or dead. So do you know what your civilized white people did to him? They heated their bayonets in the fire, and they burned his legs, and when he protested, they shot him for trying to escape. It was not enough. They cut off his head, and they boiled it in a large pot. Do you understand? They boiled his head. But now you would sit there, and you would tell me that I am savage?"

She wasn't sitting, she was kneeling, in exactly the position in which he had pressed her. She was trembling, shaking like a leaf blown in winter, and she was praying that Jamie would arrive and rescue her.

But of course, she didn't know if Jamie was alive or dead. He had faced Chavez in a knife fight, and she couldn't know the outcome. And now she was facing an articulate Apache who seemed to have reason to want vengeance.

"You speak English exceptionally well," she said dryly.

He did not appreciate her sense of humor. He wrenched her to her feet and pulled her against him.

"You will find no mercy with me," he assured her. "Do not beg."

"I—I never beg," she said, but the words came out in a whisper. She wasn't certain if they were defiant or merely pathetic. It didn't matter. He pushed her forward, then tossed her over his shoulder again.

"No!" she protested wildly. She hit his back, but he did not notice her frantic effort. She braced against him and screamed, loudly... desperately.

Jamie...

Dear God, where was he now?

Perhaps it did not matter. Perhaps there was no help for either of them anymore.

Chapter Eleven

Nalte moved through the darkness so swiftly that Tess had little idea of how far they traveled. She felt as if they twisted and turned relentlessly, but slowly she realized that they were moving downhill. She tried at first to reason with him, but he ignored her, and it was painful to try to talk when she was held so tightly against him. She was exhausted, and the words she had said to Chavez were true at the very least. She wanted to be free from Nalte, but she did not feel the same loathing for the man that she had felt for Chavez.

And now she knew Jamie was alive. Or at least he had been alive. He had gone to battle Chavez, but now she had hope, if nothing else.

Hope . . . Could he come for her against Nalte? Could he slip out in the darkness and come furtively against the Apache? She didn't know what to think anymore. She hadn't thought that Nalte would speak English, but he did so, very well.

He halted suddenly, letting out the cry of a night bird, and was answered in kind. He started to walk again and they descended a final cliff to a clearing where tepees rose magically against the night sky, and where camp fires burned with soft glows, where only the movement of shadows could be seen.

Nalte set her down and let out the soft sound of a bird cry once again.

From the shadows a man emerged. He was dressed as Nalte was, in a breechclout. He wore high buckskin boots and numerous tight beaded necklaces, and carried what appeared to be a U.S. Army revolver. He began to speak with Nalte very quickly, and Nalte replied. Then the man turned and disappeared into the shadows. The Apache camp was sleeping, Tess thought.

"Come," Nalte told her, catching her arm and leading her across the camp. She saw more shadows. The camp might sleep, but men were on guard.

She started to shiver, realizing that now she had no defenses. She had enjoyed a certain safety with Jeremiah and David, so much so that she could even be sorry that Jeremiah had been killed so coldly. But now...

She had come here as Nalte's prize. That had been von Heusen's plan. The darkness lay all around them, and Nalte was leading her toward the largest tepee. It glowed in moonlight, and she could see the designs and colors upon it, the scenes of warfare, the furs attached to the flaps. Smoke rose from the hole where the structure poles met at the top indicating a fire within the tepee.

"Get in," Nalte said, thrusting her inside.

She nearly fell, but she regained her balance and stood quickly, ready to fight him whatever came. He let the flap fall over the entryway and crossed his arms over his chest and stared at her. She moved backward, noting the amusement that flickered in his dark eyes. She stumbled upon something, looked around and saw that blankets and packs of clothing were neatly rolled against the sides of the tepee and that there were several cooking utensils by the fire that burned in the center of the tepee. Its smoke escaped through the high hole.

There was a woman in the tepee already. A young, very pretty woman, who stared at Tess with wide eyes. Tess stared in return, coloring as dread filled her. Nalte had wanted a blond woman. He already had a wife. He intended to rape her here in front of his first wife.

He took a step toward her. She tightened her fingers into fists at her side. There was no escape here. This was not a place like the haphazard Comanchero dwelling. If she could escape Nalte she would only be caught by his warriors.

Jamie had been so close! Rescue had been within reach. But now she couldn't even hope that he would come against the Indians. Nalte would kill him.

Tess gazed from the young woman to the Indian. "You are a savage!" she shouted. Tossing her hair, she stared at him defiantly. "I don't want you. I don't want to be here! I was kidnapped for your entertainment! And now here sits your poor wife, and you think that you're going to...that you're going to...No!" she shouted, for the flicker of amusement had deepened in his eyes, and he was striding toward her.

She lashed out wildly, her fists pummeling his chest. He seemed to barely notice her effort, and bent low to pick her up and throw her on a blanket roll. She opened her mouth to scream, but he did not come close to her.

He stepped back, watching her. "This is not my wife. This is my sister. And because of her, you will be safe from me this night. With the light we begin the ceremony that makes her a woman." He smiled at the woman, and there was deep affection in his gaze, but it faded when he looked at Tess again. "It is an important ceremony, a religious one."

He turned and found another blanket roll. He had dismissed her entirely, Tess thought. She stared from the warrior to the young woman, longing to bolt for the opening.

Nalte was already stretching out comfortably on his blanket.

The woman tried to smile at Tess. She patted the ground, indicating that Tess should sleep.

Tess swallowed, keeping a wary eye on Nalte. She pulled out a blanket and carefully lay down on it. Stretching out, she pretended to close her eyes. But she kept watching Nalte. When he slept, she would try to escape. If she could return to the trail in the mountains, she could possibly find Jamie.

Was he alone? she wondered. Or was Jon out there somewhere with him?

She was exhausted, and tears threatened her eyes. No matter how hard she tried, or how she fought, she never seemed to escape the fate that von Heusen had intended for her. Jeremiah and David were dead, and she could pray that Chavez was dead, yet it had done little for her. She was where von Heusen had intended she should be, and she was certain that men braver than she and far more knowledgeable of the rugged terrain could not escape the Apache.

Nalte was finally sleeping. She rose very carefully and tiptoed across the dry earth flooring of the tepee to the slit. She glanced at Nalte again. His eyes were closed, his features immobile. She started to slip beneath the flap.

A hand wound around her ankle, bringing her down hard upon the floor. In seconds the fierce warrior had crawled over her. His eyes were ebony in the night. "You have courage," he told her. "But you are stupid!"

"You speak of our savagery!" she charged him. "You deal with the despicable Comancheros, you buy rifles and women from them!"

"My sister is my only family," he told her in turn, "because the others were killed. Killed by white men. Beaten, skewered, broken and left to die. My mother died this way, my sisters. Babies, little babies. I have not brought you here to kill you. Not unless you force me to."

"You are holding me against my will."

He touched a long strand of her hair. He seemed reflective for a moment. "You will come to understand me," he told her. "You will learn our ways, and you will be happy here."

"I cannot be happy!" she told him desperately.

"We are not savages!"

She shook her head, moistening her lips. "No, no more so than we. But I am not what you wanted. I—"

"You are more than what I wanted," he interrupted, and he was smiling. "Now go back to sleep or I will forget that I keep a sacred vigil this night."

"Nalte, please—"

"Go back. Now."

She felt the tension in his arms and saw the fierce glitter in his eyes and she knew that his warning was not without good reason. Hastily she retreated. She curled into her blanket, pulling it around her ears. She shivered. She didn't hate the Indian, but he didn't understand that. She was not repulsed by him, but she had to be free, for she was not part of his society. She wanted revenge. She wanted von Heusen hurt as he had hurt her.

And she wanted Jamie. She was in love with him, and that hurt more than anything else. If it weren't for him, she could bear anything that happened . . .

But he was out there, somewhere. And she could never forget him.

Morning came, and the blanket was pulled away from Tess's shoulders. She gasped and opened her eyes, expecting to discover Nalte, but it wasn't him. Several women stared at her. They spoke to her, but she didn't understand them.

They pulled her to her feet. She protested, but was ignored. Nalte's little sister smiled at her encouragingly. She had little choice, for the women set upon her arms and drew her along with them. They left the tepee to enter the family clearing. The sun was just beginning to shine down upon the camp. Men and women were busy, moving around. Some cleaned their weapons, others watched her with curiosity. The women moved around with buckets of water or with bowls of food.

A soft word was said to her, and she was moved forward. No one was cruel to her, but she couldn't have escaped the women who were determined to escort her.

She heard the stream before she saw it, as they walked a trail that brought them through trees and dense shrubs. From the trail she could hear the tinkling melody of the water, reminding her that she was very thirsty, and that there was a certain personal necessity she had to take care of. She was glad to be with the women, even though she flushed when they tugged at her buckskins, indicating that she was to strip and bathe.

Still, she felt better once the water was against her skin and once she had swallowed huge mouthfuls of it. She realized that the women were disappearing between a bank of trees, and she was certain the trees had to be the latrine. She followed them, and thought longingly once she was done of disappearing into the brush, but even as the thought came to her, she saw that two of her keepers had come for her. Again, they were not cruel, but the women with the ink-dark hair and the huge dark eyes placed firm hands upon her and took her to the stream.

There they ignored her. It was Nalte's sister who gained everyone's attention. Once she, too, had bathed, she was dressed in a soft, pale buckskin dress with shades of yellow coloring on it. A yellow paint was smeared over her face, and her hair was lovingly combed out and let loose to fall beneath her shoulders. Necklaces were placed upon her, beautiful pieces of beads and silver cones, and one rawhide strand with a claw upon it. She smiled during it all, flushed and lovely.

It was her ceremony day, Tess remembered. And then she realized that she had not been forgotten after all. A woman called for her from the bank of the stream. She had no choice but to crawl out and let them stare at her. They whispered over her nakedness and she flushed, backing away when they would have touched her. Her pale skin was very different from their own, she knew. But it was her hair that seemed to fascinate them most—both that upon her head and that upon her body.

They didn't tease her long, but gave her a new outfit to wear. It was a soft, pale buckskin much like Nalte's sister's dress, but with no yellow on it. It fell just to her knees.

Her feet were still sore from her barefoot treks over the mountain trails, and she had hoped that someone would give her soft doeskin slippers to wear. But nothing was supplied for her feet, and when she tried to ask one of the women, the Apache shook her head. They were preparing to go back to the village, and Tess was to go with them.

Tess wondered again about her chances of escaping, but she had heard that the Apache women could be every bit as fierce as their men. The women were excited about the young girl they had dressed so carefully for her rite, but their eyes were still upon her. She walked along, weary and desolate, trying to focus her thoughts on her hatred of von Heusen so that she wouldn't be able to fear her own future, and to wonder desperately about Jamie Slater.

Her eyes were lowered, her head was down when they came into the village. She stumbled and looked up to see where she was going.

Looking across the compound she saw that four Indians were in curious costumes with huge headdresses, obviously preparing for the rites to come. But the Indians were staring across the compound at a stranger who had come among them. For a moment he looked very much like Nalte. Tess narrowed her eyes, watching the man, trying to figure out why he looked so familiar. He was dressed in buckskins from head to toe and he wore a cap adorned with eagle and owl feathers. His hair was black and straight as Nalte's, but worn shorter. Even as she stared at him, he turned slowly, pointing her way.

She gasped, stunned to see that the newcomer was Jon Red Feather. He smiled at her briefly, a sign of encouragement, she thought, then his expression quickly sobered again, and he continued to talk to Nalte.

The tall Apache was dressed for the ceremony, too. He wore a fringed buckskin shirt, buckskin pants, high, laced boots and eagle feathers in his hair. He was also adorned with a turquoise amulet around his neck, and silver studs and beads upon his bonnet and shirt. He was listening to Jon Red Feather—and watching Tess gravely as he did.

Nalte nodded, and Jon let out a whistle.

Then Jamie rode into the clearing. He was in calico shirt, denim pants, knee-high boots and a Western hat. He didn't glance at Tess, but lifted a hand to Nalte. When he reached the chief, he slipped from the horse instantly and approached the man, speaking quickly.

She felt as if her heart slammed hard against her chest. He was a fool! she thought. He didn't know Nalte, he didn't know how the Apache chief hated the white man, nor did he seem to realize the things that had been done to the Apache by the cavalry. Fool! She wanted to scream to him, but she couldn't breathe, she could only pray that Nalte wouldn't slay him right on the spot.

Nalte shook his head violently.

Forty warriors suddenly drew their weapons, facing Jamie.

His Colts were around his waist, but he didn't make a move to touch them. He spoke calmly once again, and Nalte called out something sharply. Guns and war clubs were lowered.

Frightened still, Tess cried out, shaking off the hands of the women around her and racing toward Jamie. She pitched herself against him, but he caught her shoulders hard and thrust her away.

Thrust her away—straight into Nalte's arms. Her eyes widened with alarm and fury.

"What in God's name are you doing?" she gasped. She couldn't move. Nalte's dark fingers were a vise upon her.

Nor did Jamie seem to want her. His eyes flashed upon her with dark fury. "Stop it, Tess."

"But—"

"Stop it! Shut up!"

"Damn you, Jamie—"

He switched into the Apache language, addressing Nalte. At the last, he spoke English once again. "Nalte, may Jon Red Feather take the woman away so that we may speak without interruption?"

"Speak without interruption!" Tess flared.

But Nalte was nodding.

"Tess, come!" Jon called to her.

Apparently she didn't move quickly enough. Jamie reached for her arm and thrust her toward Jon. He pulled her away even as she protested. "Jon—"

"Tess, he's trying to negotiate for your return."

"They were going to shoot him! I had to do something." She tugged free of Jon and turned back to watch Jamie, still talking with Nalte. "What are they doing now?"

"Talking about prices."

"For what?"

"For you, of course," he told her with a crooked smile.

"How can Jamie pay Nalte?"

"Well, he can't pay him…not very much, that's why he's arguing that you aren't worth the price."

"I'm not worth the price!"

"Tess—"

Tears touched her eyes. "He shouldn't be here to begin with! He must not understand Nalte—"

"Nalte would have killed most men by now. He is seeing Jamie because he knows about him, he knows that Jamie has always been fair. Tess, keep your mouth shut, all right?"

She wanted to keep her mouth shut, but she was still in terror that the Apache would betray Jamie, as they had been betrayed so many times themselves. She was deliriously glad to see him and Jon, and she wanted to know about Chavez, but she was afraid to ask. Her temper was rising because she was so desperately scared of what was to come.

Before she could say more, Nalte came striding by with Jamie and his guard behind him. Jamie cast her a fiercely warning glare; Nalte barely glanced her way. They entered Nalte's dwelling.

"What are they doing now?" Tess demanded.

"Negotiating," Jon said briefly.

She started to shiver. Nalte didn't need to negotiate. He could kill Jamie and keep her. He had all the power. He could do anything he wanted to do.

"There's no hope!" she whispered.

Jon set his hands on her shoulders. "Courage, Tess. There is every hope. Nalte's little sister begins her puberty rite today. The rite goes on for four days. The woman over there will be her sponsor. She is of impeccable character, and she will stand for the sister. The man there with the buffalo horns upon his cap and the white eagle feathers, he is the shaman, the medicine man, and he will add the sacred religion to the ceremony. The girl is dressed for her role as White Painted Woman or White Shell Woman, a sacred maiden and one of the most important of the Apache supernaturals. She will pray to the sun. The dancers with the headdresses, they are the Gan, or Mountain Spring Dancers. It is an expensive ceremony, but Nalte is a great chief, and he has supplied much for his sister's rite. The Gan dancers symbolize the four directions. They are elaborate.''

Tess watched the dancers as they prepared for the day. They were painted black and white, and they carried huge fan racks and wore buckskin kilts. They carried wands. On their arms were trailers made of cloth and eagle feathers. Their huge masks had false eyes. The fan racks portrayed snakes and other creatures.

She shivered, grateful that Jon was there to assure her that the dancers were involved in a ceremonial rite and were not preparing for war. She looked into his green eyes and realized that he had kept talking to ease her mind from worry, and she was grateful to him.

"He must be furious to be disturbed today!" she whispered.

"He is not disturbed. He will make his decision quickly," Jon told her.

An Apache warrior emerged from Nalte's tent. He spoke briefly with Jon and took Tess by the arm.

"Jon!" she cried.

"Go with him," Jon ordered her. "He isn't going to hurt you. I'm wanted with Nalte. And you are not."

She didn't want to let Jon out of her sight, but he moved away resolutely, and she had no choice but to accompany the warrior who took her by the arm. Seconds later she was thrust into an empty tepee. The fire that had burned in the center was nearly out. On rocks beside it were corn cakes and dried meat. She hadn't been told she could, but she was alone and she was starving, so she helped herself.

She had barely bitten into the food when she became so nervous she couldn't chew. She set the food down and began to pace. After a while she sat again and looked sadly at her tender and torn feet. They would never be the same again.

Moments later, she heard a rush of air. She catapulted to her feet, staring toward the opening of the tepee. Jamie was coming in. She gasped softly, then raced toward him, flinging her arms around him.

He quickly untangled himself, staring fiercely into her eyes. "We're going to get out of this. If you can manage to behave."

"Behave!"

"Listen to me!" He shook her so hard that she felt her teeth rattle. Indignantly she tried to jerk away from him, but his grip on her was firm and he wasn't letting go.

"You're hurting me!"

"I'm hurting you! We're in the midst of a fiasco like this—"

"It wasn't my fault!"

His jaw twisted hard. "I know. It was mine. For being so damned determined to try to understand you.

She felt the color drain from her face. The planes of his face seemed very lean and hard. He was more bronze, tauter. There was a fresh scar upon his cheek. She wanted to touch it tenderly, but he was holding her with too great a vigor. And the smoky anger in his eyes told her he did not want her touch.

He had come for her. He had survived both von Heusen's guns and his fight with Chavez to come for her. But now she realized that he had come only because he considered himself responsible for what had happened to her. She paled, trying to pull from his grasp, but he wouldn't let her.

"The puberty rite for Nalte's sister will last four days. He will not attend to any other business during that time. Jon and I are to be his guests. You are to stay here, do you understand me?"

"Just stay here...for four days?" she whispered. "Can't I be with you?"

He swore, vehemently. "You were purchased, Tess! Damn it, don't you realize that? And not for your talents with a newspaper."

"Jamie, don't you start with me—"

"No, don't you start with me," he said heatedly. "You can manage yourself, and you can manage a lot, and you probably are a damned good rancher and newspaper woman. But if you try anything here, Tess, we'll both probably die. Do you understand? We're walking a very narrow line here. I've tried to explain von Heusen to Nalte. He has a sense of honor; there is a chance he will return you. But I can't do any of this if you interfere. Do you understand?"

She wrenched free of him at last. His hands fell upon his hips and his hat brim tipped over one eye, yet she could still see the silver glint in the other. She swung around and walked with her shoulders stiff and straight, then she sat Indian fashion upon a blanket roll. She mustn't let him see how hurt she was.

He didn't say anything else to her, but started to turn to leave. She couldn't stand that, and called out to him.

"Jamie!"

"What?" he demanded impatiently.

"What—" She paused, licking her lips. "What happened to Chavez?"

"He's dead," Jamie said flatly.

"And the Comancheros—"

"The Comancheros never saw me," he said. "But if we're going to get out of the mountains, we're going to need an Apache escort. So don't create problems."

"Me!"

"You," he said succinctly, and he was on his way out again.

"Jamie!"

"What now?"

She hesitated a second. "Thank you. Thank you for coming after me. Thank you for risking so much."

"You don't need to thank me. I owed you this."

This time he stayed, staring at her. But she couldn't speak anymore because sudden tears were welling behind her lashes and threatening to spill over on her cheeks. He owed her this. He had come for her because he owed her. She had dreamed that he was falling in love with her.

Maybe she was proving to be too much trouble. She had traded half her land for a hired gun. But she had never told her hired gun he was going to have to go after Comancheros and Apache as well as von Heusen's men.

"I'll remember to thank Jon," she said coolly. "He didn't owe me anything."

"You do that," Jamie told her. But still he didn't leave. He stood by the entrance, and she sat across from him, her knees crossed, her shoulders and back very straight, her hands resting upon her knees. The distance between them seemed immense, and yet she felt the touch of his eyes as if it was fire.

It was he who spoke this time, lightly, softly.

"Tess?"

"What?"

"Did—did any of them—hurt you?"

She knew what he meant. Her cheeks burned and her lashes fell over her cheeks. "David was a monster, and he probably would have killed me. Jeremiah wasn't so bad—he wouldn't let David touch me. I was sorry to see Jeremiah killed." Her voice faded slightly. "Especially the way he was killed. And Chavez... Well, you know about Chavez, because... because you were there."

"Yes, I know about Chavez. What about Nalte?"

She shook her head. "He let me be. Because of his sister."

She started, hearing the long, ragged exhalation of his breath. She thought, for a moment, that he would cross the distance between them and take her into his arms. He did not. She could scarcely breathe, longing to leap to her feet once again. But he had already set her from him. She wasn't going to touch him again.

"You're still Nalte's," he told her harshly.

She gazed at him, wondering what he meant. Then she realized that he would not touch her until he had completed his negotiations with the Apache chief.

He didn't say any more. He swung around and left, and she knew that even if she had called his name then, he would have left her.

The day wore on endlessly. Tess could hear the ceremonial drums beating and the chants of the puberty rite, but she could see nothing, and she was involved in nothing. She tried very hard to be patient, and to understand that everything rested upon negotiation.

Late in the afternoon, Jon came in. She almost leaped into his arms, but he was carrying a dish of food for her. He set it down, and she did hug him, fiercely.

"Eat," he told her. "You may need your strength."

She nodded and sat and looked suspiciously at her bowl. "What is it?" she asked.

"Something exotic and Apache," he told her, "beef. Probably from cattle taken in a raid. You should not worry. The Apache are very finicky about what they eat. They will not eat snake, for they believe that the creature is evil, and they will not eat evil meat. Here they are close enough to the plains to seek out the buffalo. They also hunt deer, antelope, elk and bighorn. Their food is quite safe, I assure you."

She flashed him a quick smile and ate the beef with her fingers. It was delicious.

"How does the ceremony progress?" she asked.

"The girl has been taken to the ceremonial tepee with her shaman. She has knelt down on the buckskin and lain prone to be massaged by her sponsor, and she has run in the four directions. Tonight she will dance in the ceremonial tepee, and others will dance in the center of the village."

He paused, looking at her. "I am leaving tonight. Nalte will not let you go until this ceremony is over, and we think it is important that I hurry to Wiltshire with the news that you have been found."

"Oh!" Tess said, setting down her bowl and staring at him. Then she moved across the tent and hugged him close. "I don't want you to leave. I'm so afraid for you."

"The Apache will see me past the Comancheros, as they will do for you if they choose to let you go."

"If—"

"When!" he assured her.

She pulled slightly away, staring into his deep green eyes and feeling as if she had found a friend she would cherish all her life. In his buckskins he appeared very much the Indian, but his words were those of the white man who knew her society and understood her fears.

"Oh, Jon, be careful!" she pleaded with him.

"I'm quite sure he will be."

Jamie's deep drawl startled them both. Tess stood quickly. Jon came to his feet more slowly, staring at Jamie.

"Sorry, I didn't mean to interrupt," Jamie said drily. He ducked beneath the flap and was gone.

Tess instinctively ran after him.

Jon caught her before she could leave. "You cannot go to him!" he ordered her hoarsely. "He has explained to you. You are still Nalte's. You remain here, untouched, until a decision is made."

"But he—he misconstrued what he saw!" Tess wailed.

Jon offered her a dry smile. "Perhaps he deserved to, eh?" She didn't smile in return, and he hastened to reassure her. "He is my friend, and I am his. He knows we said goodbye and nothing more." He didn't let her answer, but gave her a quick squeeze. "I'll see you in Wiltshire," he whispered, then he was gone.

And she was left alone. Outside the light was fading. Darkness was coming, and despite the summer heat of the day, the night was coming with a chill. Tess shivered and wrapped her arms around herself, staring miserably at the center of the tent where the fire burned no longer.

Jamie walked almost blindly into the growing darkness of the night. Soon, the evening ceremonies for the young girl would begin, but at the moment, there was a lull as preparations were made. This puberty rite was one of the most important for the Apache. It was a structured society, a social one, and respect and honor were tremendously important.

The anger that seethed through him lightened for a moment as he thanked God that Nalte happened to be an exceptionally honorable man. Nalte had known when he first bargained with von Heusen that the man who intended to sell a blond woman to him had to be somewhat of an outcast in his own society. But he had not imagined the things Jamie told him. Jamie explained that von Heusen had made war on Tess and had tried to make the people around him believe it was the Comanche or the Apache who had carried out the raids. That had infuriated Nalte, and it had almost given him Tess.

Almost . . .

Nalte wasn't quite ready to let go.

Jamie clenched his teeth and his fists as he hurried past the circle of tepees and into the night. He wanted to reach the stream, to bathe his face in its coldness.

Yet even when he reached the stream, the water could do nothing to soothe him. He could not forget Tess's eyes—huge, violet and luminous upon his. She had been so straight and rigid, and yet she had seemed so very small and vulnerable when she had talked to him in the tent. She had explained the past few days with a simple dignity, and he had been so relieved to discover that she had received a minimum of abuse that his knees had gone weak. He had wanted to wrap her in his arms and promise her everything would be all right, that no one would ever hurt her again.

But he hadn't been able to do that. He couldn't make any promises. He didn't even dare touch her lest the emotion or the passion tear him apart and lead to Nalte's fury. But he had never hungered more deeply inside for her. She was always fighting; she was always strong. She had endured so much that she could be no less than strong. And yet now she had that air of vulnerability about her. She did need him. And he wanted to be all things to her.

He splashed more water on his face, and his temper cooled. He owed Jon so much—and not his anger. Yet he had been angry, seeing her trustingly in his friend's arms, seeing the tears in her eyes, the emotion within them. He wanted her. He wanted her in his arms.

He closed his eyes, and saw again the picture of the young woman with the luminous violet eyes and the soft storm of golden-red hair falling over her shoulders and down her back. So quiet and still, and somehow achingly soft in the bleached white buckskins. There'd been a strange serenity about her, a serenity she could not possibly be feeling. He'd felt impotent to be just standing there talking to her. He was her gun, her hired gun. He'd said that he'd protect her, but he hadn't been able to. Others had descended upon her, and she had endured fear and suffering at their hands. He'd been praying for a miracle. Praying that she hadn't been so abused that he'd never manage to live with himself again.

He'd never felt good about killing a man. Never. Not during the war, not after. But he'd wanted to kill von Heusen's men when they had taken her. He'd wanted to do more than kill them—he'd wanted to tear them limb from limb and watch them die in horrible agony. Chavez had taken that away from him. For the good of his soul, maybe it was just as well. It was hard for a man to live with that kind of hate. He knew. He'd watched it fester in his brother Cole, and it had nearly cost him his wife, Kristin.

Then there had been Chavez.

He'd never seen Chavez, except from the mountaintop. And watching the Comanchero shoot the men in cold blood had kept him from feeling the least remorse when Chavez had fallen beneath his blade. The fight between them had been cold, both men knowing that it was life or death. Jamie had been a little quicker, and Jon had managed to come around with the horses before the Comancheros knew that their leader had been visited, much less killed. The bound woman on the bed had never moved, and she hadn't seen anything. They were done with the Comancheros—for good, he hoped.

He smiled suddenly. He would have to ask Tess how the woman had come to be bound and tied on that bed. It would surely be an interesting story.

But when they had fled the Comancheros camp, Tess had been nowhere to be seen. They had tracked the trails up and down all night, calling softly to her. He hadn't been willing to admit that they had helped her elude the Comancheros only to send her into the arms of the Apache. But Jon knew the territory, and he knew something of Nalte. And in the end they had decided that the only way they could deal with the chief was to lay their cards on the table. Jamie was going to have to count on his reputation with the Indians.

Jon would change into his buckskin attire to approach Nalte first, then Jamie would ride in. It had been risky for them both. The Apache were a warlike people, and Nalte was known to hate the white man. But he had a reputation, too—one for upholding his own sense of honor and hospitality. Besides, it was obvious from the outskirts of the village that some big ceremony was going on, and a chief like Nalte didn't usually like blood on his hands during such an occasion.

And so they were here, and still waiting.

Darkness was falling upon the water. The moon glittered gently upon it, and the easy melody of the running water was gentle. It was a beautiful sight, this valley within the beginning of the fierce mountain ranges.

A beautiful place to die, Jamie thought.

Nalte had promised his decision about Tess as soon as the festivities for his sister had ended. Jon seemed to believe that the Apache chief had already determined he would return Tess, at some cost, of course, but he would return her.

But what if he did not?

Jamie knew he would never leave without her.

If Nalte decided against him, he would have to fight the chief. And if he won, the Apache would probably slay him in vengeance anyway. He might well die in this beautiful place, then there would be nothing more that he could do for Tess.

I'm sorry! he thought. I never should have become so involved. Falling in love with a beautiful angel has surely been the downfall of many a man. I couldn't let you go that morning. I had to make you see that the thing between us was right and that you couldn't turn away from it by the morning's light.

He hadn't had the edge he had needed, the edge that had kept him alive through so much.

So now they were here, and their fate rested on the decision of an Apache chief.

He liked Nalte. He had a keen intelligence, was well-versed in his own language and in English, well-aware of the world around him . . . And fighting to maintain the inheritance of a people despite an encroaching world. He was not so bad a man, Jamie thought. Rather he die and leave Tess to Nalte, than leave her to trash like David or Chavez. Nalte would never hurt her.

He clenched his fists and swore to the night sky. Then his thoughts raced as he sank on his haunches to stare at the rippling, moon-kissed water once again. I will not die here! Come heaven or hell, I will fight, and with every edge, and I will bring her home with me!

"Jamie!"

He thought he imagined the voice.

But then, as he stared into the water, her reflection was caught by the glow of the moon almost magically on the surface before him.

"Jamie..."

She was there. She was wearing the white buckskin dress he had seen before. Her hair was flowing, rich and waving, paler than usual in the water's reflection. Nor could the water catch the color of her eyes, that violet that was so extraordinary and so compelling, so quick to flash with anger, so deep when touched by her emotions. Nothing could catch that. No words, no mirrored image.

But the water did catch the softness he had glimpsed before, and he knew then why he had been falling in love with her so swiftly and so completely. She had great strength, she would never tire, and she would never cease to fight, for herself, for others, for the glory of all the great causes that caught her heart. She could not bear injustice, and she would never falter to overcome it.

But never could she be less than a woman, beautiful, giving, enwrapping all with the passion of her soul, and of her life. Once he had wanted only her smile to touch him. Once he had been enamored of the silk of her flesh, and the sweeping curves and slim angles of her form. Once...

But now he knew what it meant to love. It was desire, but more than desire. It was needing the smile as much as the passion. It was wanting to lie down by the still waters as much as to weather the tempestuous storm. It was wanting to share a lifetime together.

"Jamie..."

Once again, she whispered his name. He turned slowly, and saw that she did stand just behind him—no image, no dream, so much more than a reflection. In her bare feet with her bare calves, her dress falling just above her knees, she seemed exceptionally innocent.

The color of her eyes was true, deep as the night, dark as the desire that suddenly swept over him. He wanted her in his arms—but he dared not touch her. Not until Nalte made his decision.

He swallowed hard and came to his feet. He stared at her and hoped that his scowl was menacing. Yet he didn't even know if it remained upon his face, for he couldn't deny the moonlight or the strange, mystical sensation that seemed to touch her. She seemed to be of the supernatural, too beautiful to touch, an angel, a spirit, the spirit of life that pervaded the mountain.

"What are you doing out here?" he demanded harshly.

She smiled, a slow curl of her lips that touched her eyes to deep, shimmering radiance. She took a step toward him, shook her head slightly.

And reached for him.

Her arms came around him, giving, soft. She pressed against him. She was naked beneath the buckskin, and her breasts were full and flush against him, the hardened peaks seeming to rake his flesh despite the layers of clothes between them. Sparks tore into him, igniting great fires, ripping through his limbs, thundering down to his groin.

And then she kissed him. Her teeth grazed his lips, and the tip of her tongue encircled his lips, touched the roof of his mouth, swept into his mouth. There was a pounding so fierce he could not deny it.

He touched her. Touched her almost violently, his arms sweeping around her, his lips seizing hard upon hers, his tongue returning each sweet torment she had cast upon him.

He swept her from her feet and carried her to the soft embankment. He pressed her to the earth, his mouth still covering hers. He felt the soaring temptation of her nails raking lightly against his back, drawing new, shimmering sensations of deadly heat within him.

This was madness.

He drew his lips back from hers, and her eyes met his. Violet, beguiling, with a touch of fire, a touch of innocence. Sweetly wicked, she smiled again; she touched his cheek. Her lashes fell demurely, sultry, sensual against the pale marble beauty of her cheek.

She had come to seduce him.

He groaned aloud.

It was madness.

Nalte might well kill them both if he came upon him.

But the fire had spread throughout his limbs. Tension and desire pervaded his heart and his mind and knotted fiercely at his loin, driving him to madness. How could she smile so hauntingly, knowing that she invited him to doom...

He swore softly, and he touched her lower lip in the moon glow, meeting the wild violet beauty of her eyes.

"Lead me to death then, if you would, Miss Stuart. I cannot leave you now."

And he seized her lips once again with his own. The rich, verdant scent of the earth and stream surrounded them, and he was lost.

Chapter Twelve

Die?'' Tess whispered against his lips. Desperate to be near him that night, she had hardly believed the good fortune that had let her come to him, and now, in the magical splendor of the night, he was talking of dying in her arms.

He was so tense above her. His eyes raked over her with a hard edge, and his voice was harsh, but still she felt the depth of his longing. It was luxurious to be so coveted and so desired. And yet she wondered at his words, her eyes widening to his.

"Nalte," Jamie said, leaning high above her. "He would kill me in seconds if he found me with you. Is that your plan? To seduce me to my doom?"

She didn't reply right away. She smiled wickedly and smoothed his hair back from his face. "Would you really die for me?" she whispered softly.

He caught her hand where she touched him and drew her wrists together high over her head, staring down at her. She didn't know if he loved her or despised her in those seconds, but she did know that he wanted her. Tension constricted the length of his body, and muscles convulsed at his throat and within the tautness of his features.

"Is that what you want?" he demanded.

He wasn't smiling. She knew that she had probably tested him beyond endurance, so she whispered softly to him in the night. "No, I do not want you to die for me. Nalte knows that I am here."

"What?"

"He came to me and told me that I could go to you, that he had made his decision. We are to stay here until the ceremonies are complete for his sister, then the Apache will see that we are given an escort out of the mountains."

"Nalte...knows?" Jamie repeated.

She nodded solemnly. "He said that you told him I was already your woman. He also said that you were either a fool or a very brave man to have come for me, and that a brave man deserves the respect of other brave men. And so he told me that you were here, and that I could come to you."

He stared down at her, his grip hard upon her wrists as he tried to understand what she was telling him. Nalte had decided in their favor. There was no need to die here. He could leave with Tess.

He could leave with her.

And he could make love to her, here, tonight, in the shadow of the Apache's mountains, at the stream where life itself and the night seemed mystical.

He cried out harshly and lowered himself over her, his lips parting before they ever touched hers. He ravished her mouth, demanding that it open to his, and he seemed to taste and find all of her, his tongue delving ever deeper, his teeth teasing her lips, his breath mingling with hers, the whole of his kiss so deep and complete and sensual that it was raw and laid her bare. It touched her on a level so intimate that the very decadence aroused her to shattering heights. Then his lips left hers, and she was bereft. The night air touched her lips where they remained damp and moist from his touch.

His fingers were upon the rawhide laces of her buckskin dress. Her breasts spilled free to his touch, and his hand cupped and caressed them, his fingers stroking and arousing her nipples. Then his mouth formed hungrily around one nipple to suckle and tease the hardening bud, to send streams of excitement and desire sweeping through her limbs. She was glad of the darkness. Flushing, she wondered how it was the searing liquid fire of his kiss touched her breast, yet sent the molten longing to swirl to the base of her abdomen, and lower still to hover and deepen at the apex of her thighs.

It did not matter where he touched. He continued to kiss her as he slowly eased the buckskin from her body. He kissed the nape of her neck, and the tip of his tongue hovered at her earlobe, then ran a trail down her spine as he shifted her body to toss aside the dress. He kissed the inside of her upper arm, and she had never imagined that a touch could elicit such wild stirrings within her. Nor did he allow his kisses to stop there.

Soon she was lying prone upon the verdant earth again, so close to the water that it lapped at her ankles. And even the touch of the water added to the wonder and the magic. It caressed her as the breeze did, as his every touch did. She was whispering things to him, things she should never have said, things about the wonder and desire he created. She struggled to touch him in return, to know more and more of him. Her teeth sank gently upon his shoulders, and her tongue laved every tiny little wound. Her fingers stroked and massaged his shoulders and trembled over every ripple and bulge of his muscle beneath her touch. She shed his shirt, nearly ripping the buttons from it. She touched his chest with her tongue, and she moved lower and lower against him.

But then she found herself prone again, and his hands and lips were moving magic upon her. His kiss touched her, searingly hot. The cool water lapped over her feet and ankles, but the whole of her was achingly hot, a fire against the water. His lips touched her bare belly, and the arches of her feet, and her knees and her thighs. And then he kissed her warmly, intimately, at the very heart of her desire, kissed her body as he would kiss her lips, demanding all and giving her ecstasy in turn.

And still the cool stream washed against her. In the end she rose against him, and they knelt together in the shallows in the night, and her breasts moved against his chest as their lips fused once again, and then the fullness of their bodies. She led him down then to the rich earth, and crawled atop him, her hair a blaze of sunset kissed by the moon, her movements smooth and sultry as the touch of golden locks swung over his chest and belly.

In the magic of the night, to the rough and urgent murmurings of his husky voice, she rode the magic of the darkness, and of the man, until the beauty exploded within them and around them, until the sweet satiation and exhaustion seized them, until they were filled with one another. Only then did she fall against him. She didn't care about the future or the past; she only knew that she had come to him because she had wanted him. And because she loved him. Nothing else mattered, for she had learned that time and life and love were precious, and this night she had all three.

They were silent together as the moon cast its gentle glow on them. He stroked her hair softly and at long last he whispered, "It's true—Nalte sent you to me?"

She nodded happily against his chest. "It's true," she whispered.

"Thank God," he breathed.

"He's very upset."

"He is?"

"He doesn't like the idea that von Heusen has been causing so much trouble. He told me that the Apache raid, and that they make war, and that these are separate things. They raid for foodstuffs and other things they need, they do not raid to kill. When they make war, they do so to kill. But they do not kill children, and they do not slaughter animals needlessly. He says there is enough trouble between the whites and the Indians. He doesn't usually have much use for the Comanche himself, and the tribes have warred for generations, but he cannot see the Comanche blamed for a white man's sins.''

''You had quite a long talk with him,'' Jamie commented.

''Jealous?'' she asked sweetly.

He grunted.

She braced her hands upon his chest, staring deeply into his eyes. ''I like him, Jamie.''

Jamie laced his fingers behind his head as he watched her eyes. ''Want to stay with him?'' he asked.

Words, gentle words, self-betraying words, hovered on Tess's lips. I like Nalte, but I love you, she almost said. But she could not dispel the memory of Eliza hanging on to him, trying to force him to love her in return. She would never do that, she swore. It was dangerous to fall in love with Jamie Slater. If nothing else, Tess wanted her dignity left to her.

She forced a smile to her lips and asked lightly, ''Trying to get rid of me?''

''You are a hell of a lot of trouble,'' he told her frankly.

''Yes, but you've already come this far.''

''So I have.''

''And I really am worth it.''

''Are you?'' His eyebrows shot up.

She nodded. Then she moved very low against him again. She let her hair float over his chest as she lowered her lips to his slick bronze flesh. She shimmied her body against him as she inched lower down the length of his body, her thighs locked around him, moving sinuously against him. She felt the quick rasp of his breath, and she let her lips linger upon the spot where she could hear the frantic beating of his heart.

Then she moved lower and lower, daring to touch him instinctively, exploring what was intensely male about him with little subtlety and tremendous fascination. Her body undulated upon his. She discovered her own prowess and power, and drove him nearly to madness. All that he had demanded of her she took in return. He shuddered violently beneath her touch, his fingers digging into the earth when she caressed him as boldly with her lips and tongue as he had done to her. He shouted out hoarsely, and she was soon pinned to the earth as he took her almost savagely, with a driving, explicit hunger that seemed to rend the very heavens.

And when the stars had exploded to dance within the night sky and go still again, he whispered tenderly against her ear, ''My love, you are worth it indeed.''

They stayed by the water a little while longer. Whatever came in the future, Tess knew that she would dream of this place as long as she lived.

She began to shiver, and he covered her in the doeskin dress once again, and then he suggested that they return to the tepee in the village.

They slept that night alone together in the tepee where she had been taken earlier that day. They slept, having shed their clothing once again, wound into one another's arms within the warm shelter of an Apache blanket.

When morning came, they were still together.

During the next few days, they were Nalte's honored guests. They attended the ceremonies for his sister, Little Flower, and Tess was amazed to find that she had discovered a strange peace here, living with the Apache. Nalte spent time with the two of them. Sometimes he ignored Tess and engaged in long conversations with Jamie in his Apache tongue. But sometimes he spoke in English, including Tess.

Once, when they were alone, Jamie having gone to join a hunting party, Nalte took it upon himself to teach her something about the Apache ways.

He explained to her about the Gan, or Mountain Spirit Dancers. In their masks, they impersonated the Mountains Spirits. They evoked the power of the supernaturals to cure illness, drive away evil and bring good fortune. They assembled in a cave, and under the guidance of a special Gan shaman, they donned their sacred costumes. They held great power, and therefore they were obliged to honor severe restrictions. They were not to recognize friends once they were in their attire, nor were they to dance incorrectly or to tamper with the sacred costume or clothing once it had been left within a secret cache. To disobey any of the restrictions could bring calamity down upon the dancer or his family or tribe. To disobey could bring about sickness, madness, even death.

"We are a people of ritual," he told her. "We celebrate the Holiness Rite and the Ceremonial Relay. For the Holiness Rite the shaman must go through arduous procedures, imitating the bear and the snake, and curing the people of the powerful bear and snake sicknesses. The Ceremonial Relay tells us of our food supply—game and the harvest of nature. Runners symbolize the sun and the animals, and the moon and the plants. If the sun runners win, game will be in plenty for us. If the moon runners win, then we will feast on the harvest of the plants."

"You live a good life here," Tess said.

"I live a good life, yes, but I fear the day when white men come to take it from me."

"But surely, here—"

"They will come, the white men will come. War will tear apart the mountains, and blood will stain the rivers. It is inevitable. But when the time comes, I will remember you, and Slater, and I will know that all whites are not the same. Yes, it is good here. Now. And you, I think that you are at peace."

She smiled at him. "I do not believe it, but yes, I am at peace here."

Nalte stared at the fire that burned in the center of the village. "You might have been happy had you stayed," he said quietly. "And maybe not. Our women are the gatherers. The first green vegetables are the yucca, and the women collect them. Then they must collect the mescal stalks and roast them and grind them into paste. We eat the mescal as paste, and as the cakes you have been given with your meals. It is a hard life."

"A ranch is a hard life. And so is a newspaper," Tess said softly. She looked at him quickly. "A newspaper—"

"I know what a newspaper is. I lived in a town for many years when I was a child. I was captured with a war party and taken in by a minister's wife. I learned a lot about your society. A newspaper is a powerful weapon."

"It isn't a weapon at all," Tess protested.

"More powerful than a gun. Be careful with it," Nalte warned her. Then he asked her if she was Jamie's wife.

She flushed as she told him that she was not.

"But you are his woman," Nalte told her.

"It—it isn't the same thing," she said.

The Indian was lowering his head, smiling, and she remembered belatedly that he had chosen to let her go because of Jamie. "When an Apache marries, he goes to his wife's family. If she lives in a distant territory, then the man leaves and joins her family. Within it he may rise to be the leader, then he may become the leader of many families, and ultimately a great chief. But always, when it is possible, he joins his wife's family. He works for his wife's parents and elders, and he is known by them as 'he who carries burdens for me.' He speaks for her, and the man and the woman exchange gifts. A separate dwelling is made for the couple. She is his wife.

"But I tell you, Sun-Colored Woman, that it is the same among the Apache and the whites. When a man loves a woman, when he claims her for his own, when he is willing to give his life and his pride and his honor for her, that is when she is truly his wife, in his eyes and in the eyes of the great spirits, be they our gods or the one great God of the whites." He touched her cheek almost tenderly, then left her.

She thought about his words for a long time to come, and she wondered if Jamie did love her. Did he love her enough to stay with her, or would he tire of her, as he had tired of Eliza?

She had made love with him always of her own volition. She had wanted him as she had never known want before. But sometimes she wished that she had never given in to the temptation, for she felt that she had tasted forbidden fruit. She had found it very sweet, but she would perish when she could taste it no longer.

Nights were theirs. She never spoke, but came to him with her skin warmed by the fire, her body bathed by the stream, her hair soft and fragrant from the sun. She lay down beside him, and she loved him, and she tried not to think of the future.

On the fourth night of Little Flower's puberty rite, when the maiden had become a woman, Jamie was silent, holding her gently, staying motionless. Tess knew that he didn't sleep, and she shifted against him, asking him what was wrong.

"We're free to go home tomorrow," she whispered to him.

"Yes, or the next day," he said absently. "Nalte has been involved with his sister and us. He may be busy with tribal business tomorrow."

"What difference will a day make?"

He shook his head, still staring toward the top of the te-pee and the poles that seemed to reach toward the stars. "A day will not make a difference. Nothing will a make a difference. That's the point. When we go home, Tess, von Heusen is still going to be there. And we still haven't any proof of what he is doing."

"But—but Jeremiah and David kidnapped me—and they left you for dead!" Tess protested.

"Jeremiah and David are dead. They can't be brought to trial, and they can't be forced to testify against von Heusen. We're right back where we started. And I know you. You'll head right back to that newspaper office of yours."

"Jamie, I have to!"

"You don't have to!" he told her savagely.

"Jamie—"

"We're going back, Tess, and we're going to fight von Heusen. But we have to do it by my rules."

"I don't—"

"That's right—you don't. You don't make a move without someone by your side, do you understand me? Things are going to get worse. Von Heusen may be thinking right now that you and I are gone. He may even have had a few moments of divine pleasure, thinking that he'd won at last. But Tess, by now he must have discovered that he can't get his hands on that property, even if we're both believed to be dead and gone. He's going to be furious when he finds it's willed to my family—and he's going to be ready for a full-scale war. We've got to pray that we're going to be ready for it."

"Can we be?" Tess whispered.

"Yes, we can," he said. But then he swung around on her, staring at her fiercely, clutching her chin with a grip so tight that it was painful. "But Tess, so help me God, you'll do it my way."

"Jamie—"

"You'll do it my way!"

"Fine! All right!" she snapped.

He dropped her jaw. Tears were stinging her eyes, and she quickly rolled away from him, furious that no matter how close it seemed they became, he still played the dictator.

And left her frightened that she was falling more and more deeply in love with a man who would wage war for her, who would risk his life for her . . .

And yet ride away in the end, when it mattered the most.

He did not reach for her, and she did not come back to touch him that night. Her back was cold, and she drew the blanket more fully around her.

She shivered in the night . . .

But the distance remained between them.

They spent one more day with the Apache, watching the sacred ritual when a young boy departed with his first hunting party. The boy's first four raids would be accompanied by ritual. This day he was instructed by the war shaman and accepted by the adult members of the party. He was given a drinking tube and a scratcher with lightning designs, and he was bestowed with a war cap.

Jamie spoke to her while they stood watching. He pointed to the war cap and told her, "It will not yet contain the spiritual power that belongs to the men. He must complete his passage before the spirits will enter into his cap." The men and women of the village were gathering around the boy to throw pollen upon him as he departed with the warriors. "It is a blessing," Jamie told her.

"And we are standing here, watching this, and these men and that boy will go off and raid some white settlement and perhaps kill our own kind," Tess murmured.

Jamie glared at her. "I'll thank you to keep your opinions to yourself. We're lucky to be leaving here alive. And,

Miss Stuart, for your information, this party is moving against the Comancheros. I don't believe you can feel too much sympathy for that particular group."

She could not, but she didn't have a chance to tell him so. He turned her around and propelled her toward the tepee they were sharing. "Go in, be quiet. I'm going to ask Nalte if we might leave tomorrow."

She didn't hear, that afternoon, whether Nalte gave his permission. She waited endlessly for Jamie to return, but he did not. When it was dark one of the Apache women came to help her rekindle the fire and to give her a plate of beef and yams and mescal cakes. She ate halfheartedly and waited, but Jamie still didn't return. Finally her impatience brought her to the opening in the tent, and she looked out to see Jamie and Nalte and the victorious raiding party sitting around the central fire, laughing, talking, enjoying some newly arrived bottles of whiskey, and apparently enjoying one another as if they were long lost friends. In a fury she went to the fire and called Jamie's name sharply.

Every man there paused and stared at her, none of them more surprised or annoyed than Jamie. Nalte shot him a quick glance and said something in Apache. Jamie was quickly on his feet. He replied casually to the chief, but two rugged strides brought him to Tess. Before she could move or react he had butted her belly with his shoulder and lifted her precariously. Her head dangled dangerously down his back. She screamed out her protest, but Jamie ignored her and the Apache laughed, enjoying the show.

Within seconds they were back in the tepee. She landed hard on one of the blankets, desperately inhaling as he stared at her furiously. She might have thought at first that he was drunk, but the sharp fire in his eyes denied such a possibility. She accused him anyway before he could yell at her.

"You're totally inebriated!"

"Inebriated—you mean drunk, don't you? I wish I were. Drunk enough to give you what you need! And what you need is a good switch taken to your hide."

"Oh!" She shimmied up to her knees. "Don't you dare speak to me like that, Jamie Slater—"

"I don't think I'm just going to speak!" he warned her, his lashes falling over his eyes so that they were narrow and dangerous. "I think I'm going to act—"

She was on her feet instantly, running for the flap in the tent with a speed and agility as fleet as a doe's. But at the flap she paused, realizing that she would be running into a group of raucous Apaches.

She spun around, certain Jamie was almost upon her. But he was standing back, watching her with supreme arrogance and amusement. He had known she wouldn't run out of the tent.

She decided to take her chances with the Apache.

She didn't make it. Jamie had been still, but he came to motion in a flash. Just as she reached for the rawhide flap, his arms swept around her calves, and she came crashing down to the hard ground. She coughed and gagged and struggled against his weight to turn around and face him. He straddled her. Her simple doeskin dress was wound high around her hips, and she was naked beneath it. Jamie didn't seem to notice. He sat calmly upon her, crossing his arms over his chest, aware that she wouldn't be going anywhere at all.

He stared down at her. "Undisciplined—brat!"

"Brat! I'm twenty-four years old—"

"An old maid! Maybe that's half the problem."

She gasped, stunned by the remark, and started to struggle furiously beneath him. Her fingers wound into fists but he was ready, leaning forward to pin her wrists to the sides of her head. "I told you—it's done my way. You may be Miss Stuart, and you may be the publisher of the *Wiltshire*

Sun, and you may own one of the finest ranches this side of the Mississippi, but you're with me now, and I warned you, it's going to be done my way! Especially among the Apache! You don't make a fool of a man in front of them!''

"But I just wanted to know what was going on!"

"I really should take a switch to you—but at some later date." The fury suddenly faded from his voice. He released her wrists, his hands massaging both tenderly and tempestuously through the splay of her hair. "Tess, Tess, what are we doing? We're going back to Wiltshire, and all hell will break loose when we get there. Let's not fight each other now."

She stared at his striking features, at the handsome and rugged angles and planes of his face, at the passion in his silver eyes. She trembled suddenly and wound her arms around him. "Hold me!" she whispered.

And he did.

They shed their clothing, and she thought that he made love to her more tenderly, more carefully, that night than he ever had before.

When the sun rose their naked bodies were entwined together in the soft shadows. She didn't want to leave, she thought. She could live among the Apache with Jamie forever.

But of course she couldn't. This was not her world, and she had vowed that she would fight von Heusen. Neither she nor Jamie could walk away now.

Jamie leaned over and kissed her lips, and she looked into his eyes.

"It's time," he told her.

He rose and dressed quickly, and she followed his example.

They did not leave with the dawn, for Nalte wanted another conference with Jamie. His sister, Little Flower, came to Tess to say goodbye. Tess had learned very little of the language, but she had been grateful for Little Flower's shy kindness. It seemed that Nalte was bestowing gifts on Tess—she was given a new outfit in which to ride, in pale buckskin, with fine tin cone pendants and beautiful beadwork. There was a long overdress that fell nearly to her knees, and beneath it, soft trousers so that she might ride easily. She was given boots at last, fine boots with rawhide bottoms and soft leggings to cover her calves. She thanked Little Flower as best as she could for the gifts, then kissed the young woman on the cheek.

Nalte came to her then. Little Flower fled, and Nalte watched Tess for several moments before speaking. "You will take the dress, too. Slater has told me that it will always be special to him."

She flushed. "Thank you. Thank you for the gifts. I've nothing to give you in return."

He shrugged. "I have gotten what I wanted from Slater. And I give you the gifts in his behalf. In our courting ritual, we exchange gifts, as I have told you."

She smiled and lowered her head, wondering what Jamie had given him. "Most of all, Nalte, I thank you for my freedom."

He grunted and looked at her still. "I understand that you are a warrior yourself."

"A warrior?" she said, startled.

"You take on men's battles."

"I didn't really intend to. I just—I had to fight back." She paused. "This man had my uncle murdered. Do you understand?"

"Yes, I understand. I will pray that the spirits will be with you."

He left her then.

Jamie returned soon after. "They are ready to ride," he told her. "Let's go."

She nodded and hurried after him. There was a small roan mare set aside for her use, and she silently accepted Jamie's help to mount the saddleless creature.

She was startled to see Jamie mounting a large paint gelding. She stared at him and said softly, "Jamie, your own horse—"

"He's Nalte's now," Jamie said curtly.

"Your horse! But you loved that horse. Why on earth would you want to—"

She broke off. He hadn't wanted to give Nalte the horse. The horse had been the negotiation.

"I'm sorry, Jamie."

"It doesn't matter," he said, and, turning his back, he rode ahead to talk to the half-naked warrior in a breech-clout at the head of the party of a dozen or so, their escort through Comanchero territory. The Indian turned and she gasped, startled to see that it was Nalte.

She couldn't ponder the chief's participation in their ride then, for cries suddenly filled the air and they were leaving the village behind at a quick pace. Jouncing on her pony, Tess turned back.

Little Flower was waving to her. Tess smiled warmly and waved in turn.

They she turned again and hugged her knees to her pony. She had thought that she knew how to ride hard, but she had never ridden with the Apache before.

She realized she was learning about a hard ride all over again, from the very beginning.

By the time they stopped for the night, she could barely dismount, and when she did she nearly fell.

Jamie was there to catch her. She widened her eyes and stared at him and she wanted to straighten and show him that she could be strong. But her knees were buckling and she merely managed to whisper, "Oh, Jamie..."

He caught her before she fell. The Apache warriors were preparing a fire, and he carried her to it. One warrior stretched out a blanket for her, and a roll was stuffed beneath her head.

She never ate a meal that night for she fell asleep instantly.

Somewhere in the middle of the night she felt a new warmth. She opened her eyes and realized that Jamie had stretched next to her, and she was curled up in the shelter of his arms.

She stared up at the stars and was suddenly very afraid. She had wanted to go home, and they were going home. But Jamie was right, it would be open war now. She didn't want to die. She was just learning how to live.

She closed her eyes and curled her fingers around the strong male hand that curved beneath her breast. "Please God, please God, please God," she whispered. The rest of her prayer formed no words, but she knew it in her heart. She wanted to survive...and more.

She wanted to survive with Jamie. The life that was now so precious to her would be meaningless without him.

She closed her eyes again, and to her amazement, she slept once more.

The Apache stayed with them all the next day and the next night. Jamie seemed concerned for them, warning Nalte that they were moving into Comanche territory. But Nalte knew Running River, and he didn't seem concerned.

Tess tried to talk to Nalte, reminding him that many whites had believed von Heusen when he said that it had been Indians who caused all the trouble. Few of the new settlers knew there was a difference between Comanche and Apache.

Nalte, however, was resolute. He and the Apache rode with them to the outskirts of the town of Wiltshire. Then he lifted his spear high in the air and a shrill, blood-chilling cry escaped him. The Apache formed behind him.

"Goodbye, Slater, Sun-Colored Woman."

"Thank you. No matter what comes, Nalte, I will always be your friend," Jamie told him.

"I believe you." The chief moved forward, and he and Jamie clasped hands. Then Nalte swung his newly acquired mount around and his men raced off behind him.

Jamie watched them disappear in a cloud of Texas dust, then he looked at Tess. "This is it. We're almost home."

"Perhaps we should go into town—"

"No. We'll head to the ranch."

"But I need to put this in the paper—"

He swore, roughly, violently. "Tomorrow, Tess! We're going home. I tried to make a few arrangements for help. You can't go into town alone, and I have to get back to the ranch! Got it?"

"Got it!" she shouted back.

They weren't far. She swung her Apache mare around and nudged her to a fleeting gallop. She raced for a good ten minutes before she pulled up suddenly, a feeling of utter joy encompassing her heart as the ranch came into view. It was still standing. No one had burned it to the ground. Smoke was spewing from the chimney; Dolly or Jane must be cooking something inside. Life had gone on while she had been with the Apache. And the people who loved her had held on.

Jamie was behind her. She turned and shouted to him. "It's still standing!"

"Yes," he began.

She didn't let him say more. She nudged the mare hard again with her heels and thundered toward the ranch. She passed the paddocks and the beautiful mares with their foals and she felt joy cascade throughout her. Von Heusen hadn't beaten them—not yet.

She reined in the mare as she came to the house. Dust flew as the little horse pawed the ground. Tess leaped down and went racing for the front door. "Dolly, Jane, Hank!"

She stood in the entryway, looking at the large desk, at the stairway leading to the second floor, at the furniture in the parlor, at the dining table. She was home.

"They're here! Someone is here!" a voice shouted.

It was an unfamiliar voice. Tess stared in astonishment as a tall, slim blond woman came hurrying down the stairway. She was followed by a handsome little boy of about five, then a second blond woman with a serene and beautiful face.

"Miss Tess!"

Tess swung around as Jane hurried from the kitchen, throwing her arms around her. "I knew you'd come back, I just knew that you would!"

"Well." The first woman had reached the entryway. "I knew that Jamie wouldn't come back without you, of course," she said. "Where is he?"

Tess stared with astonishment at the two women and the little boy. Then the door burst open behind her. Jamie had arrived, but he wasn't alone. With him were two men, both as tall as he, with the handsome but rugged features of ranchers, of men who eked their existence from the land and the elements. They were talking, the three of them were talking, the darkest of them saying something about von Heusen.

Then Dolly emerged from the kitchen, wiping her hands on her apron. "Those twins!" she proclaimed. "The little darlings are going to eat us out of cookies and cakes, they are! Oh! Oh, Tess! Jamie, Lieutenant Slater, why you're home! You're home!" There were tears in her eyes, tears streaming down her cheeks. "I knew Tess wouldn't come home without her lieutenant. I knew you wouldn't!"

Dolly flung her arms around Jamie, and then Dolly and Jane were fighting to hug Tess, and she was trying to hug them back. But she still couldn't help staring at the strangers who were suddenly filling her house.

Twins? What twins?

The two blond women were kissing and hugging Jamie. Jamie was laughing in return and thanking both for coming. Tess wasn't sure if she would lose her temper or her mind first.

"Excuse me!" she said, but there was too much noise. "Excuse me!" she shouted. The room went still. She looked around, and then said frankly, "Excuse me, but—who are you?"

"Jamie!" the taller woman wailed. "You didn't tell her?"

Tess smiled sweetly. "No. No, he didn't tell me."

Jamie stepped forward. "These are my brothers, Cole and Malachi. And their wives, Kristin and Shannon. And that's my nephew, Gabe. And I take it that Shannon and Malachi's twins are in the kitchen—"

"The little darlings!" Dolly said rapturously.

"We've come because Jamie sent us a wire about von Heusen," Cole Slater told her.

Tess gasped. She stared at them all. So this was having a family. They were so close. They knew one another so well. They were happy and content, she could see it on their faces; they were serene with their world.

She shook her head. "Thank you, but—" She swung around on Jamie. "Jamie, you can't—they could get killed here!"

"Well, ma'am, I'm not planning on getting killed," Malachi told her, tipping back his hat. "I'm not planning on it at all. You see, we came to kill them if need be."

"You don't know von Heusen."

"Oh," Kristin said cheerfully, "we have known men a great deal like him." She smiled, stepping forward. "We're family, Tess. And that's what it's all about.'' She flashed Jamie a quick grin. "My brother-in-law was always there when I needed him," she said.

"Oh!" Shannon said suddenly. "Smell that! Oh, no, Jamie and Miss Stuart have come home at last, and it seems we've let dinner burn!"

She swung around, then looked back. "Well, isn't anyone hungry?"

And Tess realized she was starved.

She glanced at Jamie. She was still amazed, still in shock. But Kristin Slater set a hand upon her arm. "Come on! I promise you, things will start to look more reasonable after a good dinner and a full night's sleep!"

Jamie shrugged.

Tess felt herself gently pulled along.

Dinner...

The perfect end to the... perfect day?

Chapter Thirteen

They had just reached the table when Jon Red Feather came in with Hank. Tess let out a startled, joyful cry and raced to Jon, giving him a fierce hug. "You did come back! You made it out, and you came back!"

"Of course," he told her. "Someone had to be here to welcome the Slaters. I mean, this is practically a tribe. Have you realized that yet?"

"A tribe!" Kristin said indignantly. "Sit down, Jon, and watch your tongue, if you will. Jamie, by the way, you should marry this girl before you find out that you've got competition on your hands."

Jon laughed, and Tess flushed. She wasn't sure about Jamie's reaction. Kristin Slater started calmly doling out food into the numerous plates on the table.

It was a good thing it was a big house.

Uncle Joe, you would have loved to have seen this! she thought.

"If everyone would come sit down," Malachi said, pouring wine into the glasses around the table, "I think that Jon has something to tell Tess and Jamie."

"Yes, I do, as a matter of fact." Jon walked to the table and picked up a glass of wine. He smiled at Tess and Jamie. "Cheers," he said, raising his glass to his lips.

"Will you all please sit!" Cole said emphatically.

Tess sat at her own dining table—as she had been so politely ordered. Jamie sat beside her, and they stared at Jon, who looked at them.

"I have discovered why von Heusen is so particularly eager to seize hold of your land, Miss Stuart."

Tess gasped, and she and Jamie stood.

"Why?" Tess demanded.

Jon smiled, swirling his wine. "The railroad."

"Oh, my God!" Jamie said, sinking into his chair.

Tess stared at him. He obviously understood completely what was going on, but she didn't have the least idea.

"What?"

"Miss Stuart," Cole Slater told her, drawing out a chair and sitting back in it, "the railroad is coming through here. That means that this property is going to go sky-high in value. If you wanted to sell some land straight, it would be worth a small fortune."

"But there's more," Jon Red Feather told her softly. "If you do sell just the necessary land, the rest of your property will still go sky-rocketing in value—you'll be able to send your produce right out from your own doorstep. Tess, you're sitting on the best land this side of the Mississippi. And that's why von Heusen has been so desperate to get rid of you. With this property in his hands, he could really control a good percentage of western Texas."

Tess smiled slowly, looking at Jamie. "But—but he can't touch any of it now. He must know that! Half of it is in your name, and even if we hadn't returned—"

"Ownership would have come to Cole and me and our families," Malachi supplied for her.

"Well, he must know that."

"He does know that," Jon said. Gabe was sitting beside him, and he tousled the lad's brown hair to be rewarded with a fascinated smile. Jon smiled in turn, then gave Tess his attention again. "I let it be known that Jamie had found you and that he'd be bringing you home. I also went to see Edward Clancy and had him print up the arrival of Cole and Malachi—and I stressed the ability of the Slater brothers with their small arms."

"A couple of von Heusen's men rode out here the other day. But we uninvited them quickly," Kristin said, heaping mashed potatoes on a plate to pass to Jon.

"Cole or Malachi scared them away?" Tess asked.

"Oh, no, Shannon did," Kristin said. "She's an ace."

"I'm a decent shot," Shannon said demurely.

"She can hit a fly's eye at a hundred yards," Malachi said drily.

They all laughed, but Cole sobered quickly and spoke to Jamie in low, even tones. "The point is, this von Heusen knows that scare tactics aren't going to work with Miss Stuart anymore. No one can quite fathom what he'll pull next."

"Well, he'll have more to worry about after tomorrow," Tess said firmly. "I'm going to go to the paper and I'm going to give Clancy another front-page story. It's going to be all about David and Jeremiah and Mr. von Heusen's orders to see that I never returned."

"There might be a few problems with that," Jon advised her.

"Why?" Tess asked.

"Because Clancy and your printer gave in at last. Someone shot a few windows yesterday, and by last night, Clancy had thrown in the towel. He wanted you to know that he was sorry."

Tess inhaled and exhaled. "I can do it myself," she said.

"You won't have to do it yourself," Kristin corrected her, sitting at last with her own plate. "Dolly and Jane can keep the children here, and Shannon and I will come in and help you with the press. If you give us directions, we can surely follow them. The three of us will go into town first thing in the morning—''

"No!" Jamie said emphatically.

"I have to," Tess began, turning, ready to give battle. "Jamie, I've told you—"

"The three of you aren't going anywhere alone," he interrupted harshly. "It isn't safe. Dammit to hell, Tess! Don't you understand yet?"

"I understand that the newspaper has always been my major weapon."

"But right now it isn't enough. Okay, we'll go. You'll do your damned article, but we'll go together. Tess, what do I have to say to get through to you? When von Heusen attacks again, it's going to be all-out war."

She wanted to retort. She was furious. He was right, of course, but she still wanted to yell at him.

Fighting desperately to hold her tongue, she looked at Jon. "How did you find all this out?"

He shrugged. "I was still in buckskins when I came back, and I didn't change before I made a visit into town. Von Heusen had one of his guns follow me. I knew it, so I doubled back and got hold of him. As it happened, Cole and Malachi had been riding in to meet me."

"And," Malachi said, grinning, "Jon just happened to be dressed for the occasion."

Tess was still confused. Kristin sighed and explained. "Cole and Malachi convinced von Heusen's hired goon that Jon was scarcely more than a raw savage and that he actually delighted in human flesh. Between the three of them they barely had to touch the fellow before he was spilling everything he had ever known in his life."

Tess smiled and glanced at Jamie.

He was not smiling. She looked away quickly, pushing a piece of roast around on her plate. They were a lot alike, the Slater brothers. Cole was the darkest, with golden eyes—his little boy had those eyes, even though he had his mother's soft blond hair. Malachi was a golden blond with blue eyes, and Jamie was sandy-haired with his smoke gray and silver eyes. But the planes of their faces were similar, strong and hard and weathered. She realized suddenly that she would trust any of the brothers with anything she had.

And she didn't really mean to keep fighting Jamie. It just kept coming out that way.

He stood up suddenly, his chair scraping back. "That was a fine meal, Kristin, Shannon—Dolly?"

"We all contributed," Kristin told him.

"Well, thank you, but I think I need a little air. You got a good cheroot on you anywhere, Cole?"

"Sure," said his brother, rising as well. He stopped by his wife's chair and kissed her tenderly at the base of the neck before following Jamie out.

"Seems like we're splitting up here," Malachi said.

"Well, don't stay on my account!" Shannon told him.

He laughed, shrugged at Jon, and the two of them left. Hank followed them and the women were left—Jane, who had barely said a word, Dolly, who was unbelievably quiet, and Shannon and Kristin and Tess.

"All this to make a meal, and then it's just wolfed down, and then everyone runs—"

"Ma," Gabe suddenly interrupted from the end of the table. "I cleaned my plate. Can I go join Pa?"

Kristin threw up her hands, and Tess felt some of the tension leave her as she laughed.

"Go!" Kristin told her son.

He smiled, excused himself politely to Tess and ran out of the house.

"We might as well pick up," Shannon said.

"Might as well."

Things went quickly with five of them to do the clearing, the scraping, the washing and the drying. Shannon asked

Tess what it had been like with the Apache, and by the time she finished with her story about Jon and Jamie appearing at just the right time, they had finished the dishes. Jane and Dolly kissed Tess again and went to bed. Shannon and Kristin and Tess made tea and then sat around the kitchen table, staring at one another.

"And then this Nalte let you go—just because Jamie asked for you? He let you go to Jamie?" Kristin said.

Tess felt herself flush, wondering how to avoid saying the very thing the Indian chief had so clearly understood. "He, uh, he..."

"Oh, for God's sake, Kristin, they've been sleeping together and this Nalte man knew it!" Shannon exclaimed.

"Shannon!" Kristin protested.

"Well, all right, I'm terribly sorry, but Kristin and I both married Slater men. I know. They're so easy to want to shoot, but at the same time..." Her voice trailed away and she was really beautiful as she grinned. "Well, they are easy to sleep with. Seductive."

Tess knew she had to be a thousand shades of crimson.

Kristin sighed. "He's very much in love with you. I'm sure we'll see a wedding any day."

"I'm not terribly sure about that."

"He called us here. To protect your interests. He must love you."

"I've turned over half the property to him. It's his own property he's protecting."

"Um. Did he bargain for anything else?" Kristin asked her.

She didn't know why she was being so honest except that somehow she felt she had known the two women all her life.

Maybe it was because they had all become involved with Slater men.

"Maybe they just don't marry easily," Shannon suggested.

"But you're both married," Tess began.

"Cole had to marry me," Kristin said.

"Oh, the baby?"

"No!" Kristin laughed. "There was a horrible, horrible man after me. The war was going on and the only way he could count on some protection from some old acquaintances was to be able to say that I was his wife. He fell in love with me slowly; it took him a long time." She smiled sweetly at Shannon. "And Malachi had to marry Shannon."

"Well, he didn't have to," Shannon protested.

"The twins?" Tess asked.

"No, a shotgun," Shannon explained ruefully. They both laughed, and Shannon took a deep breath and tried to explain that Kristin was her sister, and that Kristin had been in trouble. She and Malachi had gone after her, and a kindly old couple had decided the two of them had to be married.

"But they'd been in love for years. They wouldn't admit it, of course, because they were too busy gouging one another's eyes out."

"Oh, it never was that bad!" Shannon protested.

"No, it was worse!" Kristin said. She stood up. "I think that we need a drop of brandy to go with this, too. Girls?"

Shannon and Tess both agreed. Then Tess yawned and complained that her buckskins were filthy and that she felt as if half of Texas was covering her. The sisters quickly had the hip tub out and filled, and Shannon was racing upstairs for French bath oil, and before she knew it Kristin was presenting her with a lilac nightgown that matched her eyes.

"I can't take these things!" Tess protested.

"But you can. It's all in the family," Shannon told her.

Tess shook her head. "I heard Jamie once. He said that no one would ever make him get married."

Kristin shrugged. "They can't force him—but he just might choose to do so on his own."

"Do you want him?" Shannon asked her.

Tess felt her heart beat hard and she closed her eyes. Yes! Yes, she wanted Jamie desperately. She had wanted him since his eyes had first fallen upon her, since he had killed the rattler, since he had told her in a soft voice that she was beautiful.

Since that day by the stream before the nightmare had begun and he had touched her and said, "I think I'm falling in love with you . . ."

But that had been before they had nearly been destroyed, before he had lost his beloved cavalry mount to retrieve her. She was trouble. He had told her that again and again. He had walked out at dinner because he had been so furious with her that he hadn't been able to stay at the table.

"Do you?" Shannon persisted.

"Yes," Tess admitted softly. "I want him. For keeps."

"Then forget the arguments. Even forget the fact that you'll probably never get along. I have," Shannon said cheerily. "Forget von Heusen, forget everything, and cherish what time you have together in peace."

"And get in the tub with the rose oil," Kristin suggested drily. "There's just nothing like a very sweet smell."

"And a see-through lilac gown to match your eyes! Aren't they beautiful eyes, Kristin?"

"And she's not jealous often," Kristin said, laughing.

Feeling loved and protected, Tess stepped into the water and felt the steam surround her. It was good to be home.

"I'm more worried now that I know just what this man is after," Jamie said.

He was sitting on the rocker on the porch. Jon was perched on the railing with Cole, and Malachi was seated across from him on the swing. It creaked slowly in the night air.

Jamie exhaled. He looked at his brothers. "Thanks for coming. I'm just wishing right now that I hadn't had you bring Kristin and Shannon."

"Jamie, you've known the McCahy girls a long time," Cole said drily. "And you should know at this point that they wouldn't have it any other way."

"I just don't know what this man might plan. I do know that he keeps twenty to thirty hired guns on his property at all times."

"We've met up with bad odds before," Malachi reminded him.

"God damn it, don't you understand what I'm trying to say? I don't want you, your wives or your children killed on my account."

Gabe came out then. He glanced at his father and it was obvious he had heard some of what had been said. He went straight up to his Uncle Jamie and took his trail-roughened face into his hands.

"There's right and wrong, Uncle Jamie, and you know that. And my pa and my ma, they say you have to fight what's wrong, because if you just give in, it'll bury you in the end. I don't mind fighting. Not if it's the right thing to do."

Jamie lifted his nephew and hugged him tightly.

Cole smiled. "I rest my case."

"Malachi, those twins of yours aren't quite three years old. You think they feel the same way?"

"Jamie, we're here, and that's it," Malachi said flatly. "Now, what about Tess?"

"What about her?" Jamie scowled. "She's the hardest creature to tangle with I have ever encountered, Yanks and Indians and rattlers included."

"Think you're going to marry her?" Malachi asked pleasantly.

"If he doesn't do so soon," Jon Red Feather supplied, "I will."

"Damn you, Jon—"

"I'll have to, to keep the poor woman honest."

Jamie groaned. "You know, the lot of you, you may be a man's kin and his best friend, but I'm telling you—"

"She's beautiful, very bright and has the will of a wild-cat. Besides that, she's worth a damned fortune. He's already absconded with half her property," Malachi said.

"Wait a damned minute!" Jamie protested.

"The least you could do is marry her," Cole said.

Jamie threw up his hands. "Thank you, one and all, for coming. And now I'll thank you, one and all, to mind your own damned business. Good night."

He set Gabe on the rocker and headed into the house. He was halfway up the stairs before he realized he didn't know if he had a room in the house. His brothers and Kristin and Shannon and even the kids seemed very happily moved in.

But where the hell he was supposed to be, he didn't know.

He headed for Tess's room, wondering what her reaction was going to be. If she threatened to scream and bring the house down he thought he'd throttle her.

He tapped on her door, then pushed it open. "Tess?"

"Jamie?" She said his name softly, sweetly. Her voice touched the air like the fragrance of roses that seemed to be all around the room, light as stardust. Her whisper was sultry, as if he had awakened her.

He strode across the room then paused, seeing how the moon entered through the window and glowed upon her. Her hair was shining with greater splendor than any sunset, and it was spread out behind her as if each strand were a glorious ray of the sun.

She was dressed in violet, a shade that matched her eyes in the darkness of the night. A shade that was barely concealing, a shade that managed to enhance every beautiful line and curve of her body.

"Tess, where the hell—" He paused, clearing his throat, wondering why the hell he was getting so damned angry. "Tess, where am I supposed to—oh, the hell with it!" he growled.

He didn't see her smile as he dropped forcefully upon her, sweeping her into his arms. He didn't really see anything except the color of her hair, entwining and tangling around him. He breathed in the clean, sweet scent of her, and he could barely contain his longings. The Apache had kept them apart for the last two long nights. He hadn't realized how badly he could need her after such a short time, how much he could crave her. She was like a sweet a man thought he tasted once, and yet wanted more and more once he knew the exotic taste...

He kissed her fiercely, and he kissed her long, and he felt the frantic rise of her breasts against his hand as she lost her breath. Only when she trembled and gasped did he raise his head and stare at her. "I'm staying here. We're doing it my way, remember?"

She returned his stare. Her arms wound around him, and she pressed her lips to his, then she shoved him slightly away from her and started to open his shirt buttons. Slowly, achingly slowly, she opened them one by one, pressing her lips against his flesh. And when his shirt was cast aside she tenderly nipped and kissed his shoulders while she tugged at his belt buckle. She inched his pants slowly down his hips. Boldly, possessively she touched him, stroked him and trembled, her fingers shaking as he came hard as steel to her ministrations. Then he could stand no more of the sweet torture and she was on her back, with his lips savoring her body beneath the gauze of the lilac gown. He tasted her breasts and the valley between them and her navel and her upper thighs and teased her more intimately still until she was thrashing and calling his name to the moon-dusted night, begging that he come to her.

With the deepest pleasure, he obliged, and the feeling of being where he belonged within her was almost as great as the pure sexual excitement of being so tightly, so erotically sheathed. He shuddered with the force of his desire, and stroked deeper and deeper until they exploded as one. Then he took her tightly into his arms, glad of her lips pressed to his chest, her head burrowed against him.

You're mine, he longed to tell her. You were mine when I first found you, and mine when I came to Nalte to ask for you. You are mine this night . . .

And if we can only survive, you will be mine forever.

His thoughts gave pause, and he added silently: even if you are the most ornery and troublesome female in the western world.

In the morning his troublesome female was up and almost dressed by the time he had pulled on his trousers.

"Afraid of my family?" he asked her.

Tess looked his way curiously and shook her head. No man could be a finer lover, tender and tempestuous, but in the morning his temper always seemed to leave something to be desired. "I don't care what they know, if you're talking about our sleeping arrangements."

"I see. You think my older brother will insist that we marry."

"No one will ever force you to marry, Jamie. You said so yourself."

"So you're not planning on marriage."

"I try not to plan on anything."

She was at her dresser, brushing her hair. He slipped behind her, his chest still naked, and pulled her against him. He whispered against her ear. "What if you're already with child?"

She turned and faced him, looking him up and down. "You're nicely built, intelligent, I think, and your brothers don't seem to have too many flaws. If I have a child, it should be a darling one." She swung around to continue to brush her hair.

He laughed as he donned his shirt and socks and boots. "Tess, you are a hellion," he told her.

She smiled sweetly. "I just do the best I can with what I've got, Lieutenant. I'm going down for breakfast. I'm sure Dolly and Jane got things started very early with all those little children to feed. And I do want to be at the paper by eight. I've got to teach Kristin and Shannon how to work the press."

"I'm right with you," Jamie told her. But when she would have exited the room, he pulled her back. "We do things my way, remember."

"I remember," she said coolly.

"Everything."

"Meaning?"

"I'll tell you later," was all he said.

He stepped past her and hurried down the stairs. She followed him, convinced that he had only stopped her to prove to her that he could be down first.

Dolly and Jane were busy with the children, and they seemed like a couple of doting old aunts. Dolly beamed at Jamie. "I just can't wait until it's one of your little bundles I'm holding, Lieutenant!" she said. Of course she wasn't really holding Shannon's daughter—the child was squirming away, ready to chase a little string ball that was rolling across the floor.

"Yeah, soon enough, Dolly," Jamie said sweetly. To Tess's surprise he winked at her.

"Coffee!"

A cup was shoved into her hand by Malachi. "Jamie," he said, "I've told Hank to take Dolly and Jane and the children down to the storm cellar once we've gone. They're invisible there."

"Fine," Jamie said. "Dolly?"

"I understand, Lieutenant, I understand perfectly."

"I'll watch them," Hank promised. "Me and the hands, we'll stay in and down in the cellar with the children."

"Is everybody ready?" Jamie asked. He swallowed his coffee and set the cup on the table, then everyone was hurrying out. The children were taken to the cellar, and Dolly waved a cheerful hand to Tess. "You take care, missy, you hear?"

"Yes, Dolly, I promise! Thank you!"

Dolly disappeared into the storm cellar, and Hank followed, closing the door over them. Cole and Kristin stamped the dirt around so the opening was invisible.

By then Jon was coming around with the wagon, and Kristin and Shannon and Tess climbed up with him. The Slater brothers mounted their horses. Tess was aware that each was wearing a gun belt with two Colts. Each also had another gun attached to a saddle. They were well-armed, but managed to remain nonchalant.

Tess froze, praying that she wouldn't bring about one of these men's deaths. It was her fight. Her own. She had no right to get these men killed.

Maybe nothing would happen today. Maybe von Heusen would lie low. Maybe he would take his time to attack her again. She had written the truth once. After today, maybe more people would believe her. He couldn't kill everyone.

"Why don't you explain the press while we ride?" Jon suggested to her.

Tess gave him a grateful smile. If she talked, she would relax. "It's a small press, really, compared with many of the innovations they're coming up with today. But it's a small town, and we're a small paper. We set the type in a box called a chase. We tap our letters and words in with wooden mallets, ink the set type, then roll the papers through. It's very simple." She was just warming to the subject when Jon's voice interrupted her softly.

"The town is quiet today."

It was quiet. The streets were deserted. Not that it was usually busy at this time of the morning, but there was no one around. No one at all.

"Well," Tess murmured. "There's, uh, there's the paper over there. See, *Wiltshire Sun*. The place with all the windows broken out," she added drily.

"Well, you can set to typing your story while Kristin and I sweep up," Shannon said.

Tess nodded. There was a giant lump in her throat, though. Why was the town so damned deserted?

Jon stopped directly in front of the paper. Jamie had already dismounted, and he was watching the silent buildings for any sign of movement. Malachi came to the wagon and helped the women down.

"Get into the office," Jamie ordered curtly.

Tess didn't argue but did as he told her. Shannon and Kristin followed her.

"Will you look at this mess!" Kristin said, clicking her tongue.

"I should help you," Tess said.

"Will you please go type! We can handle this," Kristin said.

Tess nodded and walked to her desk and typewriter. She dusted fragments of glass from her chair and blew it from her papers and rolled a blank sheet into her typewriter.

She stared at it for just one second, then her fingers began to fly. She had a lot to say. A hell of a lot.

Time moved quickly. Kristin and Shannon moved around the room competently, and their presence didn't disturb Tess in the least. She was just getting to the part where Jeremiah and David had admitted their involvement with von Heusen when she heard a shout in the street.

The three of them froze. The shout came again.

"Tess! Tess Stuart! We know you're in there! And you're under arrest."

"Under arrest!" Tess gasped.

Then she heard Jamie respond from beyond the window, his voice harsh and firm as he met the threat.

"It's the sheriff, I think!" Shannon said, peeking around a broken window.

Tess joined her beside the window, and nodded.

"She's under arrest for what?" Jamie demanded.

"Slander and murder."

"Murder!"

"She killed two of Mr. von Heusen's men. She tricked them out into the open fields. I've witnesses to that effect. Then she shot them down cold."

Jamie let loose with a flaming oath. Then he was striding out to meet the sheriff face to face. Tess gripped the window frame.

"This is bull, and you know it. Von Heusen set you up to this. You're just a hired gun, like any other of his thugs."

"You shut your mouth, Slater. You're under arrest, too."

"For what?"

"Conspiracy to commit murder."

"Well, I'll tell you what, Sheriff, you just try to take me in."

Tess was never quite sure what propelled her, but before anyone could stop her, she was racing out to the street, streaking toward Jamie. She caught his arm and faced the sheriff, furious. "Don't you even think it! Don't you even try to drag him down into the mud and mire that you've created with von Heusen! Arrest me if you want to so damn badly—"

"Tess, damn you!" Jamie swore, swinging her around behind him. "What the hell are you doing out here? I told you—"

"Slater, shut up," came a new voice.

It was von Heusen. He came striding out from the saloon, his pale eyes shimmering with hatred, his white hair touched by the breeze. "Miss Stuart," he said, addressing Tess, "you are ever valiant. But I can't wait to hang this Reb. I just can't wait."

"You aren't ever going to hang me, von Heusen," Jamie said. "And you aren't ever going to have that property for the railroad."

Von Heusen's brows shot up. "So you know. You're quite a detective."

"I travel in good company," Jamie said with a shrug.

"It doesn't matter. The sheriff is my man. Aren't you, Harvey?"

"Von Heusen, don't say that," the sheriff began uneasily.

"Why? Who is going to stop us now?" von Heusen said. "I own the sheriff, and I own the magistrate, and I can damned well bet you I'm going to own the executioner. You're dead, Slater. As dead as a doornail."

"No. You may own the sheriff, but I've got a few guns around the place, too, von Heusen."

"Yeah, your brothers and that half-breed friend of yours. It's not enough. I've got guns all over this town."

As if to prove it, and obviously uncaring that he was about to commit murder in broad daylight, von Heusen raised his pistol and aimed straight at Jamie's heart.

But he didn't have a chance to fire. A gun cracked, and von Heusen grabbed his hand, screaming. And the streets came alive. There was a fearsome pounding of hooves, and war cries tore the air.

Jamie, astonished, bent low and whirled around. "Jesus!" he breathed.

The cavalry. The cavalry was coming, Sergeant Monahan in the lead. Nor were they alone. They were traveling, curiously enough, with a small band of Indians.

Apache.

"Jamie!"

Tess screamed his name and he swung around again even as the horses came tearing down the street.

Von Heusen had Tess. His right hand might be crippled and bleeding, but he held his pistol in his left hand, and the muzzle was pressed against her temple. He was backing toward the saloon.

"One more step and I blow her to kingdom come!" von Heusen warned Jamie.

Gunfire was spitting all around him. From behind a water barrel by the *Wiltshire Sun* office Cole was picking off von Heusen's men from the rooftops around them. Malachi and Jon were positioned behind the wagon, which they had overturned.

And the cavalry and the Apache were rushing in to the fantastic sound of a bugle call. It was quickly obvious that von Heusen's men would not be enough.

Except that von Heusen had Tess.

He disappeared through the swinging doors of the saloon. Jamie caught his breath, hearing Tess's screams as the man dragged her upstairs.

"The roof, Jamie! The roof!" Cole called to him.

He looked up. He made a leap toward the railing and swung himself up to the roof. A shot nearly made him trip and fall. He heard someone groan and saw a man fall to the ground. He looked across the street.

Cole smiled, blowing the smoke from his gun. "Dammit, Jamie, go get the girl!"

Jamie grinned and gave his brother a thumbs-up sign. Then he felt his blood run cold again. He was going to have to kill von Heusen if he wanted to live himself.

"You, Miss Stuart, have been a bloody thorn in my side since the beginning. You should have died in that raid on the wagon train, and if you'd had any damned sense, you would have stayed with that bleeding Apache."

Tess winced. Von Heusen's hold on her arm was vicious, and she could feel the cold steel pressed hard against her temple. She swallowed. If he killed her now, she was still the winner. She had to keep telling herself that, so she could keep fighting him.

"That bleeding Apache, as you call him, is here to kill you, von Heusen. The Apache and the cavalry are riding together. Just to kill you."

They had come to the top of the stairs. Von Heusen burst open the door to one of the rooms and threw her inside. Tess staggered across the room as von Heusen closed and bolted the door, putting a chair across it.

"What now, von Heusen?" Tess demanded.

He cast her an evil glare with his near colorless eyes, and she felt fear creep along her spine. He strode across the room to her, wrenching her by the hair. "You foolish, foolish little girl. You could have lived as that Indian's squaw, but now I promise you that you're going to pay dearly. One wrong move, and I'll scalp you myself. What a beautiful trophy that hair would be, eh, Miss Stuart?"

She spat at him. He pulled on her hair so hard that she was certain half of it left her head and, despite her efforts to choke back the sound, she cried out. She saw him smile at her pain, and it sickened her, and she realized that he liked hurting people, that killing gave him pleasure.

"What now? Now we wait. We wait for your ever gallant young cavalry hero to come running up those stairs. Then I shoot him dead. Then I use you to escape this town, and then maybe later I'll let you go, but more likely, I'll kill you. I'll kill you slow. I'll have you first, and I'll humiliate you every way I know how, and then I'll kill you bit by bit . . ."

She managed to jerk away from him, backing toward the window, staring at him. "You bastard! Why don't you just kill me now? I'll make your life a living hell. I'll never take a single step with you. Unless . . ."

"Unless?" He drew out his knife, a wickedly sharp and long bowie knife that glinted in the fraction of sunlight that entered the room.

"You leave Jamie alone. We'll go out by the roof right now and I'll come along without a protest—"

"How touching."

"If you kill him, I won't make a move."

"Oh, but I can make you," von Heusen told her softly. And maybe he could. He was walking toward her, his knife before him, twisting in his hands. "I'll just make you bleed a little now, but you'll feel it," he promised her.

She was going to scream or faint. She wanted desperately to fight, to be brave, but all she could see was the glinting steel. He was coming closer and closer, and she didn't know how brave she could be once that steel touched her.

"I'll make you bleed!" von Heusen promised again.

He was almost on top of her. She could see the razor sharpness of the blade, aimed toward her face.

The window shattered behind her, and a man came bursting through. Booted feet connected with von Heusen's chest and he was sent flying into the room. He landed hard and turned, ready to throw his knife straight at Tess's heart.

Jamie fired his Colt without hesitating, without a flicker of fear or remorse.

And von Heusen stared at him, startled. Then his color-less eyes closed for the last time, and he slumped to the floor.

Jamie strode over to Tess.

"Are you all right?" he demanded.

She nodded, her throat dry, her heart pounding.

"Dammit, Tess, I told you that this had to be my way."

"I—I was trying to do it your way!" she said. But then she looked at von Heusen again, and back to Jamie. And she passed out cold.

With a tender smile, Jamie lifted her into his arms and held her very close. He didn't look at von Heusen. He carried her into the light of day.

Chapter Fourteen

It was really amazing when one looked around, Tess thought.

She was having a barbecue. Well, the ranch was hosting a barbecue. Huge sides of beef were being roasted all around the property, the wine and beer and whiskey were flowing freely and all manner of entertainment was going on.

She was having a party—and the cavalry and the Apache and the townspeople and even the whores from the saloon were in attendance.

Nalte was her honored guest. She and Jamie had discovered that the Apache had never intended to leave the area, that he meant to find out about the man who would betray so many people. It was Nalte who had called in the cavalry, taking a tremendous chance when he had sent a messenger to the fort.

Tess was glad of the party, and she was grateful to feel a part of a huge family. She didn't have to be the only hostess. Kristin, always calm and capable and serene, was handling most of the social duties.

Still dazed from the events of the day, Tess wandered through the crowds rather aimlessly, welcoming the men who had been her friends after the wagon train had been raided, keeping the peace when it seemed that the rowdy Indians were getting too close to the rowdy whites. But she didn't need to take care of much of that. Cole and Malachi and Jon seemed to have a good eye on things, and Hank knew how to take care of the place.

She had just wandered into the kitchen when Jamie caught up with her.

As always, he didn't stand on ceremony, but caught her hand and told her bluntly that he wanted to talk to her.

"But Jamie, we've people—"

"Now, Tess."

She was alarmed when he started to drag her up the stairs, and she tugged on his hand. "Jamie—"

"Tess!" He groaned. She was too slow. He turned and swept her into his arms and ran the rest of the way up the stairs.

"Damn you, Jamie Slater—"

"I told you, Tess. Things were going to go my way today!"

They reached her room. Setting her down firmly upon her feet, he closed and locked the door and leaned against it. She backed away from him distrustfully. She moistened her lips. She still hadn't really talked to him. There had been so much commotion when she had first come to. Kristin and Shannon had insisted on taking care of her, and she hadn't realized until tonight that they had won not just a battle but the war.

"Thank you. Thank you for saving my life."

"You're welcome," he said briefly, striding across the room for her. "It seemed the least I could do."

"Yes, well, it's done now."

"Damn you, stand still."

"Jamie—"

He caught her. He caught her arms and he pulled her against him. He buried his face against her neck and he murmured softly. "Just think, you could be carrying a child. And it would be a fine child. Cute, beautiful, just like my brothers' kids.''

"Jamie—"

He moved away from her, his eyes flittering silver as they met hers.

"I told you, we're doing things my way today. And we're going to get married."

She gasped, stunned. "Wh—what?"

"Married. Now."

"But why?"

"Well..." He touched her cheek, softly, gently, studying the movement of his fingers upon her face as if he were seeing it for the first time. "Well, for one, I'm damned afraid that if I don't, Nalte will determine to ride away with you again. He'd already warned me that I really better make you my woman in truth."

She stiffened. "Jamie, I heard you say yourself that no one could force you—"

"Then there's Kristin and Shannon. They'll never give me a moment's peace."

"Jamie—"

"Then I'll be damned if you'll be having any children of mine without me being present."

"But we don't even—"

"Then there's this," he said softly, and his lips touched hers more gently and tenderly than she had ever imagined possible, as if the moon itself touched her. She closed her eyes and she was back, back to a beautiful valley where they had made love beneath the moon, where their love had seemed so very right. Where magic had touched them despite all the odds.

"And this..."

He touched her forehead with his kiss. Then her cheeks, and her throat, and her lips again. "And most important, there is this. I love you, Tess. I love you. I want to marry you. I want to be beside you from this day forth, and I want to cherish you forever. Of course, I still want to throttle you. But most of all, I want to love you, and I want to be loved by you. I want to know your strength and even fight it sometimes, and I want to know your tenderness and your love and hold tight to them forever. How is that?''

"Oh, Jamie!" she whispered. Words failed her. She came up on her toes and kissed him. She teased his lower lip and his upper lip with her teeth and tongue, and she met his hunger with a fever of her own. A dizzying fire swept through her limbs, and she thought she could sleep beside him tonight, and every night, and she could feel his arms around her.

"Slater. Tess Slater." She sampled the name, but then tears touched her eyes and she threw her arms around him and kissed him again. "Oh, Jamie, I love you! I've loved you for so long now, and I thought that I didn't dare to believe in forever—"

"But you believed in yourself, Tess. Now you've got to learn to believe in me, too."

"I've always believed in you!"

"Then believe in this. I love you, and I will do so forever."

"Jamie . . ."

She would have lain down with him then. She would have tasted his flesh and savored his kiss and given him all and anything he wanted. She would always lie down with him anywhere, in any wilderness, and love him, and feel the sun or the moon upon them. It would not matter, as long as they were together.

But he was clutching her hand again. "Don't tempt me!" he warned her. "We've got to get downstairs and do this now. Before Nalte leaves."

"What?"

"We're getting married now, Tess. The chaplain is here, and Nalte is here, and my brothers are here, and I just can't think of a better time."

"Married? Now? Tonight?"

"Yes!"

They were out the door and he was pulling her down the stairs.

She tugged hard upon his hand. "Jamie!"

"What?"

"Today I promised to do things your way. I really can't promise to do that every day."

"Fine. I'll keep you in line," he said, and tugged her again. They reached the landing, and he shouted, "Cole! Tell the musicians and get the chaplain. She said yes!"

A rebel cry went up from the Slater brothers. The cavalry didn't seem to mind—in fact they joined right in. There was another sound, and Tess recognized Apache war whoops.

She tugged on Jamie's hand again, but he didn't notice. He kept walking. Kristin and Shannon and the children and Dolly and Jane and Jon and everyone were wishing her luck, and she was suddenly standing in front of a cavalry man wearing a chaplain's insignia.

"Jamie!" she whispered. "I'm really sorry about your horse."

"Don't be. Nalte gave him back to me as a wedding present."

"Oh! You're marrying me just to get your horse back!"

"Say, 'I do,' Tess."

She stared at the smiling chaplain and she heard the words but she didn't hear them. Oh, they would be cherished in her memory forever, but right now all she could think of was the feel of Jamie's hand upon her, and the promise of the security of it. It was time, and she said her vows. Then she was wearing a thin gold band, and everyone was wishing her luck once again. There were toasting and dancing, and she kissed Nalte, a huge sloppy kiss on his cheek.

But then she discovered herself in her new husband's arms again, and she was heading up the stairs again, and she didn't know if she was drunk with champagne or with happiness or with desire for this man who had come into her life and given her everything.

"Jamie!"

"What?"

"We've still got guests downstairs."

He groaned long and low and kicked open the door to their bedroom and walked determinedly over to the bed after kicking the door shut behind him.

Then he smiled wickedly. "My way, Tess. Everything is my way today."

Then he cast himself down upon her. He kissed her slowly and with seductive force, and she knew that there was nowhere she would rather be. When his silver eyes rose above her she smiled sweetly and breathlessly.

"Your way," she promised.

And he smiled, and he kissed her again.

And indeed, the night was delightfully passed . . .

His way.

* * * * *

Especially for you,
Christmas from
HARLEQUIN HISTORICALS

An enchanting collection of three Christmas
stories by some of your favorite authors captures
the spirit of the season in the 1800s

TUMBLEWEED CHRISTMAS by Kristin James

A "Bah, humbug" Texas rancher meets his match in his
new housekeeper, a woman determined to bring the spirit
of a Tumbleweed Christmas into his life—and love into
his heart.

A CINDERELLA CHRISTMAS by Lucy Elliot

The perfect granddaughter, sister and aunt, Mary Hillyer
seemed destined for spinsterhood until Jack Gates arrived
to discover a woman with dreams and passions that were
meant to be shared during a Cinderella Christmas.

HOME FOR CHRISTMAS
by Heather Graham Pozzessere

The magic of the season brings peace Home For
Christmas when a Yankee captain and a Southern heiress
fall in love during the Civil War.

Look for HARLEQUIN HISTORICALS CHRISTMAS
STORIES in November wherever Harlequin books are sold.

HARLEQUIN'S "BIG WIN"
SWEEPSTAKES RULES & REGULATIONS
NO PURCHASE NECESSARY TO ENTER OR RECEIVE A PRIZE

1. To enter and join the Harlequin Reader Service, scratch off the pink metallic strips on all your BIG WIN tickets #1–#6. This will reveal the values for each sweepstakes entry number, the number of free books you will receive and your free bonus gift as part of our Reader Service. If you do not wish to take advantage of our introduction to the Harlequin Reader Service but wish to enter the Sweepstakes only, scratch off the pink metallic strips on your BIG WIN tickets #1–#4 only. To enter, return your entire sheet of tickets intact. Incomplete and/or inaccurate entries are not eligible for that section or section(s) of prizes. Not responsible for mutilated or unreadable entries or inadvertent printing errors. Mechanically reproduced entries are null and void. Be sure to also qualify for the Bonus Sweepstakes. See Rule #3 on how to enter.

2. Either way your unique Sweepstakes numbers will be compared against the list of winning numbers generated at random by the computer. In the event that all prizes are not claimed, random drawings will be held from all entries received from all presentations to award all unclaimed prizes. All cash prizes are payable in U.S. funds. This is in addition to any free, surprise or mystery gifts that might be offered. The following prizes are awarded in this sweepstakes: *Grand Prize (1) $1,000,000; First Prize (1) $35,000; Second Prize (1) $10,000; Third Prize (3) $5,000; Fourth Prize (10) $1,000; Fifth Prize (25) $500; Sixth Prize (5000)$5.

   *This Sweepstakes contains a Grand Prize offering of a $1,000,000 annuity. Winner may elect to receive $25,000 a year for 40 years without interest totalling $1,000,000 or $350,000 in one cash payment. Entrants may cancel Reader Service at any time without cost or obligation to buy (see details in center insert card).

3. Extra Bonus Prize: This presentation offers two extra bonus prizes valued at $30,000 each to be awarded in a random drawing from all entries received.

4. Versions of this Sweepstakes with different graphics will be offered in other mailings or at retail outlets by Torstar Corp. and its affiliates. This promotion is being conducted under the supervision of Marden-Kane, Inc., an independent judging organization. By entering this Sweepstakes, each entrant accepts and agrees to be bound by these rules and the decisions of the judges, which shall be final and binding. Odds of winning in the random drawing are dependent upon the total number of entries received. Taxes, if any, are the sole responsibility of the winners. Prizes are non-transferable. All entries must be received by March 31, 1990. The drawing will take place on or about April 30, 1990 at the offices of Marden-Kane, Inc., Lake Success, NY.

5. This offer is open to residents of the U.S., the United Kingdom and Canada, 18 years or older except employees of Torstar Corp., its affiliates, subsidiaries, Marden-Kane, Inc. and all other agencies and persons connected with conducting this Sweepstakes. All Federal, State and local laws apply. Void wherever prohibited or restricted by law.

6. Winners will be notified by mail and may be required to execute an affidavit of eligibility and release that must be returned within 14 days after notification. Canadian winners will be required to answer a skill-testing question. Winners consent to the use of their name, photograph and/or likeness for advertising and publicity in conjunction with this and similar promotions without additional compensation.

7. For a list of our most current major prize winners, send a stamped, self-addressed envelope to: WINNERS LIST c/o MARDEN-KANE, INC., P.O. BOX 701, SAYREVILLE, NJ 08871.

If Sweepstakes entry form is missing, please print your name and address on a 3″ × 5″ piece of plain paper and send to:

In the U.S.	In Canada
Harlequin's "BIG WIN" Sweepstakes	Harlequin's "BIG WIN" Sweepstakes
901 Fuhrmann Blvd.	P.O. Box 609
Box 1867	Fort Erie, Ontario
Buffalo, NY 14269-1867	L2A 5X3

© 1989 Harlequin Enterprises Limited   Printed in the U.S.A.

LTY-H119

Wonderful, luxurious gifts can be yours with proofs-of-purchase from any specially marked "Indulge A Little" Harlequin or Silhouette book with the Offer Certificate properly completed, plus a check or money order (do not send cash) to cover postage and handling payable to Harlequin/Silhouette "Indulge A Little, Give A Lot" Offer. We will send you the specified gift.

Mail-in-Offer

OFFER CERTIFICATE

Item:	A. Collector's Doll	B. Soaps in a Basket	C. Potpourri Sachet	D. Scented Hangers
# of Proofs-of-Purchase	18	12	6	4
Postage & Handling	$3.25	$2.75	$2.25	$2.00
Check One				

Name _____

Address _____ Apt. # _____

City _____ State _____ Zip _____

Mail this certificate, designated number of proofs-of-purchase and check or money order for postage and handling to:

INDULGE A LITTLE
P.O. Box 9055
Buffalo, N.Y. 14269-9055